A TOOTH-CLENCHING MOMENT

"Ladies and gentlemen and et cetera . . ."

At this, there was a chuckle all around, as people like to chuckle when there is something familiar, even if there is nothing particularly funny about the familiar thing. Yes, it can get annoying, but people will keep on doing it.

Grimfir continued, "Allow me to present to you the amateurish and therefore charming, not to mention thought-provoking, magical derring-do of my squire-at-arms, protégé, and errand boy, the somewhat inimitable Charley Tooth!" He took a step back and to the side, propelling Charley forward.

The room was silent. All eyes were on Charley, except for Charley's, which were on everybody's. Charley had not felt this much at a loss since he was mistakenly enrolled in Advanced Chemistry as a freshman, and showed up to Mr. Blatt's class in the midst of seniors. On the first week's test, he received a 22% and an invitation from Mr. Blatt to explain his poor performance in front of the class. Once it was discovered that the registrar had made the error, Charley was very neatly moved into Ms. Vaneer's Health class, where Charley proved to be a slightly above-average student.

But these people wanted him to "entertain" them!

THE ADVENTURES OF CHARLEY TOOTH

L. B. RICHARDS

VORTEX

VORTEX®

September 2004

Published by

Dorchester Publishing Co., Inc.
200 Madison Avenue
New York, NY 10016

ISBN 0-8439-5136-2

Printed in the United States of America.

Visit us on the web at www.dorchesterpub.com.

My thanks go to:

*Chris Keeslar for his strange patience
and constant encouragement.
Jonathan Howe and David Vaughan
for various inspirations.
Fritz Blanchette for tremendous help throughout.
My family for everlasting support.*

*Dedicated to Charley O. Bernstein,
whose presence I will never forget.*

THE ADVENTURES OF CHARLEY TOOTH

Book One:
THE REMOVAL

CHAPTER ONE

"Ah, look, everyone is here!"

And he appeared to be right. There was no denying the crowd was complete and completely drunk. Riboflavia Gumchewie was leaning heavily into Sir Dorchester the Beggar, who, though interested, was still trying to play a hand of whist through with Baggo B. Winnebago. Observing them with snide indifference was Ulmuth Wagonspack, Jr., who was known for coming to every party and remaining snidely, indifferently observant of all that went on. Had he been not so odorous, he might have made quite a go of it as a gossip, but the more pleasantly scented, arrayed, and de-warted Kyly Dewdropsonton was the rumor-mongering darling at such gatherings, even if her reports tended to be completely factual and therefore not even a third as interesting as Ulmuth's. By the window were The Sisters Yippie, each of them casting a line for Leif the Pasty, whose erstwhile lover, Lips O'Leary, had recently been seen watering the geraniums with a substance that distinctly was not water but rather something more solid altogether. The Abbot of St. Orson, a thin, small bore of a man, was in the process of constructing a banjo out of odds and ends he had been able to remove from the pool house, which included a lot of netting and some filter pipe. Flafalf and Son looked on bewildered, as Flafalf the Senior had just agreed to pay the good abbot for swimming lessons, even though his water allergy made that kind of thing difficult.

Off by the double bookcase was Flossy the One-Eyed Jerk, surrounded by the usual types of thoroughly unsurprising people who feel the need to associate themselves with those of physical uniqueness or loudly repugnant personalities. These odd sycophants tended to include Dame Jeffrey Mangirl and Duke Riebald, as they did this very minute, except that Riebald was under the sofa. On the sofa sat, more or less on top of each other, Tonsil Grinblar, Beytore of Beytore, Jarsan son of Nisan, Lightwing the Diseased, and The Tiny Smippens, who, at this point in his life, was noticeably thick around the middle, and the top, and the bottom. These five were discussing whether experience is clouded or clarified by language, though Beytore believed them to be discussing the need for some more salmon-and-artichoke slivers. Incidentally, Beytore was the only one of them who would go home satisfied that night.

Singing, or apparently singing, by the piano were Lady Footslip, Mucker McFlugle, Yorgad, HrYlgYr, Glubdort Minxer, and Slusie Crinfaber. That none of them played the piano was of little deterrence, though HrYlgYr's lack of a mouth caused some consternation when the group tried for harmony. Sitting on the stairs, head in hands, was Trynl Flinzhum.

Next to him was the always startled-looking Kwuito Karbelbammer, who possibly had not yet figured out why she was there. There were more people, creatures, and beings pocketed away throughout the rooms, so that it certainly did seem as though Grimfir Boldrock was correct when he said,

"Ah, look, everyone is here!"

And it would've been presumptuous of our Charley Tooth to argue, not knowing a single one of them, though it's true that Tandor Ovenheat had one of those faces that looked familiar to just about everyone.

At this moment, up glided the magnificently splendorous hostess, Hololo Summersweat, and grasped Grimfir by the hamhock, as her sixth and ninth tentacles were low about the floor.

"Hullo, hullo, my dearest dear of a Boldrock, Grimfir! Aren't you the dear! Such a dear! And who is this dear with you, at your side, in accompaniment?"

With a stiff, seemly bow, Grimfir nodded toward Charley and said, "With me is my squire, Charley Tooth."

"Oh, how remarkably and breathtakingly dear!" said Hololo Summersweat, her smiley mouth full of white and blue teeth, many of them hers. "Perhaps he can entertain us until Onnser the semi-Magnificent manages to find his way out of his dear little carriage?" Several of her tentacles warmly and clammily prodded and hugged Charley, who stood still as a fish, were fish to stand still.

"A fine idea, my fine lady," nodded Grimfir, who then took a tray of salmon-and-artichoke slivers from the passing waiter, thereby temporarily thwarting the slightly distressed, slightly overdressed, Beytore of

Beytore, still on the sofa. Grimfir began to eat and grunt, as was his wont.

"Attention, please, my dear and fellow ladies and fellows," said Hololo Summersweat, "but this dear Charley Tooth will be entertaining us until the entertainment comes and arrives to entertain us. Applause, please, applause."

The guests turned their attention to the doorway, in which stood Hololo, Grimfir, and Charley, all of them more or less wrapped up in Summersweatean tentacles. Expectancy was in their eyes, but luckily not much of it. In nearly every world, being overeager is something that is wisely looked down upon, especially at fancy parties. On the other hand, uncomfortable silences are also looked down upon, and that is where the crowd at Hololo Summersweat's Gala Fete Ball Party found themselves with Charley Tooth. Grimfir looked sternly at Charley and grumped, "Well?"

Charley felt Hololo's tentacles squeeze him, though it was hard to gauge whether it was encouragement or coercion. "Entertain away, my dear boy," she said. Charley, looking as uncomfortable as a fish trying to stand still, which we've already touched upon, glanced around and said:

"May I use the bathroom?"

There was silence, and then a lot of laughter led by, of all partygoers, Tandor Ovenheat. But then there was more sudden silence, led, as much as silence can be led, by HrYlgYr, who still had no mouth and wouldn't for many years to come. Then there was some laughter, a bit limp here, a bit forced there, mostly led by the arguers on the sofa. Hololo Summersweat, ever consummate, laughed lightly and flapped several of her sucker-bearing arms in appreciation. Invariably, this gesture made people (and we shall use that term quite generally) feel at ease—the undulating iridescence of her purple-and-green skin, shimmering slowly in the light, was pacifying. The effect was something like an aquatic, scaly peacock shimmying to a slow easy-listening tune, perhaps underwater.

"On you go, dear boy, up the stairs and to the left and to the right and to the left and back to the right, on the right."

Charley clambered over Trynl Flinzhum and Kwuito Karbelbammer, who introduced herself and said as Charley passed, "Your show was nearly magnificent," to which Trynl responded morosely, "Kwuito, that wasn't even Onnser." Inwardly, Trynl was shaken to recognize, somehow, that he would repeat this phrase to Kwuito throughout the rest of his life. Abashed, Kwuito hurriedly made up for her error by calling after Charley, "Then I really didn't like your show, I mean." Charley climbed his way upstairs and, in making a variety of combinations of rights and lefts, found himself in the bathroom, or *a* bathroom.

Though he wasn't bothered by Kwuito not liking his show (okay, he was a little bit bothered—it wasn't as though they had given him time to prepare; sure, he might be no Onnser the semi-Magnificent, but then again, Charley didn't have any idea who *was* Onnser the Magnificent), there was something wrong here. First, Charley was not a squire. And not Grimfir Boldrock's squire, on top of that. Charley didn't even know who Grimfir was, or what he was. To be more than honest, Charley wasn't even sure that he knew what a squire was, exactly—he imagined it to be someone with a bad haircut and tights who held a master's quiver or leashes to the greyhounds. And the strange party guests were, well, strange. Hololo Summersweat, while charming and fine, was not the kind of hostess Charley was prepared to feel at home with. Sure, she had tentacles, but that was not what made Charley uneasy—after all, he could see no reason why she shouldn't be allowed to be a fine hostess with tentacles; it even made sense, after a fashion—but it did seem somewhat out of place.

Which is exactly where Charley was.

Charley looked in the mirror. He looked the same. That is, different—Charley was a bit tall for his age, at fifteen. He had red hair and more red hair. Not the bright, shiny red hair that is associated with bad tempers, but rather dark red, curly, thick, and a little untamed. Hair that grew as though it had never really learned where it was supposed to grow. Charley, looking at himself, breathed a bit easier once he realized that he was still Charley. Then he breathed harder again, as he then realized this whole scene might make more sense if he actually weren't Charley anymore. That lady, or what-have-you, had tentacles and talked and threw parties. As his memory caught up with him, Charley thought that more than half of the beings downstairs didn't look human at all. Which, when you come from a nice little place such as Connecticut, is a bit startling. Charley was clearly out of place, or else all the other people here were. As few others appeared as uncomfortable as Charley, he quickly and correctly deduced that yes, he was the one not where he should have been, or at least where he used to be.

"How did I get here?"

He asked himself, but not aloud. He answered himself with another question, this time aloud:

"How did I get *where*?"

And then a more relevant question muscled its way forward.

"What do I do now?"

A good question. At that exact moment in time, that exact same question was being asked internally by Grimfir Boldrock, who had to keep eating salmon-and-artichoke slivers in order to avoid addressing the odd entrance he and his squire made, and he wasn't even all that hungry, truth be told.

It was also being asked by Hololo Summersweat, who had a party to run.

It was being asked by Kwuito Karbelbammer, who wasn't sure if she should keep talking to cover up her gaffes.

It was also being asked by Beytore of Beytore, who was increasingly hungry and confused by the sofa conversation.

It was being asked by HrYlgYr, who was gamely trying to join in on the third verse of "Who's That Riding My Cow?" but still confounded by a lack of oral aperture.

It was also being asked by the Abbot of St. Orson, who was quite at a loss at how to proceed in banjo-making with his makeshift materials.

It was also being asked by Flossy the One-Eyed Jerk, who had run out of flip remarks to say about Duke Riebald, who was also asking himself that very question as he was trying to negotiate a dignified way out from under the sofa.

Riboflavia Gumchewie and Sir Dorchester the Beggar were each asking themselves that very question, as poor Riboflavia needed to choose between making her move or passing out, and Sir Dorchester the Beggar found himself in the unusual position of not having to beg.

Charley had asked himself this question at the cash register in his school's cafeteria, shortly before he found himself at Hololo Summersweat's door.

Chapter Two

Connecticut can be described in two ways. One is Quaint.

The other is Boring. What is quaint is extremely quaint, in the good sense, and what is boring is extremely boring, not in any good sense. Whatever you get, you get in heaps.

Charley was sick of heaps. Not that he was unhappy, but he had the feeling that there was something more out there. Why even call it a feeling? He knew there was more out there, but there he was, in Connecticut. Life was normal. Mr. and Mrs. Tooth were normal yet weird. In fact, they were almost embarrassingly normal yet weird, in Charley's opinion, as everyone's parents are invariably embarrassingly normal yet weird.

Charley had an older sister, Cynthia Tooth, and a younger sister, Tabitha Tooth. The Tooths (or Teeth, depending) had a dog, Shiny. Charley had named the dog, resisting Cynthia's push for the more obvious, though doubly fit, name of Canine. Tabitha wanted to name the pooch Buck, but the rest of the family thought it too much. Charley was not like the rest of the family. For one, his appearance was different from that of the rest of his kin. Cynthia was nearly brunette, Tabitha nearly blond. His mom had darkish hair, and his dad had been gray as long as Charley could remember looking at his dad's hair. Charley was also a good half-foot taller than his father, who was the same height as Cynthia, who was a half-foot taller than Mrs. Tooth, who was the same height as Tabitha. Charley was the only one in the family who liked tuna. Not including Shiny.

Shiny was a good dog. Most dogs are, as long as you treat them well, and the Tooths or Teeth certainly did. Shiny was in fact a very good dog, exceedingly so, and it is a shame that he doesn't figure in to this story more.

Charley was a good boy. One could describe him as both curious and inept; in fact many people did, often at once. It would be wrong to say he was luckless, but it would not be completely wrong. A math teacher at his school, Ms. Formfal, actually used the word "bobulous" to describe him, even though it is not a real word (she was a math teacher, not an English teacher, remember). And, to be fair, bobulous was not far off the mark. To illustrate: Charley once, as a joke at school, pretended as though he were about to fall down the main staircase. He ended up actually corporeally falling down the stairs, accidentally taking with him Grace O'Malley, who broke her arm in the fall. Surprisingly and laudably, Dr. and Judge O'Malley did not sue a soul—not the Tooths (Teeth), not the family of Clint Ryder (who was the intended and appreciative audience of the spectacle, and, as some said, the one who dared or pushed Charley), not the school and Mr. George the principal, not Ms. Hall the monitor, not Vitz Construction who made the staircase, not HyperShoe, makers of the sneaker that Grace was wearing that clearly did not provide enough Non-Slip-Grip® traction, and not the good folks at Mother of Mercy Hospital who correctly diagnosed and treated Grace's broken arm. The O'Malleys were clearly good people, and Grace was a wonderful girl. We wish that Charley would someday marry her and be happy, but she ended up marrying a man by the name of Keller Kellog who was a decent fellow and good provider, even if he was a bit uninteresting. I suppose that's what happens if you are like Charley and don't act on a crush, even if you realize that you are far too young to be thinking about marrying and such. Grace Kellog had four children, and only the male offspring turned out to be bratty.

What is still missing is how Charley was transported from more-or-less-present-day-Connecticut to more-or-less-present-day Nivalg, which is the name of the world in which Hololo Summersweat's party was occurring. Even in retrospect, Charley couldn't quite pinpoint the details of the event. He himself acknowledged years later through several aides, "I would pinpoint for you the details of the event, but I won't, because I can't." This much is 50% certain: Charley was in the school cafeteria. Though he had had a full lunch earlier in the day—a gyro, a chicken-patty sandwich, and a carton of fries—he had two free periods in the afternoon, and the cafeteria was as good a place as any to spend the time. It was a

Thursday, and on Thursdays the seniors played cards in the cafeteria in their late-afternoon lunch periods. Charley joined a game and found that in no time at all he had lost most of his money. He was also incredibly thirsty, having had a rather rich snack before he joined the older guys in the card game. Back in the lunch line, he found himself at the cash register with a carton of chocolate milk, an ice cream sandwich, and a dollar in quarters. The dollar would not cover the cost of both. A dilemma faced him. He could steal one or both of the items, he could buy the chocolate milk and call it good, or he could buy the ice cream sandwich and then use the rather unclean drinking fountain for some free water. He quickly dismissed the idea of stealing. He knelt down to tie his shoelace and buy some time while he thought, "What do I do now?" And that was the last thing he remembered from Earth.

Mrs. Tooth was at home. She had been doing crosswords all day. She had finished maybe thirty of them. Yes, thirty. Practice makes perfect. You still might think that's a lot, but remember that there are those common clues that end up with words like *ewer* or *olla*, hockey names like Orr, and so on. Once she got the hang of it, she was quite adept at filling in all of the boxes, in pen (the only way to do them properly). She was a professor on sabbatical, which is really a good deal, and she had been doing research for the past week and a half, so she took this particular Thursday off. So many things happen on Thursdays.

Why is it that Thursday is such a day of conflict? It's not quite the weekend, but then again, it doesn't deign to be part of the regular week's weekdays. At some point, weekends begin and end on Thursdays.

It seems that schools try to thwart this, to everybody's dissatisfaction. So many things meet Monday, Wednesday, Thursday, or Tuesday, Thursday, making Thursday the most overused and underutilized day of the week.

Mr. Tooth was at work, at Amalgamated Boesing, Inc. No one seemed to know what it was that Amalgamated Boesing did or represented—it fell into that category of "work" that defied any normal categorization that would have led to a completely normal childhood for Charley. Mr. Tooth could easily have been anything from a bricklayer to an engineer to some sort of banking manager; it is entirely possible and probable that even he did not know what it was that he did. Whatever his job was, he did it well, sometimes even with gusto, so that he was well respected within his mysterious industry. This Thursday he would be leaving work early for the airport to take a business trip to London.

It took Charley a full day of psychological exercise to prepare to fly on a plane. A day of preparations—redoing his very own will, reconfirming that, though his life was full (overly full) of regrets, he was, all things considered, more or less, or even less than that, ready to die. That's what flying was—the preparation for death; the willingness to sacrifice the idea of control to the idea of faith. Nothing could be more religious than flying, and Charley did not like flying. When he broke it down, religion felt to him like an arrangement of precepts that govern behavior within a rigid set of boundaries. When Charley got on a plane, he felt as though he were in the most fundamental of leaps of faith—that of commending your life to something larger, more terrible, and more amazing than anything that could be piloted by a force outside the self. To be sure, Charley's instant journey to Nivalg would, in retrospect, be a complete extinguishment of the idea that uncontrollable travel was a test of faith. Sure, it might be for you or for me, but here Charley was, quite suddenly, in a foreign world populated by strange beings, with all sorts of expectations expected of him. If these are the times that try men's souls (and perhaps they are), Charley found himself in the times and places that try men's souls, ideas, bodies, actions, and patiences.

CHAPTER THREE

One of Charley's first thoughts, upon finding himself in so improbable and unbelievable a situation was, "Could there really be a god that allows such a goings-on?" But shortly thereafter—within seconds—his more pertinent question was, "What the hell is going on?" After this question repeated itself a number of times, Charley set it aside in favor of, "What do I do now?" And that is where we just left him, upstairs in Hololo Summersweat's villa, staring into what approximated a bathroom mirror. When he first entered the bathroom, the double-toilet caught his attention, but he had other pressing issues to consider (and his curiosity about the toilet was satisfied later in the evening when he saw that Lightwing the Diseased was double-buttocked. Or perhaps more accurately, quadruple-buttocked, depending on if you consider a single buttock as one or two). "What do I do now?" It felt very nearly like a palindrome, and Charley suddenly desired a pen and some graph paper.

There was a knock at the door just then, and Charley had the undeniable feeling that on this world, he could merely wish for something and it would come to pass. He opened the door to find that he was mistaken—Ulmuth Wagonspack, Jr., and Kyly Dewdropsonton had not knocked in order to deliver the desired pen and graph paper.

"Hello," said Charley, as disappointed as he was nervous.

"I hear that you are Grimfir Boldrock's squire." Kyly smiled, searchingly.

"According to my sources, you are the secret lover of Yartha the Platinumed Voice, Siren of Star Seven," said Ulmuth, causing Charley inexplicably to blush, though partly it was due to the odor Ulmuth released from his mouth.

"Word has it you are the Crown Prince of the Universe," countered Kyly.

"Some say you can see into the future, but only when the future is horrible," chirped Ulmuth, not to be outdone.

"There are pictures of you eating your own weight in sand," claimed Kyly, taking an entirely different and ineffective tack.

"You two must be rumor-mongers, because I am just Charley Tooth," said the only one in the room who was qualified to say such a thing.

"I suppose," said Ulmuth, "in a sense, we both are prone to hearsay, which is quite different from heresy. And as that is true, perhaps you would be so kind as to oblige us with some dirt with which we might maintain our livelihoods?"

"I don't do anything, and I haven't done much,"

said Charley, again blushing at the thought that he might be letting down these two honest gossips.

"Good Boy," cried Kyly, "there certainly doesn't need to be much truth in it! Just enough detail about yourself that might conflate the probable with the possible with the preposterous!"

"Well, I am not from this world, and I have no idea how I got here. I am an average student on Earth. I don't much like basketball, but I play it for school. I like drawing. I have two sisters. We have a very good dog named Shiny. I got sucked away from school about ten minutes ago, I think." Charley hoped to win over these first beings to talk to him.

"That is silly," said Ulmuth Wagonspack, Jr., who promptly turned and left.

"Grimfir and the rest of the party are still waiting for you. I wouldn't keep them waiting. You know how Grimfir is," said a disappointed Kyly.

"But I *don't* know how he is," said Charley, but Kyly had already left, unhearing. And suddenly Charley thought that maybe it wasn't so hard to guess how Grimfir was.

Just about two minutes ago, Grimfir had finished the platter of salmon-and-artichoke slivers, and was now standing idly by, trying to ignore the pressing pressure facing him from the party guests. Now, two minutes sounds like a short time, but if you were to put this book down right now and stand still for two full minutes—by the clock—with a crowd of people waiting for you to do something, you might begin to appreciate the growing feelings of perturbation that were bombarding Grimfir at this moment, and he doesn't even have your amount of patience. Also, a minute on Nivalg is several seconds longer than a minute here on Earth.

The party was mumbling and murmuring, with the exception of HrYlgYr, who, still having no mouth, could not do much more than muffle. Grimfir, a profound sweater, was now sweating profusely, which would seem odd here on Earth, where the reptilian sorts don't perspire. But there was Grimfir Boldrock, stout, thick, husky, solid, and constant, semirefined, and sweating. Grimfir was dark green and lizardly, and when out in high society, he was given to wearing lots of ruffles, though he had a hard time keeping them clean. Though not young, he was certainly still a brute, and he delicately chose to ignore the thinning bumpy scales on the top of his head that ran down to the nape of his neck.

"Where is that dear Charley Tooth dear of yours, my dearest Grimfir?" asked Hololo Summersweat, who was understandably eager for the party to continue. Her purple velvet dress had a small dark stain on it— even a lifetime of being multi-tentacled does not mean that there isn't an increased probability of spilling.

"My young squire has a stomach wound to which he must attend, and I have no doubt he will be along in no more than a matter of seconds," gruffed Grimfir, giving what he believed to be a charming edge to his voice and stepping over to the bar, where there was an ugly ice sculpture presumably meant to be of Hololo Summersweat herself.

Now, it is worth discussing Grimfir's answer, which was not true. Grimfir was not an intentional liar, as far as he knew, and as far as we know. However, in times of error and awkwardness and uncertainty, rather than flaring eyespots or changing colors,

Grimfir above all valued saving face. What he said in this case to Dame Summersweat was partly to cover for himself and his squire—Grimfir was protective of his own—and partly because Charley had indeed looked queasy. True, using the word "wound" was misleading, but who among us has not exaggerated here and there a bit? I know that I did once. Charley was queasy, but that's partly because that very day, as a snack before he played cards at the seniors' table, he had decided to buy a can of chocolate frosting and a jar of peanut butter, and then see how far he could make it through the two of them together. He made it farther than you would have thought, if you have ever undertaken such an endeavor.

Descending the stairs, Charley once again had to negotiate the obstacle Trynl and Kwuito created with their seated selves. The two of them were perhaps slightly more irked than the rest of the party guests, as they had needed to adjust to accommodate Charley's going and coming, as well as Kyly's and Ulmuth's. Regardless, the atmosphere downstairs was fraught with antsy anticipation. The crowd did not exactly hush as Charley reentered the fray, but there was a dip in the register of the sound they had been producing, approximating the most quiet many of them had ever been. Please remember this was a noisy bunch. Everyone turned an eye or similarly sighted appendage in Charley's direction, but as it was pretty clear that he wasn't about to volunteer any-thing, the focus shifted back to Grimfir.

"Ahem."

Charley stopped where he was, on the last step, and looked at Grimfir, who continued:

"Ladies and gentlemen and et cetera . . ."

"Wait!" cried Trynl, "We can't *see* from back here!"

Charley, Grimfir, and the ladies and gentlemen and et cetera turned to look at Trynl and Kwuito, who indeed were sitting smack-dab behind Charley, not able to see the pallor in his face, the sweat on his brow, or even the flap of salmon on Grimfir's slightly disappearing chin.

"See what?" grumped Grimfir, unhappy to be interrupted, especially before he got anywhere with his speech.

"The entertainment, of course! Your squire's performance! And what of his stomach wound? We're stuck behind him, and what's the point in that?" replied Trynl, perhaps in a more offended tone than Grimfir's.

Grimfir might have been second-rate in all his professional endeavors (indeed he was), and he might have been awfully bristly much of the time without good cause (also true), and he might often have ignored other people's advice, criticism, and warnings (he was proud of it, in fact), but in spite of this bullishness, he always had a strong tether to his heart that yanked him when matters of audience were involved. Nothing could spring Grimfir to action, give him that quick, warm spread of joy, or lash him sharply like the reaction of an audience. And for a slightly overweight, slightly middle-aged lizard, he was almost frighteningly adroit at changing gears without blinking.

"A million apologies, Trynl and Kwuito, on top of a thousand acts of contrition. Boy! Come over here! Show the kind crowd your awkward features and featherless arms!"

Charley crossed to Grimfir, wondering with each

step if it was the right thing to do. He slowed a bit as he drew within a few feet of the formally dressed reptile.

"If nothing else," he supposed to himself, "this Grimfir seems to be associated with me, and therefore probably on my side. Besides, what else is there for me to do?"

And then, a second later, "What stomach wound?"

Grimfir placed a sweaty, scaly hand on Charley and turned him to face the eager assembly of odd beings.

"I have no idea about anything that's going on," whispered Charley to Grimfir.

"You can do this. You *have to*," replied Grimfir from the side of his mouth, gripping Charley tightly with the last two words.

"Do what?" said Charley, practically not bothering to lower his voice.

Grimfir took a step forward, hand still on Charley, and made a swooping flourish with his other hand.

"Ladies and gentlemen and et cetera . . ."

At this, there was a chuckle all around, as people like to chuckle when there is something familiar, even if there is nothing particularly funny about the familiar thing. Yes, it can get annoying, but people will keep on doing it.

Grimfir continued. "Allow me to present to you the amateurish and therefore charming, not to mention thought-provoking, magical derring-do of my squire-at-arms, protégé, and errand boy, the somewhat inimitable Charley Tooth!"

Grimfir took a step back and to the side, propelling Charley forward a couple of steps at the same time.

The room was silent. All eyes were on Charley,

except for Charley's, which were on everybody's. Charley had not felt this much at a loss since he was mistakenly enrolled in Advanced Chemistry as a freshman, and showed up to Mr. Blatt's class in the midst of seniors. On the first week's test, he received a 22% and an invitation from Mr. Blatt to explain his poor performance in front of the class. Once it was discovered that the registrar had made the error, Charley was very neatly moved into Ms. Vaneer's Health class, where Charley proved to be a slightly above-average student.

"I don't know what it is you want me to do," said Charley, finding that his current circumstances had instilled in him the initial reaction to be instantaneously honest.

"I hope and hope that your stomach wound is quite much better, my precious dearie," said Hololo Summersweat with a smile.

As instantaneous honesty didn't figure into this query, Charley quickly reverted to a time-tested response, "Humm, well."

"Of course he's fine!" said Grimfir grandly.

"Do something!" cried Flossy the One-Eyed Jerk, completely in character.

"I don't know what it is you want me to do," reiterated Charley, who found himself suddenly thinking about when he was twelve years old. Summers seem to last forever when you are twelve. Thick, hot nights with hazy fireflies outnumbered the heavy days of sickeningly sweetly scented honeysuckle. Long, long days were spent at the neighborhood pool, where Charley played Marco Polo, Corner Tag, and Kickboard Baseball with kids about whom all he knew was their first names.

Cassie Sullivan was an exception, and an exceptional girl. She was the best swimmer of all the kids, and in Sharks and Minnows she could hold her breath for a full four minutes, allowing her to spend an entire round underwater, almost impossible to catch. Charley knew her, like most of the kids, only from the pool, as she went to a different school. She practically lived at the pool, and Charley often thought of one hot day, the sky close with purple and grey clouds, when he was at the pool and a thunderstorm struck. The pool had been slow and thinly attended that day, anyway, due to the crouching storm, and the water had been too tepid to enjoy. At the first crack of thunder, the lifeguards headed into the snack bar, but Charley and Cassie sought refuge behind the check-in desk, which, though covered, was still exposed to the rain. Cassie curled up on the fresh white cotton towels under the desk, towels folded into long triangles and still retaining warmth from the dryer.

Charley, too tall even at twelve to cramp himself into the towel slot, sat Indian-style on the smooth concrete floor. The two of them talked the afternoon away, and it was the first time that Charley felt as though talking to a girl made his chest too tight. Cassie had zinc on her nose, despite there not being a drop of sun the entire day, and her normally curly, curly dark blond hair was still wetly smooth and brown from the last lap she had taken, when the rain began to pockmark the water. Charley felt closer to Cassie that afternoon than he had ever felt, ever ever, to anyone else in his life.

Two days later was the next time Charley saw Cassie. Again, they were at the pool, and the bad weather still lingered, though maybe a dozen kids had turned out, having nothing better to do, as it was too wet for fireworks. Charley was playing Pickle on the strip of grass next to the pool, and Cassie was competing against Gorey and Little Joe to see who could go farthest underwater without kicking. There was a sudden commotion as Charley left base, and he turned to see kids pulling Gorey out of the six-feet-deep section of the pool. The on-duty lifeguard was in the snack bar getting a grilled cheese. Gorey apparently had pushed his limits, staying under longer than he could, and was now light blue, his nipples dark brown. Charley felt the wet tennis ball smack him in the chest, leaving a red mark that would endure for two days. The kids ran over to the side of the pool, where Gorey was dumped, unconscious, in a heap. Everyone stared, but no one moved toward the quiet body. Rory and Dave, who had pulled Gorey from the pool, even moved back into the anonymity of the crowd, having done all they knew to do. Clearly something horrible and unforgettable was happening. Cassie, who was the last one to know, having of course been able to make it the farthest underwater and missed the developments, came panting through the mass of people.

"Do something!" she cried. "Someone do something!"

Efren, the oldest kid there, stepped forward and rolled Gorey completely onto his back. Charley and Cassie made eye contact, and Charley was scared of how wild her face looked and how great her body looked, water still dripping from her broad shoulders, running down her pronounced lats. Just then, Tracy the lifeguard sprinted up and began CPR. Charley could see around her mouth and on her chin bits of cooling cheese from the sandwich she had been eating. Gorey turned out fine, but after that day, Charley could never look at Gorey or Cassie again. He and Cassie seemed to have come to an immediate understanding that they didn't know each other, and though they saw each other occasionally through the years until Charley's departure from Earth, they never again even said hello. But Charley could always hear her, imploringly shrill, demanding, "Do something!" Then, as now, Charley did not know what it was that he was supposed to do.

"Please understand," Grimfir interjected, "that young Mr. Tooth is not a professional with a pre-set pre-formance, a confident bag of tricks, a repeatable show. He is, as I have pointed out almost to an embarrassing degree, an amateur. He does not know what it is you want of him, meaning that he is open to requests. Penny magic, intermediate spells, and occasions of brilliance are the menu. A showman's boy, Mr. Tooth will astound and entertain, though please accept his apologies for his humble background and talent. Requests? Requests? Requests? Parlor tricks and party laughs? Requests?"

The Abbot of St. Orson spoke up quickly. "Show us how to make a banjo from nothing!"

Baggo G. Winnebago jumped in. "Make four aces appear out of nowhere!"

Riboflavia Gumchewie slurred, "How do you get someone to make the move on you before you pass out?"

Pointing at where his mouth would be, HrYlgYr gestured hopefully for the trick that would give him some means of oral expression.

Charley stood silent.

"Friends and Strangers, we shall indeed build the evening's climax around these requests, but please allow Onnser the semi-Magnificent, our featured headliner for the evening, the decency of the more elaborate feats of magic. Mr. Tooth shall warm us all up with some fire-snapping and image manipulation. Charley, the floor and very air are yours. . . ."

Grimfir, so saying, took another grand bowing step backward, leaving Charley once again the object of fixated eyes.

"Hum, well, um," began Charley, trailing off as he searched his pockets for any little bit or trinket that he might be able to use to distract the crowd.

"Those are magic words," whispered The Tiny Smippens, entranced by the occasion.

"All the good magicians have their own," replied Lightwing the Diseased, with a slightly phlegmy cough.

Charley fingered in his pocket a warm quarter. He pulled it out, rolling it in his fingers. He noticed everyone staring at his hand. He held the quarter up flatly between his left thumb and forefinger. This was a trick Charley's painfully punning biology teacher, Mr. Klumidia, tended to show his class every Friday afternoon. Charley had tried it only four times before. This same Mr. Klumidia would often ask, "Is Charley Tooth abscessed today?" instead of "absent today?" And he would only ask when Charley was, in fact, present.

He swept his left hand from across his body to the full extent his shoulder would allow, pointing at his clasped fingertips with his right hand. He kept his left arm extended, hand held in the "OK" gesture, but parallel to the ground. He brought his open right hand smoothly over to his left hand, and made to grasp through the circle holding the quarter. Here, he lost his focus as he tried to draw his left fingers in to his palm as his right hand swept down, making it appear as though he had grabbed the quarter with his right hand. Charley suddenly realized the quarter was no longer in his fingers. Nearly panicked, he tried to sense where it was, but to no avail. Still, the trick could work, as long as the quarter, secreted wherever it was, didn't ping to the floor. Best to go on with it. Charlie drew his hands apart, his right hand now in a fist. With his left hand, he pointed at the right, and slowly opened the fist, finger by finger. His hand was empty, of course.

Kwuito Karbelbammer, still seated on the stair, gasped in astonishment. "Magic!"

Hololo Summersweat's tentacles softly flapped on the floor in polite, hostess-ly appreciation.

Ulmuth Wagonspack, Jr., spoke up loudly, "Let's see the other hand!"

Charley felt a rush of righteousness now, having completely lost track of the quarter but now being able to show his left hand was empty, quite uncharacteristic of how the trick was designed to work. He slowly unfurled his left hand to reveal nothing. The crowd looked to Ulmuth, who heretofore had been looking rather smug. At the empty sight, Ulmuth raised his glass to his lips, taking a long, long drink without ever removing his eyes from Charley. The crowd looked back to Charley, who stood with both hands outstretched, palms open.

A sharp, sudden pain in the center of his palm forced Charley to cry out and crumple his palm so tightly he could feel his fingernails dig in. With his right hand, he grabbed his left wrist. Slowly, he opened his hand, which had felt like it was giving birth (or what Charley imagined a hand giving birth might feel like, knowing full well it was a hard thing to imagine and really not a fair comparison to imagine in the first place). There, in the smack-dab middle of his left hand, was the missing quarter, plain as day for all to see. A murmur went up from the crowd.

"I knew it! I *told* you the gold was in his left hand!" crowed Ulmuth, relieved to see that he was sort of correct (and incidentally assuming the coin to be typical of the region: a gold piece depicting on one side a hedgehog-like creature caught in a cyclone, with the other side showing a blizzard).

Charley, understandably astounded at the appearance of the quarter, and still stinging in the heart of his palm, jerked his hand, sending the quarter through the air, landing at the feet of the group of erstwhile singers, who backed a bit away from the magical talisman, as though it were burning hot and wicked, which it was not (it was, in fact, just a quarter).

Predictably, it was HrYlgYr who was the most audacious one, first picking up the quarter—after all, he had the least to lose, as the others still stood to lose their mouths. And so, it was HrYlgYr who first noticed that the quarter was not a Nivalgian gold piece. He examined it closely, first because of the suspicious magic they had all just witnessed, but then a second time due to the grimier carriage of this silver-colored circle. He tried to get the attention of his companion singers, Lady Footslip, Mucker McFlugle, Yorgad, and Glubdort Minxer, (Slusie Crinfaber had unwittingly eaten some hruckney, which disagreed with her, and she was therefore otherwise engaged at the moment). Mucker finally realized that HrYlgYr had something interesting to indicate about the coin. Mucker looked at it, then looked up and said loudly, "It's no longer gold!"

It wasn't a "What?" that came out from the single voice of the crowd, but the sound that did arise was similar in tone and intent.

Mucker spoke again, "He has turned gold into silver!"

"I bet it's not real silver," countered Ulmuth, though he was visibly bewildered by the stunt Charley had just pulled. For that matter, so was Charley.

"I think it's actually made out of nickel or something," said Charley.

"Not gold!" exclaimed Hololo, who had not been paying attention to the trick but rather was showing the appearance of being enraptured by it. She said it half-worried that the guests had discovered some element of her party was not of the proper quality, and nothing scared her more.

Grimfir took to the middle of the hubbub, holding up his clawed hands. "Thank you, One and All, for the warm response to young Tooth's first trick of the evening."

Behind him, HrYlgYr was quietly pressing the coin to the featureless area below his nose, apparently in the hopes that the magic might somehow rub off.

Tandor Ovenheat stepped toward the speaker.

"Hold a second, my good Grimfir," he said. "I don't think this first trick is quite over. After all, if it's amateur night, we are certainly both surprised and impressed at the opening trick. But shouldn't we have had the opportunity to inspect the gold *before* the trick, to ascertain whether it was in fact a gold piece to *begin* with? In most polite circles, that is considered standard etiquette."

"Tandor," Grimfir replied, "we all know that you have a certain education in white and black magic, and that your family is well-respected in its support of legitimate sorcery as well as its debunking of the frauds. In our particular case, though, I kindly ask that you keep in mind that these are parlor tricks of a novice, and therefore should not be taken too seriously, and the poor boy certainly doesn't need too heartless an eye with heavy hands upon him tonight."

"Of course, Grimfir, of course, but doesn't a neophyte such as Charley Tooth here, someone looking to make a name for himself in a career of diablerie, need to have critical feedback early on, so as to prune back bad habits before they set? Just as a sword being formed needs a hammer to temper it to perfection, this young wizard needs to have the kinks in his presentation pounded out of him. Rather than shielding himself from such scrutiny, he should actively seek it out, no? That is, if he wants to be a good magician. I take it that is what you both want, isn't it, Grimfir? Do you want him to become a good magician, or even a great one?"

"Yes. Yes, of course," replied Grimfir, with the sinking feeling he was about to be bested, or that it had just happened already.

Tandor took the coin from HrYlgYr, and looked at it closely.

"And you, Charley Tooth, what kind of wizard do *you* want to be?" he asked, though he looked at Grimfir.

"Well, um, I'm really not much of a wizard really," stammered Charley.

"No, not yet, I don't suppose, but I asked you what

kind you want to be—in the future."

Charley stood silently, not sure of what to do, yet again.

"Answer the man!" yelled Flossy the One-Eyed Jerk, clarifying the situation and reminding all of why he bore his particular sobriquet.

"Why don't you show us another trick, then, so we can perhaps get an idea for ourselves?" said Tandor.

Charley hadn't anticipated a second trick. Somehow, he had innately believed that things would revert to normal or the attention would be drawn to someone else once he had performed that first bit of sleight-of-hand. The fact that Charley was not thinking ahead explained why he was not a very good chess player, much to his father's quiet—unspoken, even—disappointment. However, Luck or Fate or Fortune, perhaps even Skill or Hardian Hap, had ingrained in Charley's character the ability to act nearly without thinking, to stall for time, to have the motor click almost automatically.

"Well, my next trick, you see, would also be in the same vein as the tricks that have gone before: full of magic and import, carrying in it the vestiges of the mysticism that has been passed down, Originator to Disciple, coming to fruition in what might be considered by many—many magicians, many people, many nations—as nothing less than a life-altering way. Almost a kind of new science, a breaking of the mold, a new crushing idea of how the mind and body work in the physical world . . ."

His mind was racing as he waited for his hands to pick up the slack on their own. He was not disappointed. Well, not entirely.

He found himself doing the thumb trick. Yes, that

very selfsame trick. His right hand, palm facing out, two fingers closed over the tip of his right thumb, moved to meet his left hand, palm hidden, thumb folded.

Quickly, almost cartoonishly but more circus-like, Charley's hand did the detachable thumb bit three or four times, ending with him flexing his left thumb, as though to ascertain its maneuverability after such an undertaking. The room was silent.

A silent reception from a room of spectators means exactly one of exactly three things: 1) they loved it; 2) they hated it; 3) they had no idea what the hell just happened.

To cheat just a little bit, in what could be considered a subset of the above, it could happen that there is a mixture of the three things, and it could all be frosted by people who are in such disbelief at the inanity or obviousness of the presentation that the only appropriate reaction, in the absence of an appropriate reaction, is thunderous silence. Such a silence met Charley and his enchanted thumb.

Grimfir, who had been suitably impressed though superiorly critical of Charley's oral presentation, spoke into the void.

"Thank you, thank you, one and all, for your stunned silence." Here, he faltered.

"What a seemingly magical thumb!" commented Hololo loudly, supporting her evening's entertainment.

Tandor smiled a too-kind smile. "What a lovely rendition of the detachable-thumb trick. Truly, a nearly practiced event."

"Did you see that?" broke in Flossy, who had been waiting his whole life to be convinced of something.

"He entirely disconnected his thumb and then reattached it in working order again!"

It was this sort of response that went a long way to justify Grimfir's belief in the ultimate salvation found in people's gullibility. He turned to look at Charley, this time with a warning flash in his eyes.

"Grimfir!" called Kyly Dewdropsonton, "tell us again the charming story of how you became a wizard!"

Grimfir smiled and gave a slight bow. "Of course. It was a complete misunderstanding. Not long after I was born, my parents took me to the District Registrar, who was an old man, hard of hearing. When I was presented, my mother said, 'He will be a great lizard.' The Registrar recorded in my file that I was due to become 'a great wizard,' and so my path was laid clear.

The audience responded with laughter, even those who had heard it before. It reminded Charley of *The Pirates of Penzance*, his mother's favorite musical. Charley smiled at the thought of it and looked to Grimfir.

"Oh? Are you the very model of a modern merry something something something something and so on?"

Everyone looked at him strangely. Grimfir held his hands out to the crowd.

"Excuse my protégé, please. Opening-night jitters. However, I am sure we could coax him into performing another feat of magic for us?" Grimfir began clapping, and the audience joined in. Using the sound of the applause to mask his words to Charley, he recommended that Charley do something truly dazzling or be finished, socially, forever.

Adding further nervousness to repeated embarrassment, Charley struggled to think what other magic he
knew—anything at all. He never was successful at
pulling off card tricks. He thought quickly and
painfully, and then he struck upon the only extended
bit of "magic" that he had ever presented.

"Ladies and gentlemen, ladies and gentlemen," he
began, "I would like to bewitch you with a short presentation on 'The Magic of the Pyrenees.' Stretching
over two hundred fifty miles from the Bay of
Biscay...." A purist, or perhaps even a passing amateur, might argue that Charley was not performing
magic, and that person would be correct. Charley
was, in fact, reciting a discourse he had to give that
year in Speech and Communication class. It had
nothing to do with magic, other than in the title. To
be sure, Kwuito Karbelbammer found it interesting
that the highest point in the Pyrenees, Pico de Aneto,
rose to 11,168 feet, but that was hardly magical by the
standards most of the listeners were prepared to
accept. Charley had just finished talking about baux-
ite mining and was about to go into "The Peace of the
Pyrenees" of 1659, which ended the Franco-Spanish
War, when there was a terrific boom from outside in
the driveway. Mercifully—not only for Charley but
also for the entire audience—the commotion was
enough to draw everybody outside, even those people
who would otherwise do their best to avoid going
toward a sound such as an unknown explosion.

Out in the driveway there hung a dissipating cloud
of smoke over the carriage that was drawn up by the
front door—Onnser the semi-Magnificent's carriage.
It was boxy and black, with silver slivers, spangly
shiny, swooping down from high in the back to low in

the front. The horses were white with black legs, manes, and tails. The carriage driver's name was Vang, though at the time only Onnser knew it, and it wouldn't have helped anyone particularly if they did know it. Vang was trying to get the door open for Onnser to emerge, but the last fifteen minutes of effort had been with no result other than to make Vang's fingertips raw. Inside, Onnser could be heard speaking encouraging words to Vang, but the door remained locked. All of the guests had come out of the Summersweat Mansion to see what the excitement was about, excluding Riboflavia Gumchewie and Sir Dorchester the Beggar, who, inside, continued their descent into what would be either love or slumber. The Abbot of St. Orson, though he accompanied the group outside, quickly made his getaway into the night, unable to face up to his failure at constructing the banjo he had bragged about.

The Abbot of St. Orson stole away, crossing the driveway, darting among the cars, carriages, and other vehicles until he made it to the woods. From there, he picked his way lightly through the dark under- and overgrowth, remarkably adept at finding safe passage with minimal light from the moons—as though this was not the first time he had found himself absconding in the middle of the night in order to save himself from further embarrassment. Forty minutes in the forest, including through two streams and one drainage that was now no more than mud, the Abbot came to the edge of the trees, which was coincidentally the edge of Lake Fritz, a rather large mess of a lake shaped like a wild head of thick hair. On the other side of the lake was a footpath that leads up to the Monastery of St. Orson, home to the good Abbot.

All he had to do was swim across the lake, and it would be a mere fifteen-minute amble to the sanctuary of his own room. We might as well remind ourselves—if only to contribute to the universal snickering at his expense that the Abbot was feeling at this very moment—that swimming was beyond his power. So, the night weighing him down, the Abbot of St. Orson set off along the perimeter of the lake, sticking through mud holes, tripping over hidden logs, and wrapping his shins (unintentionally) in more than plenty of nettles (more than one nettle is plenty, and there were more than more than one). After about twenty minutes of this misery, equaling about one quarter of one quarter mile, the Abbot suddenly remembered the pouch he had in the inside pocket of his robe. He sat down, scratched his legs furiously, and pulled out the leather bag, which had once been kind of rough but was now worn smooth along the seams, as well as along the neck. These smooth patches caught the light of both of the moons that were out. There was another shiny spot the Abbot had not previously noticed, about the size of his thumb. He rubbed this particular spot, feeling how the material moved ever so slightly, back and forth in brisk unison. He judged the weight of the pouch in his hand, and sniffed at the rich deep smell of the leather. Slowly, he shook the pouch and undid the leather lace at the top, careful not to spill. Into it he dipped two fingers and scooped a bit, much as you or I might do with sunscreen, were we to carry it around in convenient leather pouches. You may argue the degree of convenience; I will not.

The pouch, and its contents, had been a gift from The Historic Ganka, one of the most renowned magi-

cians on the planet. The Abbot had taught The
Historic Ganka how to draw in three dimensions—
simple cubes, cylinders, vanishing points, and such.
Not anything complicated, to be sure, but Ganka had
spent so much time developing his magic that he
missed out on all the discoveries that come with doo-
dling with your classmates, copying pictures out of
comic books, or attempting to eat a can of chocolate
frosting in one sitting. And so, once the Abbot had
imparted the basic knowledge to Ganka (thereby
allowing Ganka to complete his masterpiece book,
The Magic that Is and Maybe Isn't), Ganka presented
him with this magical bit of stuff. The Historic Ganka
had a justified reputation as a magician's magician,
but he had fallen out of favor with the Ruling Powers,
so that now people had to whisper his name, or not
even refer to him at all, lest the prying eyes and ears
of the authorities exact punishment. In fact, The
Historic Ganka had been officially stripped of his definite article ("The"), and instead was to be known by
an indefinite article. The trouble was, much to the
credit of the sinister cleverness (or clever sinisterness)
of the Ruling Powers, nobody knew if it was proper to
say A Historic Ganka or An Historic Ganka, and the
punishment was therefore all the more successful and
severe—people stopped saying his name pretty much
altogether because of this uncertainty.

The Historic Ganka was short, heavy, clean-shaven,
and tended to wear a sort of long Nehru-jacket-type
of garment.

The Abbot of St. Orson sat on a damp log by the
edge of the lake, fingers covered in the softly glowing
goo from the pouch. He examined it closely, noticing
again that it looked like tiny, tiny thistles threaded

together in fuzzy blue syrup. Though they were in fact tiny, tiny thistles threaded together, the fuzzy blue syrup was not really fuzzy blue syrup; the magic simply gave it that appearance, as it fit in with the perception of what the stuff should look like, according to exhaustive market research done by legions of apprentices. The Abbot removed his sandals and began gooping up his legs, starting with the soles of the feet and ending mid-calf. Like many men of superstitious habits or vocations, the Abbot always began addressing his body right side first, then left. Whether it be putting on socks, shoes, and pants, or taking them off, he always started with the right side. And so he slathered his feet in this mystical slime. By the time he had wiped his hands on the bottom of his robe and tied his sandals together, the Abbot could feel the potion begin to burn. Quickly he stood up, hopped to the lakeside, and tottered. Always he tottered, readying himself for that baffling first step, and then he took it. Right foot first, he strode out flat-footed, full of shaky faith in what he was doing. He was always tempted to slide the first step onto the water, but the fear of scraping off his hydrogen dioxide protector forced him to take that giant first step, encouraging him to put the whole of the bottom of his foot, toes splayed wide, solidly onto the water. The water gave somewhat, and the burrs of thistles knitted about his foot furiously, racing to and fro, nearly humming with activity. The first ten or so steps were all about establishing balance, which the Abbot did. He found his water legs, and a short couple of hops led him into wide-legged stomps, tip-toed mincing bites, and one-footed leaps from which he nearly toppled, time and time again. A smile as bright as the moon creased his pallid face.

You might be thinking that this is unusual. You're right—most abbots know how to swim and don't need to rely on magic to cross a lake (especially one that isn't more than six feet deep and is warm all year round).

The problem, of course, being that once you can rely on something like magic to get the job done, there is no real motivation to learn how to do the task on your own.

He delighted in this water dancing, the feeling of the water slightly giving way to his feet as the charmed goop swirled with activity, keeping him afloat. Lightly making his way across the lake, for a moment forgetting why it was that he was fleeing secretly away through the night, the Abbot was as happy as he had ever been. A little over halfway across he remembered that he made a fool of himself at the party, that he made promises he could never keep, and that he ignominiously stole away when everyone was drawn to the trouble at the carriage.

The Abbot stopped his traipsing, and he slowly bobbed up and down in the water as the potion worked furiously not to let him sink. Overcome with guilt, he quickly walked all the way back to where he first stepped onto the lake. He walked ashore, and sat down upon the same mossy log as before. With a stick, he began to scrape at the magic on his legs, and he was successful at peeling it off in strips. He untied his sandals, put them back on, and walked off into the thickets, picking his long way home. By the log he left two glowing messy heaps, looking like fallen elastic-less socks, slowly fading into the earth. By the time he made it home to the monastery, his legs and arms were criss-crossed with red lines from the thorns and branches. He was tired and miserable, but felt slightly better at not having taken the easy way home, just this once.

Back in the Summersweat driveway, the party guests had gathered semicircularly around the right side of Onnser's carriage, giving it a wide berth first of all because it contained a semi-magnificent magician, and secondly because something seemed to have gone wrong.

Vang paid next to no notice to the throng who had been summoned by the explosive but unsuccessful attempt of Onnser to undo the stuck door from the inside.

"Hello, my dear brilliant Onnser," called Hololo. "It's me, Hololo Summersweat. Is everything all right and okay, my bright friend? I didn't realize your show would be starting in the out-of-doors tonight! Ah ha ha ha ha . . ."

"Ah, Madame Summersweat!" cried the unseen Onnser from within the coach. "My unmatched hostess! Alas, I am not even out-of-doors yet, which is precisely the trouble."

"How charming, you gifted man! Is this the beginning, then? Where it all starts?"

"No, my lady, this is me stuck in the carriage, rather unrelated to the show I had planned for the evening. I cannot imagine what the problem is, but perhaps there is someone else out there who might be able to assist me?"

"You seem to have regular difficulties with your carriage door. Perhaps it is time to have a locksmith refurbish the lock?" said Ulmuth.

"A capital idea, sir! However, that useful advice does

nothing for the present moment! I seek immediate assistance!" came the reply from within.

"Your coachman is already hard at work, Onnser, semi-Magnificent," said Tandor.

"Yes, Vang is always hard at work. But no shame on him, this door is quite locked. I smell something of the magical persuasion out there. Who can help, who can help?"

"Well, Master Onnser the semi-Magnificent, Grimfir Boldrock, the entertaining magician, is here with his squire. These two may be the handiest around for the difficulty that constrains you," replied Tandor somewhat coolly.

"That is outstanding!" said Onnser. "I do believe that Gromfir and I have crossed paths time and occasion in the past, and now the present, and presumably the future!"

"It's Grimfir, sir," snapped Grimfir, feeling ornery mostly at being put more or less on the spot by Tandor Ovenheat, but also due to Onnser getting his name wrong.

"Ah, so there you are, and of course it is Grimfir, for how could you be any different, or anyone else! Now, as you can see, I'm in a slight fix, and your capable maneuverings would be most in order, and most appreciated. My hope and faith lie in you, so what do you say to getting me out?"

Grimfir felt a reptilian chill creep through his naturally cold blood.

"Well, sir, I am flattered beyond flattery that you would select someone as humble as I am humble for such a noble task, such a fruitful partnership, such a boundless adventure—"

"I say, Grimfir, the speech is lovely so far, but life is

in action. Let's have at it, shall you?" came the semi-amused voice of the semi-magnificent man within.

"Yes, excellent idea," said Grimfir, stung, thinking to himself that he would no longer so generously throw around the deferential "sir" with Onnser so much. In fact, right then and there Grimfir decided to emphasize the "semi" in "semi-magnificent" when addressing this particular wizard. He approached the door and peered closely at the lock. He stuck a dark-green-almost-black claw into the keyhole. He blew a short blast of salmon-flavored air into it. He gauged the smoothness of the side of the carriage with his hand, and then stepped back.

"You are correct, Onnser the *semi*-Magnificent. This particular situation can easily be fixed. I would therefore like to bring forth my squire, one Charley Tooth, who has of late been performing feats of magic for these kind people, and who could not only benefit from the furthering of his meager reputation, but also the furthering of his practicing of magic. I therefore bequeath this opportunity to perform to him."

"Your generosity is simply astounding," said Onnser from within.

Charley, thinking that he had already dodged the bullet of attention, now found himself back in the crosshairs of the party's focus. He quickly rose to the occasion:

"Whump?" he said, or asked, or exclaimed, depending on any number of things, but nonetheless sounding like a walrus being hit by a rotten watermelon.

"Well, boy. Don't just gawk about and make sounds like a moggler being hit by a wet cabbage," said Grimfir. A moggler is the Nivalgian version of a walrus, but Grimfir was quite wrong in describing the sound as involving a wet cabbage. He just wasn't the best at descriptions. "Get to it, and use the external. . . unlocking . . .spell I've been asking you to practice."

We have already touched upon Grimfir's rather lax adherence to what many of us would term "The Truth." But here, again, he was not lying. Not completely. In fact, for the last two minutes or so, Grimfir had indeed been asking Charley to have practiced this particular spell. He had been asking this of Charley over and over, to himself, as soon as he gauged the situation with Onnser's carriage. Charley, and the rest of the non-telepathic world, might not have known it, but Grimfir had nearly been *praying* that Charley had spent some time practicing this spell, despite the fact that Grimfir was quite certain Charley had not exactly ever in his life ever performed anything remotely similar in sight, sound, or smell to what would be ever termed genuine magic, prior to this evening. But then, what is life without hope?

Grimfir glared at Charley, trying to convey not only this hope but also a substantial amount of threatening insistence.

"Perhaps what Tooth needs is some encouragement," asked Tandor, who turned to the crowd to elicit a response.

"No, no encouragement! No encouragement!" said Charley immediately, as he really didn't like this kind of public encouragement from strangers, one of whom seemed a little too interested in the qualifications that Charley did not have to be a magician.

Tandor and Grimfir both eyed Charley keenly, with some surprise.

53

"I do not ask for encouragement," Charley recovered, "but I ask that everyone focus his or her . . . its . . . energy on the matter of the lock, to help me direct some magic its way."

Both Grimfir and Tandor smiled at this, but for different reasons. Grimfir thought to himself that the boy was a natural showman, quick on his feet, who, for his odd ways and lack of experience, might have a few good ruses and crowd-pleasers that Grimfir himself could ably use. Tandor, all the way on the far other hand, smiled because he saw that Charley was a natural showman quick on his feet, but clearly covering for the fact that he had no idea what he was going to do, magicwise. Sometimes, when a hunter sees his cornered prey scrambling desperately to stay alive, he can't help but smile to know that the chase is over. He also recognized that, though Charley knew the right kind of words to say in this particular situation to create a diversion, he did so with a characteristic lack of confidence, the same lack of confidence that kept him from ever asking out Grace O'Malley or Cassie Sullivan and a number of other girls we have yet to discuss and with whom, at any rate, Tandor Ovenheat was completely unfamiliar.

Not being a complete fool, Charley first tried the door himself, half-prepared for this to be some royal prank with the door already unlocked, or not even a door at all but an impenetrable wall. But it was a door, and, as his tugging demonstrated, it was locked. Though Charley couldn't see it, inside Onnser grinned at the attempt. Charley took a step back.

He felt like he did when he was playing basketball; that is, awful. The attention was focused on him, as people were looking for the magic, just as being tall meant that he was always passed the ball and expected to score, and he really didn't know what to do. He looked around, hoping for some way out, someone to pass to, or something to help him. He espied Grimfir's belt, in which there was secured some sort of handled weapon. Charley made a motion to Grimfir and said, "Grimfir, would you please hand me the tool that looks like an ice pick you have on your belt?"

Grimfir obliged, visibly wary that Charley would resort to something so mundane. Charley, not noticing, quickly looked at the object, which had a skinny yet sturdy metal shaft that tapered to a point like a pencil set into a solid wooden handle that resembled that of a quality screwdriver.

"What is this?" asked Charley.

"An ice pick," replied Grimfir, curtly yet deferentially, as though all his life he were accustomed to patiently yet acerbically having to point out the obvious to those who were in authority to him. Not that he felt Charley was superior to him, but he felt that Charley was acting as though he thought *he* was.

This identification of the ice pick surprised Charley more than anything else so far since he had arrived on Nivalg. Somehow, finding himself suddenly in a strange world, with a variety of strange creatures who managed to talk, dress, and eat in a variety of strange ways, with a plethora of strange accoutrements, had all been so abrupt and complete that it almost made sense, as a dream follows its own outrageous logic, but then the sheer mundanity of this Earthly ice pick, which, to be fair, is not even all that mundane a thing to encounter on Earth, suddenly struck Charley with how far away he was from his former real life, with what risks he now faced that were completely unimaginable in his hamlet-lived life within Connecticut. A strange sense of nostalgic nationalism and repugnance at such patriotism seized him at that very moment, corporeally, physically, psychologically, creasing his stomach into thick folds within and upon themselves, as he held that bizarrely out-of-place instrument.

Charley tested its point, and then turned to the lock. His hope was that this horse-drawn carriage would have a lock technologically similar to that of the footlocker he had used when he went to Green Creek Camp for two summers, where, incidentally, he first tried tobacco, learned striking profanities, and mastered nearly professional control of flatulent, eructal, and expectorant abilities of the body; that is, farting, belching, and spitting. The trunk he was remembering smelled always of dampness and mold and bark, and he distinctly remembered how gray the day was when Vince Butler, his own cabinmate, took Charley's trunk key and ran out to the lake, Lake Pejota, with it. Charley, who had been sharing Howard McCord's care package of white-chocolate-covered pretzels and raisins from Howard's sister, dashed after him in pursuit, and came up to Vince, who stood about halfway from the end of the diving dock. Vince had that vicious delight to his face that you only find among adolescent boys looking for a way to engage in any sort of behavior that might somewhat provide an alternative to out-and-out violence. Charley came to the front of the dock, and knew that the next step would mean Vince would hurl the key into the lake. So, he stopped.

"Vince," he began, "before you . . ."

And Vince, gleefully, turned and sprinted toward the end of the dock. About ten steps from the edge, his body turned slightly sideways, more so in his torso than hips, his sinister arm came back, his hips swiveled, cocking into place for just a kinetic instant, and then his whole body unfurled, with his arm uncoiling last, releasing in a final five-fingered delta of energy Charley's footlocker key, sending it high and far out over Lake Pejota.

Charley had to admit to himself, quietly, all these years later and for the rest of his life, that it was indeed a beautiful throw. The key's trajectory delineated a perfectly symmetrical arc, and though it was a gray day, the silver key glinted in the available sunlight, flashing its rotation, until it plipped into the unhealthy green waters of the lake.

Charley never saw the key again. He never even tried.

The loss of the key meant that Charley had to act delicately when locking his locker, leaving the latch loose enough not to catch but tight enough to fit the padlock through the metal loop. For a while, he borrowed Jerry Newman's key after Jerry discovered that one key worked as well as another. But, understandably, Jerry got tired of being the doorman to Charley's trunk, and Charley had to experiment. He noticed that within the lock there was a thin band of metal visible that, manipulated instinctively by a set of Swiss Army Knife tweezers, would spring the lock. After the inevitable rusting of the tweezers left them inevitably cemented within their slot in the knife, Charley discovered that merely inserting the awl into the trunk's lock and turning it clockwise would open it. It was a revelation in workmanship.

Quickly doing the math and history, Charley figured that footlockers probably appeared at about the same point in time, or even after, horse-drawn carriages. It occurred to him that footlockers might even have been invented as the luggage designed specifically for carriages. Therefore, he thought, it stood to one line of reasoning that the locking mechanisms could be of the same caliber and intricacy, which is to say, low and low. He bent to examine the lock and saw nothing in particular. He again probed the tip of the ice pick. The crowd continued watching. Grimfir, still displeased with Charley so quickly resorting to use a tool rather than the appearance of magic, forced a yawn that he then pretended to try to stifle.

Charley inserted the pick into the lock until it wouldn't go any further. He withdrew it just slightly, so that it wasn't scraping against the back plate. He rotated it and encountered no resistance. He angled the pick, rotating his elbow in order to scope out fully the interior of the device. No luck.

"Is that some sort of a magic wand?" whispered Hololo to Ulmuth.

"I doubt it," replied Ulmuth. And then, a moment later, "Though it might be some sort of enchanted stick."

Charley withdrew the pick, feeling a sinking in his stomach that nicely complemented the rising sense of panic in his head.

Tandor stepped forward, and upon seeing this, Grimfir stepped forward even more quickly, hoping to avoid anything that might further embarrass Charley, or more importantly, Grimfir.

"All right, boy, give me back the ice pick and stop fooling around." He turned to the rightfully skeptical crowd of onlookers, who looked on skeptically. "Young Tooth is also a budding comic, as I see that you all understand."

Kwuito, hoping to be among the first to show how astute they were, laughed quickly and loudly, though singly. Flossy the One-Eyed Jerk, who considered himself to be something of a jokester but more accomplished as a heckler, coughed once and said, "Tell us another one," and basked in the polite if uncomfortable laughter that Dame Jeffrey Mangirl and Duke Riebald provided.

Grimfir half-turned to Charley so that he could half-address the crowd, half-address Charley, half-address Tandor, and half-address Onnser the semi-Magnificent. "And now, Charley Tooth, with absolutely no further ado or distraction, will open the carriage."

It is interesting to note at this point that Grimfir was not even thinking about the fact that he well knew Charley was no magician. Being caught up in the situation and desperate not to be shamed, he lost sight of the fact that he was trying to dig them all out of the hole he had already dug for them by digging further—sort of pushing on through to the other side, as it were. In his defense, though, it meant that he did, in a way, believe implicitly that Charley would be able to free Onnser.

Charley looked at Tandor. Tandor looked at Charley. Physically, this action was the same for each of them. There was, however, an ostensible difference—Charley looked at Tandor in a mixture of fear and imploring, and Tandor looked at Charley with the kind of look that one man might give another before pushing him in front of a train with considerable amusement.

Charley turned back to the carriage. He had no idea what to do.

He reached out and ran his hand along the handle to the door, and then along the door itself. He traced a bit of molding that ran through the carved, deeply dark, almost black wood of the door. His hand moved back to the lock, and Charley realized he wasn't even thinking of anything at all, if such a realization is possible and not some second-rate paradox that only someone really annoying would find worthy of arguing the validity of using the term "paradox."

His finger ran along the circle of metal that formed the outer plate of the lock, and then he rested the tip of his index finger over the keyhole. He pressed his finger against it harder, to feel the impression that was the void of the hole. As he pressed, he felt the cool sharpness of the rim, but then he felt that something was giving—that his finger wasn't really stopping. This was, in truth, what was happening. At the same time, Charley felt as though the soles of his feet were drawing up and in, as though they were withering or very, very gradually imploding. This was, sort of, what was happening.

Charley felt his finger continue to drive into the lock, almost like his digit was turning to liquid, or perhaps thick pudding, or even stiffish bread dough. It was exhilarating and uncomfortable, and he at once wanted to pull away quickly but also to keep pushing further and further. The choice was nearly out of his hands, and quite literally. His finger kept right on draining into the lock, maintaining its sensate capabilities, until Charley could understand the lock, until he could feel at once all of the pieces and nooks and spindles within it, like having the ability to perceive all sides of a sphere simultaneously.

Also, the impression, or rather depression (or was it withpression?) of diminishing, of withdrawing in his foot increased, until it felt as though his shoe housed merely the tent of the structure of a foot.

Instinctively, before the lock was filled up completely, Charley stopped the slow seeping of his finger. He examined his hand, and it looked as though he had buried his index finger up to the middle knuckle, with skin bunched like an old sock where it met the carriage door. Charley was reminded of the time that he broke his wrist, in an incident entirely separate from the one in which he had broken Grace O'Malley's arm, though Clint Ryder was a factor this time as well (having been the one who possibly dared or pushed Charley that day, as has been mentioned previously).

Like many people, Charley fractured his wrist accidentally during a game. Unlike many people, the game that did in Charley's wrist was cards. Poker. And no, not in a brawl over the pot or the dealing or the table talk. It was, in fact, after the best hand of poker that Charley had ever played, or would ever play, save two. At the table in Mattie Cohan's basement were Mattie, Charley, Abe Minney, Dave Clark, Vic Feliciano, and Clint Ryder.

The pot was up to nearly $76, and there were three players left in the hand—Charley, Abe, and Clint. Abe was a solid second-place finisher on poker nights, Clint was king, and Charley was generally out most of his cash. This time, however, Charley had thrown his usual anxiety to the wind and chosen to stick it out to the bitter end, not so much with the thought of winning but because he decided that, this time, he would not be the first loser, the first one out.

Not that Charley was afraid of being the first one out. In fact, he was almost the vanguard of many things he did in his life, by virtue of the mere fact that he never quite got why everybody was so very, very interested in fitting in to the point of discomfiture and unhappiness. He had been the first one to quit band and to quit softball, and he was the first one to sign up for the Gaming Society. He was the third to quit it, but the youngest to do so.

But here he was, with a pair of jacks and a pair of fours, playing for the big pot. The night had been cool, ready to frost, but they all wore T-shirts and occasionally sneezed in the dampness. Abe was feeling tight and stringy, not liking the fact that he was ready to fold, but used to being the final obstacle between Clint and the pot. Charley, finding himself pleased not only at recognizing this distinct feeling but also at exacerbating it, grinned inwardly and continued to bet. Clint remained as cool and confident as ever, though there was a certain look of amused surprise on his face at Charley's insistence on staying in the game.

Clint's confidence would serve him well throughout his life. He was the first among his friends to place his hands on a girl's breasts, on the bus for the class trip to Washington, D.C., and many would remember his generosity in sharing the sweat that collected on his hand with the remaining guys who had not fallen asleep at two o'clock on that long, late ride through the blackness of the states southeast of their home state of Connecticut. Though he would disappear from Charley's life soon enough, Clint would go on to become, almost improbably, a highly successful concert pianist, with a select, devoted audience that would provide him with enough lovers to make his life one of constant upheaval, heartbreak, heartbreaking, and productively golden and black periods of inspiration.

Once the pot hit $76, Abe grew visibly uncomfortable and folded his three tens. Charley and Clint kept right on pushing, with Charley figuring, as ever, that he would just keep going until someone else made the decision to change it or end it. Clint, a keen and close observer of those around him, figured that it was more likely that Charley was bluffing than it was that Charley had a worthy hand, as Charley never quite got the game down. However, there was still that sense of danger that Charley was quite unwittingly bluffing his way with a hand that required the subtle opposite of bluffing—that is to say, the demonstration of mental acuity that bluffed the bluffing to invite the foe into the trap of calling the lower-level bluff. Clint found this unpredictable challenge too exciting to let go, and Charley could sense this feeling in him. He intuited that there was a point at which either Clint would recognize that Charley could bluff no further, or else Charley himself would reach that point at which he had bluffed too far. And so, at nearly $100 in the pot, Charley broke Clint's belief that he would continue, and called. Clint had a pair of aces. He was both surprised and impressed by Charley's Zen-like play, in which Charley had serendipitously happened upon the exact confluences of events that would bring him victory. In the end, Clint was not at all sorry to see Charley come away with the big win, especially given the occurrences that followed.

Upon Charley's realization that he won, which dawned only seconds after Clint's preemptory realization but almost three hours before Mattie, Abe, Dave, and Vic were to understand, he stood up quickly and banged his fist down on the card table. The table, being one that Mr. Cohan had salvaged from a church-bulletin-flea-market-gone-bad, was flimsy enough that the impact of Charley's fist caused it to simultaneously half-crumple and half-jump up, giving completely under Charley's force, throwing the glass mug of root beer into his face a split second before it dropped Charley facedown to the floor, knocked Vic backward over in his chair, and made the other cohorts laugh shortly as they jumped back in surprise.

Here, the aforementioned bobulousness of Charley Tooth.

The only distinct sensation Charley recalled from the incident was that of the mug banging painfully against his left front tooth, hitting him hard against the lip, and causing a split that would be remarkably painful for almost a week, and the sound of that mug, combined with chips and table clattering together as they ricocheted off of every protruding surface and then the floor.

When he sat up, he had the distinct feeling that his left wrist had fallen asleep; the small idea that it felt like the snow of an unused TV channel playing through the five inches of his arm occurred to him as he held it up to shake it out. For some reason, before actually shaking his wrist back to life, he looked at it and was immediately struck by the zigzaggedness that had actually contributed to the separation of his watchband from the watch itself.

The angles of his arm were pretty fascinating, but he also noticed a feeling of dread in realizing that shaking his arm out would not do much to improve his situation, and might actually make it considerably, loudly, worse.

"Mother of Holiness," said Abe. "Mother of Holiness."

Mattie, whose instinctual initial reaction was for the well-being of his home, said, "What the hell, Charley! Damn it, what the hell! Nice goddamn job, you idiot!" He fell quiet, though he was still visibly annoyed, upon seeing that everyone was focusing on the sad state of Charley's bone.

"I say, Exclamation!" said Clint, who was the only one still laughing.

Now, in front of the carriage, looking at the unusual state of his finger, Charley wondered what the condition of his body beneath the skin was, and there was a vague sense of unease as his subconscious dimly recollected the ensuing resetting of the broken wrist and the frustration that accompanies wearing a cast for drawn-out periods of time. This feeling fell second to that of being able to sense the entirety of the interior of the lock.

Charley realized that the draining sensation in his finger had abated, and that the withdrawing of the inside of his foot had stopped as well, and he no longer felt the liquidity of those two extremes. He also realized that to the rest of those in attendance it had appeared as though he had passed the last several minutes merely resting his finger against the lock, which did not make for much in the way of spectacle.

He looked back over his shoulder and said, "Okay, I am going to try this now, I think."

He turned his hand slowly, feeling only the slight give of flesh compressing against metal, and he felt the weight of the lock give, slowly but certainly—almost like clockwork, Charley thought, before deciding that lockwork was a much more practical and unavoidably suitable term for it. As he rotated his wrist, he felt in what had been his fingers the clicking and shifting of the lock's intricacies, and then the final resistance that fell over in a heavy click indicating the lock was now indeed unlocked. Charley stopped and took his first breath of the past minute or two. He pulled back slightly on his hand, and nearly immediately the sudden spooling of his globulated extremity coursed back into him, specifically back into the cavity of his foot, reminding him of a power cord sucking itself back into a vacuum cleaner. Within seconds, his hand was back to normal, finger resting lightly on the keyhole.

"Booooooring . . ." said Flossy the One-Eyed Jerk.

"Yes, perhaps it is time to get on with it and things," came Onnser's voice from inside the coach.

Charley turned to the crowd. Grimfir, anxiety turning his eyes deep yellow, gave Charley the slow head-nod-and-tilt-with-widening-eyes-and-jutting-lower-jaw look that indicated it was more than past the time to which Onnser referred.

Tandor, a step closer to Charley than the rest of the group, looked intent but untrusting.

"Hum, well, um," said Charley to them.

Charley faced the lock again, held his left palm in front of it, and his right hand high above his head, palm to the sky.

"Well, alakazam, flimflam shimsham, hocus pocus shishkoombah, lock be open now, please . . . hurrah."

In one quick, inwardly unconfident motion, Charley reached forward, left hand to the handle, turned the knob down, and pulled the black door open.

Chapter Four

Tandor did not blink.

Recollecting, many of the witnesses at that spectacle would swear—and believe they were telling the truth—that lightning or some sort of palpable radio wave shot out of Charley's left hand, or maybe into his right hand, or both, though Beytore of Beytore insists that the *opposite* happened, and that Charley somehow drew radio-electrical züt from the lock itself and hurled it out into the nöosphere and beyond. Some believed there was a burst of smoke, though whether it was yellow or gray or mauve was contested to the point of punches. Leif the Pasty went to his deathbed convinced that he had seen eleven horse-drawn angel-raccoons descend on an arc across Charley's frame and into the lock. (To be fair, Leif the Pasty was aggressively anemic and given to a sub-dued but effective hysteria. Also, to continue to be fair, Leif the Pasty never quite made it to his deathbed, as his life actually came to an end some time later, far from his bed, where the high seas of Glaron clash mightily with the low seas of Rincey. The moon was three-quarters full, and the clipper swift and yar, but sometimes even the ablest sailor is lost, and Leif the Pasty was not even the ablest, though he was rich.)

Whatever the speculation was, one thing was certain: Tandor Ovenheat did not blink. Nobody noticed it, and even Tandor at the moment wondered if maybe he was mistaken, maybe he had blinked, but the objective, categorical truth was that he had not, in fact, blinked. But no matter.

Though the details of the unlocking were, and to this day are, open to debate, there was no doubt that it was Onnser the semi-Magnificent who emerged from within the carriage. He stepped out, wearing his show outfit, which was comprised of a long overshirt with a loose collar, made of black silk with intricate black dragon-like patternwork; smart tan slacks; and comfortably soft, brown shoes. He was of medium height, solid but not of fat build, and bald. His shoulders sloped, framing a small chest. He clapped his hands once, and took in the spectators with a look.

"Hello," said Onnser the semi-Magnificent, "I am Onnser, the semi-Magnificent."

There was pleasant applause from the crowd, though many of them felt silly, as all Onnser had done was to come out of the carriage, which technically he was supposed to have done some time ago. But people will applaud for anything, and, if initially seated, they will give a standing ovation for anything. In this case, they had all been standing to begin with.

"And you are Charley," he said to obviously Charley.

"That was a nice bit of magic you just pulled. Has Grimfir been such a tutor? Can it be he has a quick learner? Grimfir?"

Grimfir visibly puffed out all over, glistening with instant pride.

"Yes," said Grimfir. His mouth remained open as if to continue the thought, but as there was no thought to follow, all he could do was repeat, "Yes," and loudly shut his mouth. Part of him, and it was a bigger part of him than anything else, had not thought that Charley would be able to pull off the trick. And now that part of him was wondering just what the trick was that Charley had indeed pulled off; but if Onnser wanted to give Grimfir some of the credit, that bigger part of him was wise enough to figure he might as well receive it.

The audience again applauded, this time for Charley, and as Grimfir hoped, for Grimfir, as well.

Onnser peered closely at Charley. "Well?" he said, demonstrating some less-than-magnificent teeth.

"Hello," said Charley.

"I am Onnser the semi-Magnificent," said Onnser again, but this time just to Charley. "The 'semi' is mine. As is the 'magnificent.'"

"Hello," said Charley, wondering if he was uninformed on some standard protocol of salutational interchange. He was not. This banter was unique to this particular moment and these particular personages.

"Aha, and there is Tandor Ovenheat, up front as usual. Tell me, Tandor, have you found anything remarkable?"

Tandor blushed almost imperceptibly and gave the slightest of nods in which he dropped eye contact.

"There must always be someone searching, Your semi-Magnificence," replied Tandor.

"There must always be someone searching? Searching for what, Tandor—failure? If you focus on finding failure, I am sure you will find the most singular success."

"You know I admire the truths you speak, Onnser, but I sometimes wonder how often you are deliberately twisting words to your advantage at the expense of the greater good. Pleasant turns of phrase might misdirect, but they certainly aren't magic."

"Right you are, and magic is why we are here tonight!" cried Onnser, loudly enough to make Kwuito suddenly wheeze.

The crowd burst into another round of spontaneous applause, instigated by Grimfir, who had seen Onnser enough to recognize when he was giving the masses the appropriate cues for extemporaneous admiration.

Onnser suddenly rose about six feet off the ground, emitting sparks, smoke, and moths from his feet, cuffs, or thereabouts. He clapped his hands again, this time thunderously, and then shot red confetti straight out into the gathered audience. Next came doves (or, as Charley recognized, pigeons), numbering eight, arising apparently out of the nothing that could be used to describe Onnser's shoulders. The pigeons began in a lovely chevron formation before three of them spotted the moths and quickly abandoned their predetermined flight in favor of a quick meal. Four of the remaining pigeons went after the shiny bits of jewelry that some of the ladies were wearing, and the other pigeon, smelling salmon on Grimfir's mouth, quickly decided to investigate.

Amid the confusion, Grimfir welcomed the bird into his mouth, seconds later discreetly expectorating the remaining bones, which, magically, turned into glitter when they hit the ground. By now the other pigeons had caused some pandemonium with their marked aggression toward the bedecked guests, and Onnser was trying desperately to calm everyone down.

"Calm down!" he commanded in a voice of authority, which, not surprisingly, is not always heeded. "Calm down!"

Seeing that people were perhaps not quite ready to calm down, Onnser de-levitated. He gauged the mayhem, pointed four fingers toward the most assertive of the pigeons, which was at that moment plinking at the glass eye of the corpulent and otherwise eminently agreeable Glubdort Minxer, who was overcome with feelings of not at all being agreeable, given the circumstances. Onnser released from the aforementioned four fingers a dazzle of jagged white lightning, which caught the bird completely, sublimating it into a mass of golden glitter, of which hundreds of sparkles promptly lodged themselves in between Glubdort's glass eye and its socket, causing him no end of quiet consternation—he was loath to show at such a nice party any signs of disagreeability that might prevent him from being invited back to such a lovely occasion. Onnser released similar bolts again and again, five more times, in quick succession, vaporizing all but one pigeon, who coincidentally died at the same moment of what appeared to be natural causes.

There was a small pattering of scantier applause at this display of marksmanship from those who were unruffled enough to notice—namely, Charley,

Grimfir, Tandor, Ulmuth, and Hololo, who was in truth quite ruffled (as ruffled as a featherless being can be), but as the consummate hostess, still keeping an encouraging eye on each partygoer, including the entertainer.

Onnser, looking slightly abashed, slightly annoyed, turned to Charley, who was still applauding.

"This trick has gone wrong often enough that I have become adept at zapping the birds without even having to aim," he confided, as one of The Sisters Yippie (was it Crispina?) ran by in flames, as was her wont in periods of mild panic.

CHAPTER FIVE

The evening progressed in the exact opposite manner that Charley would have predicted it going that morning, when he supposed that after school would have found him at basketball practice, and then dinner at home, followed by homework, perhaps some unfortunate and scrape-inducing bike tricks in the yard, television, some sketching, perhaps some time on the phone, and then bed. None of that was to happen, except for eventually going to bed (all sentient beings Charley had met so far slept, at some point. When he thought about it, as he was to think about it some time later, it was strange to him that beings—human, namely—needed to sleep as part of living. Why was that? Why couldn't whatever biological functions that are addressed by sleep be addressed while one was conscious? Charley would devote small portions of the rest of his life to ruminating on this particular question, but as of this particular writing, he had not answered it satisfactorily).

But tonight, bedtime was a long, unknown way away.

The rest of the evening saw a reduced role for Charley, much to his relief at first, but the longer he had less pressure on himself, the more he had the chance to reflect on what a day it had been, and what a fix he was in, if indeed it was a fix in which he found himself. After the initial presentations of Onnser the semi-Magnificent as the entertainment for the evening, the party moved back into Hololo's mansion, in which Onnser put on charming displays of magic, turning table lamps into angry, biting wolverines, and back into lamps (though two of them needed their lightfish bulbs replaced afterwards), creating a floating mouth just in front of HrYlgYr that would move just beyond his reach, making of him a Tantalus, mouth always receding from him just close enough for the trick to be viewed as cruel by those of less humorous persuasions, such as Beytore of Beytore, and sundry other tricks of ingenious if unimportant nature.

Charley ate a number of foods, or what he supposed were foods, because a fifteen-year-old, even in a foreign situation that makes no sense to him, needs a little something here and there to tide him over, or as Mrs. Tooth used to joke (rather painfully) after they would eat at Bangkok Palace, "Thai him over." Charley tried to think of his mom and how in these few hours he missed her greatly, but, as a teenager often enjoys a bit of time away from his mother, and as her dreadful pun lingered in his head as though it were squatting just above the taste section of his brain, ready to let go, he found that, for the moment, he wasn't exactly missing her, just wondering when he would next see her. It would spoil things considerably were I to tell you the answer.

Here are things that Charley noticed through the haze of the evening, the things that stuck in his memory like so many pins in a voodoo doll:

Grimfir toadying up to Onnser (the association to toad was easy, given Grimfir's scaly, vaguely damp appearance).

Annoying inquisitiveness on the part of Tandor Ovenheat, who would corner Charley repeatedly—especially, it seemed, whenever Charley was about to get a few of the cream-cheese-chutney crackers passing by on the appetizer tray. Perhaps it was no coincidence that Tandor's breath bore the remarkably strong scent of chutney.

The molting of Tonsil Grinblar. Tonsil was birdlike in appearance—downy feathers all over, some light plumage in the back, googly eyes set on either side of his head. Other than that, he wasn't much like a bird at all. And the molting was like a snake's—it worked itself off almost in a Tonsil Grinblar-shaped tube. Afterwards, Tonsil looked much like a wet chick. It transfixed Charley and, it seemed, a few others. Apparently, though, Tonsil was more prone to molt when relaxed after too many drinks, so some were accustomed to it, though it was still clearly not the most appropriate behavior in polite company.

Still less appropriate and just as memorable was Duke Riebald taking the discarded skin Tonsil left behind, hiding behind the tall plant with the pink and yellow leaves, and munching on it contentedly.

A punch fight between Yorgad and Jarsan son of Nisan. Charley had seen people fight before, mostly out of boredom (remember, he was from Connecticut), but never had he seen two beings fight for the pure reason of keeping each other awake.

Zea Yippie and Leif the Pasty kissing madly in the doorway that led to the back pantry. Charley had seen make-outs at parties before, but never was the ratio of mouths to beings more than one to one.

Eventually, Grimfir said it was time to go, as Charley had chores in the morning, apprenticeship duties, and so on. Charley, exhausted from the day (that is not to say jet-lagged), didn't think about chores in the morning any further than he would normally think about school in the morning. In fact, it would be a remarkably safe presumption that some part of Charley—an important part, or combination of parts, such as the basic areas of his brain and body—felt that sleep would reset the whole ridiculous scenario, and things would be back to the way they always were in Connecticut, and that he would wake up a little late in the morning, only vaguely recalling wisps of the dream that, by now, he should have fully realized was not a dream. Charley and Grimfir paid their respects to the principal people at the party, as well as some of the second-tier folks that Grimfir found to be promising contacts of one sort or another, as well as to the horse-like creature that had borne the tray of salmon-and-artichoke slivers around in such a dignified and magnanimous manner.

Taking leave of the charming hostess Hololo Summersweat, Grimfir said, "I sincerely hope that we shall have the honor of presenting ourselves to you in the future."

Hololo, wrapping warm tentacles around Grimfir's forearms and Charley's waist, replied grandly, "Of course but of course. I certainly would simply love it were you to come and help at any time, in any way, soon, in the future, not long from now, to entertain us so thoroughly and deliciously as you did this very evening at this very party tonight."

"Thank you, ma'am," Charley managed as she unwound him and Grimfir from her thick, sticky arms.

They said cursory good-byes to the remaining characters, and Charley even nodded at Flossy the One-Eyed Jerk. It was one of those things—the most noticeable loudmouth in a place invariably is able to draw uncomfortable yet unavoidable eye contact from the quieter ones around. In fact, that is the principle behind behaving like a nitwit: If you have nothing intelligent to say, say it loudly, and at least you will get the attention you crave but can't merit on your own, and chances are that nobody will tell you to be quiet, lest it make you louder still. So, Charley nodded politely, and Flossy, unused to such an unmitigated pleasantry, could barely manage a sneer before Charley moved on.

Onnser the semi-Magnificent stepped forward from behind the floor-to-ceiling chair and grabbed both Grimfir and Charley by the forearms.

"Charley, Charley Tooth. That's right, isn't it?"

"Yes, sir."

"Tooth, eh?"

"Yes."

"Charley is short for . . . ?"

"Um, Charles. Yes. Charles."

"You're certain."

"Yes, it's Charley for Charles."

"Hmm. I see. Not for Charlethvameernis?"

"No."

"Not for Charlmuthheward?"

"No, sir. Charles."

"Not for Frippozapocharl?"

"I've never heard of these names. Are these names?"

"Charley is short for Charles, eh?"

"Yes, for Charles."

"Why?"

"Because it's shorter. Slightly shorter. Charley is slightly shorter than Charles."

"Is it now? How do you spell Charley?"

"C-h-a-r-l-e-y."

"Not C-h-a-r-l-i-e?"

"No."

"You spell it that way, huh."

"Yes, with a 'y.'"

"Well, Charley with a 'y' has the same number of letters as Charles, which is seven. Charlie 'i-e' is the same length. Ergo, neither Charley with a 'y' nor Charlie with an 'i-e' is shorter, you see."

"Yes. But, well, I guess it sounds shorter to say Charley."

"Does it now?"

"Yes. I guess so, I think."

"I disagree. Charley, in either spelling, is two syllables, but Charles can be spoken as one. Also, Charles ends in a concrete 's,' which closes the word, but Charley concludes without concluding, with the open-ended 'y.'"

"Well. I see, but that's just not right. Not correct."

"Not correct? Isn't it? It is longer, no?"

"Yes, sir, but no, I mean no. It's shorter because . . . it's affectionate. It's what my parents and friends have always called me. Charles is too formal. It's too long because it's not really what I go by."

"Hm."

"I mean, the point of a name is to be known by it, and to be that name, right? I have a friend Jeff and a friend Geoff, and they are totally different people; though their names are said the same, there is a slight difference to how you say them. Not like a . . . a defined difference, but their names are who they are, and they are who their names . . . um, are."

Grimfir curtly broke in. "It's time we left immediately." Onnser had released them from his grasp a few moments before, and now Grimfir drew Charley rather sharply to the side, placing himself between the boy and the magician.

"Wait, Grimfir. I am certain I was not quite finished."

"I beg your pardon, Onnser the semi-Magnificent. I just know the boy is tired, and I thought it best if I tucked him away in some dirty corner so he can sleep the night off appropriately."

"Of course. I don't mean to be insensitive. While we are nominally on the subject, what is Grimfir short for?"

"Well, my proper first name is Harjkfgrimfirdfkjkdfj-Sam."

"And why do you go by Grimfir?"

"I have never thought about it."

"Ah. Well, good night to the both of you. Charley, I would like to meet with you tomorrow. That was a very impressive bit of magic you performed tonight."

Grimfir chortled loudly, as though he were sharing some sort of private magician joke.

Charley, on the other hand, flushed red as blood, feeling the way he'd felt when Ms. Werth caught him cheating on the nines of the multiplication tables in

third grade. And, analogous to that particular situation, Charley also realized immediately that, like Ms.
Werth, Onnser was not looking to turn him into the
ultimate higher authority of his parents, but just
would allow the devastating humiliation of the situation, the fact of being caught, to be enough to embarrass Charley privately to the point of mortal chagrin.
And so it was: Charley felt that before-known burning
feeling of hate, fear, and nausea; but, at the same
time, part of him conceded that there was nothing
specific in Onnser's tone that betrayed any belittling.
And hadn't Charley performed magic? Well, he wasn't
sure he had; in fact, he was pretty sure he hadn't, and
that he had just managed to jimmy the lock somehow,
and the details of the act grew hazier by the second.
But Onnser could know none of this, having been
stuck in the carriage. Perhaps there's a certain glint
to the eye, a bearing or a posture, a nod, wink, and
a handshake that genuine practitioners of conjuring
display to acknowledge each other—perhaps exhibited merely in the quality of the magic performed—
and Charley had not given the signal to Onnser, so
Onnser knew he was a fraud.

Charley got a little sore at this. After all, hadn't he
just shown up on this planet, or in this dimension, or
whatever the hell it was, without having any choice in
the matter? And he was just supposed to know the
rules and etiquette right off the bat? That was grossly unfair, and it was grossly unfair of Onnser, or
Grimfir, or anyone, to make any assumptions as to
what Charley knew. Sure, maybe he prided himself
on what he thought was a rather remarkable assimi-
lation at the drop of a hat, but he couldn't be expected to maintain that composure the entire night in this

unsettlingly bizarre place. Half of the apparent natives had displayed marked neuroses; couldn't they give Charley a little leeway?

Indignation and nostrils flaring, Charley managed only to say, "Thank you"—but in the most sardonic manner capable for his person. Unfortunately for Charley's intentions, but somewhat fortunately for his future, it came out as more tired than anything else, so few would have picked up on the bite in tone.

"Charley, I insist you visit with me tomorrow. I take it you are lodging with Grimfir?"

"Umm. Hum. Well . . ."

"Yes, he is, as a squire, an apprentice. So I provide a place to stay, food to eat, lessons to learn, and chores to accomplish," interjected Grimfir, sensing a business opportunity of some sort close at hand.

"Then I will stop by before breakfast. Well, let's say lunch instead, as he looks a bit drained, now don't you, Charley. Like you've traveled far to get here?"

"It has been a terrifically long day for me."

"Fair enough—get some sleep, and I look forward to visiting with the two of you tomorrow, late morning."

With that, Onnser the semi-Magnificent produced a small flash of light and quick-rising smoke, which, upon its rapid dissipation, revealed that Onnser was gone. Well, not gone, exactly, but about six feet away.

"That means the conversation's over," Grimfir said gruffly, taking Charley by the arm and directing him toward the door. They had not gone too far before Tandor Ovenheat stepped suddenly in front of them, with an even smile.

"I take it this means 'good evening'?" he said.

"Good night," Grimfir corrected tersely.

"I was hoping that I might have more of an opportunity to chat with Charley here."

"Sorry. The boy has a full day, and no time to talk, Tandor."

"Is that right?"

"It is, and that's why I said it, and good night."

"Well, I trust that our budding young magician will be performing in public again soon?"

"He has a lot of training to do, of course, and you can't learn to show before you've learned the skills, so don't count on a lot of upcoming performances just yet."

"But the unlocking spell or trick or maneuver certainly was a skillful demonstration, even if it was lacking in crowd-pleasing flair. It's a most useful ability, that of unlocking."

"Yes. I suppose it is."

"Oh, Grimfir, I know you *know* it is. But Charley's ability seems to exceed even that of any number of lock-breakers I have known."

Charley interrupted. "I didn't break the lock."

"Oh, no? Most interesting, wouldn't you say, Grimfir?"

"I would say the boy has a lot of training ahead of him, both magic and otherwise, and that we would like to retire for the night, if that meets with your approval."

"Of course, by all means. However, I would consider it decent of you to allow me to come see Charley in training at some point. And it would be appreciated if the two of you were to instruct me in the ways of the unlocking trick—I am keen to learn it."

Charley felt a sudden flash of sweat surge at his hairline. "A magician never reveals his tricks," he said, remembering his father's response to any number of questions Charley had growing up, and they were not necessarily all even about magic.

"But they must be passed on somehow."

Charley continued doggedly, almost desperately, "Master to apprentice, of course, how else? It's a sacred and secret bond, and not just anyone gets to witness the instruction. Right, Grimfir?"

There was a pause. A kind of long one. Charley continued to look at Tandor, having thought to direct Tandor's focus toward Grimfir, and wanting to take the opportunity to examine his antagonist, who always seemed to be examining him. This was a standard maneuver of Charley's, trying to observe those who do the observing. He had first discovered the delight and fascination of this act in a movie theater. He had gone with a friend to a movie house with stadium seating, and the mediocre movie was notable only for its occasional instances of graphic intensity. In one of these scenes, there was an audible gasp from the crowd as one character stuck a pen into the bullet hole in another character's chest. Charley, sitting far to the right toward the front of the theater, was able to turn inconspicuously to take in the other moviegoers. He saw horror and revulsion on the faces of those compelled to look. He saw shudders and cringing from those who covered their eyes or looked away. And he saw one guy, about twenty years old, wearing a gold necklace, who was aggressively trying to kiss his date, who exhibited a dismay that was difficult to attribute to a singular factor, whether that be the movie scene, her date, what her date was trying to do, a combination, or something else entirely. It was these two people who captivated Charley the most. And, in watching them, he realized that there are always people who are not interested in the main attraction at any given time, but are working a separate agenda entirely. And from this instant was born in Charley an agenda all his own—that of seeing what it is other people were looking for when everyone else was looking at something else entirely.

In this case, though, Tandor had not broken Charley's gaze. Nor had Grimfir broken the silence. Charley turned to Grimfir, who was exhibiting in his demeanor a conflict at answering, and one that it seemed he would settle on as though forced to.

"Tandor, it would be an honor to have you as a guest, and my apprentice is at your disposal anytime I am your host. Now, if it pleases you, may we go?"

"Many thanks for your generosity, Grimfir. I anticipate that I shall see the two of you again soon."

Without another word, Grimfir and Charley strode out of the party, out of the front door, and down the marble steps. And then down the sponge steps. Out on the driveway they walked, passing the various modes of transportation parked along the sides: horse-drawn carriages, car-drawn carriages, cards, aircars, spaceships, broomstick-drawn carriages, car-drawn broomsticks, animals that looked like wet combinations of such animals as giraffes with ostriches, zebras with orangutans, horses with dogs, eagles with deer, and big cats with small elephants. On Grimfir and Charley walked, silent, until they were out on the main road, which was a nicely paved ribbon with what appeared to be a sort of river in the median. Grimfir looked both ways, and then crossed with Charley to this median, which was covered by an endless stretch of opaque glass.

Closer inspection revealed that the median was not

a river, per se, but more like a moving sidewalk covered in a thin layer of what appeared to be firm Jell-O, slightly electrified. It was sea-green, and smelled vaguely of medicine. Grimfir led Charley straight out onto it, and they nestled their feet into it, about four inches deep. Charley looked down and saw that there were actually a variety of channels in the goo, of varying shades of green, blue, and brown, moving at various speeds. The two of them were in the thick brown channel.

"Keep your knees slightly bent," growled Grimfir. "The ride back to town is fast and bumpy."

Charley bent his knees to steady his balance as the goo carried them with increasing speed away from Hololo Summersweat's mansion.

"Why did you back down to Tandor? Why did you tell him he could come see me about the trick?"

"Because he asked nicely."

"What are you talking about? He clearly doesn't trust me, or you, but you said we would show him our magic tricks!"

"What is this 'our' stuff? What magic tricks do we share? Please name for me any tricks I have taught you, or any tricks you have taught me. Are you afraid he's going to learn how to do your coin trick? Do you think that's what he's interested in?"

"No, I . . . the lock on the carriage."

"Yes, a neat bit of manipulation, that. I suppose you will have to show him how you did it."

"But I don't really know how I did it."

"That's a good try, but it won't work with Tandor—trust me. How did you do it, anyway? I didn't see you palm a pick, but there was certainly something going on."

"I really don't know how I did it."

"Hmm. 'Magic,' I suppose." Grimfir chortled sarcastically.

"No, really, I don't know."

Grimfir turned his body from the waist to look at Charley. "Look, Charley, I know you're tired, and I know you had opening-day jitters, and I know that you are a thickheaded fool, but two things: You are going to have to come up with something to satisfy Tandor, and you are going to have to teach me how you did that trick. Got it?"

Charley had once read that it is useless to argue with people. Actually, that's what he thought he read, though really it was something more along the lines of it being counterproductive to argue with someone in public, as it gets them on the defensive, and then you've earned yourself an enemy, or at least someone who won't trust you. In any case, Grimfir had sharp teeth, sharp claws, and an ornery disposition, and so Charley managed a meekish "Okay."

Charley took in his surroundings. He looked up at the opaque covering above them as they scooted along the median. Even in the darkness of night, Charley could see a yellow tinge to the roof of it, like a sunroof or a covered bus stop. The yellowness glowed faintly, iridescently. Charley looked out to the left and right. The road was still on either side of them, and as they were carried along, they passed or were passed by the occasional horse carriage or hovercar, respectively. Beyond the road had been the trees and rocks and stands of what appeared to be naturally occurring rods of various metals, some right up against the road, others out on the lowlands and then up into the dark hills. As they traveled, Charley noticed these bits of nature losing their density in favor of human (or, shall we say, sentient) development. Clearly, as structures and artificial light increased, the closer they were coming to a town.

They coasted along in silence, sometimes overcoming other travelers who were in other, slower-moving channels of the Jell-O, on their way to other places than town. There were some coming the other way in the Jell-O, heading out into the darkness of the countryside, generally looking as though the late night in town had been a highly successful night out, or a highly disastrous one, depending on one's perspective. The first few beings whose paths they crossed Charley would say hello to, or acknowledge with a nod, wave, or an "excuse me." After the fourth person, though, Grimfir chastised him, saying, "Don't talk to people." But the closer they got to town, the more social Grimfir got, sharing an occasional grunt. After one almost friendly noise from Grimfir, Charley looked at him questioningly.

"Safer in the city. Only people out this late in the country are drunks and freaks."

"But *we* were out that late. I mean, we were in the country at this hour."

Grimfir did not respond, except to yawn. They were clearly on the track through the main part of town, as Charley could see residential dwellings on streets that shot off their path on either side, while their own path took them through blockier buildings lacking in the warmth of character you would expect of a home, no matter what planet you found yourself traveling on.

The buildings did not have a particular theme—some of them were sleek, smooth, and high, purely functional and with no character save that of functionality. Others looked almost Tudor, and many were what Charley would describe as avant-garde without knowing what he was talking about: strange, almost confrontational angles, bizarre materials, inexplicable pockets of space and shadow. There were a few public-park-looking areas, a large dirt field with bleachers, low obvious storefronts, and what Charley took to be a gallows, discernible even at this hour of night. As they smoothed along, Charley was able to distinguish that they were passing through the more affluent part of town, several blocks after the central plaza. There were more rough wooden structures, more flat concrete buildings, than there had been previously. To be sure, this later sector had character—the houses looked handmade and lived in, and the less residential buildings appeared to have been most creatively kept erect. About fifteen minutes into this side of town, Grimfir took Charley just above the elbow and began stepping in place, removing his feet up and down from the Jell-O, each time with a soft sucking sound almost like an inverted kiss, if you can so imagine.

"Here," Grimfir said, stepping lightly past Charley toward the solid, unmoving ground (not counting the presupposed rotation of the planet, had Charley at that moment been thinking about it. Which he was not). Charley, however, had not anticipated their arrival, and he had not traveled via this mode before, so though his reflex was to move in the same direction as Grimfir, his feet remained rather solidly planted in the gel, warm and comfortable. Grimfir pulling on Charley's rather long torso while the legs remained fixed made for an awkward maneuver.

Grimfir moved with enough purpose (that is, muscle) that everything about Charley from the ankles up lurched with him. As everything below his ankles (which is more bones than you might think, as well as a healthy dose of muscles, tendons, and probably ligaments) remained unyielding, Charley's balance was thrown completely off kilter, reminding him at once of an elderly gentleman Charley once saw fall down.

This particular incident occurred once when Charley had caught a ride home from school with Sperber Chudworth, who was two years ahead of Charley. They were about a quarter mile from Charley's house—maybe a half mile, as estimating distances in the car was never his greatest strength—at a red light, when Charley noticed a man in a brown suit walking on the far side of the street. He might not have noticed him had the man not also been wearing a brown hat, as though this were the fifties, or whenever it was that men always went about with hats on, investing in Ponzi schemes and speculating in the steel industry.

This white-haired man was not moving particularly quickly, but as his focus was not apparently on where he was going so much maybe as where he had been, he managed to clip his shoulder against a sidewalk light pole. Being on the frail side, the old man was not quite capable of absorbing the slightly embarrassing shock of such a blow with the uncaring aplomb of someone a third or a quarter of his age (and here again, thinking that he was easily a quarter of this man's age, Charley could not help but wonder how accurate his assessment was that he was a quarter mile from home: Was their age difference analogous to how soon Charley would be home compared to how soon he would be home had he been a mile away?), and the man was thrown completely off balance. Charley watched him as his arms flung straight out before coming back quick and short, bent at the elbows, and then back out again, windmilling to create some sort of air cushion that might keep him on his feet.

It did not, and the man began to spin back toward the offending pole (or was the man's body the offender? Charley sort of wondered, recognizing that the pole remained where it had been all along) in a desperate attempt to find support in the object that had enacted its loss. His hands and delicate forearms clawed and clamped at the pole, but they were not strong enough to hold up the weight of his falling body, which now had a bit of momentum to it. Charley watched the man fall quickly to the ground, and felt nauseated at having witnessed such an embarrassing event surreptitiously.

It so bothered Charley that he wondered if it would actually make things worse to get out and help. After all, perhaps the man was fine, and the ignominy of having a sympathetic stranger pull you to your feet after such an avoidable accident might have made the event, and the memory of it, all the worse for everyone involved. If nobody stopped or acknowledged noticing, perhaps some part of the man's mind could believe that nobody had in fact seen it, and he could get on with his life without ever having to dwell or happen suddenly upon the recollection of the fall. Perhaps it would not even have really happened. If an old man falls on the sidewalk, and nobody notices (or at least pretends not to notice), does it make any memory?

But the light had turned green, and Sperber drove on. Charley hadn't mentioned any of what he saw. He suddenly wondered if maybe the man had had a heart attack, and that was the reason he had hit the pole and gone down. Charley leaned forward to look in the side mirror and saw the man kneeling, leaning against the pole, ostensibly all right but visibly shaken. Feeling somewhat relieved of his guilt at not doing or saying anything, Charley closed his eyes.

All of this occurred to Charley as he himself rocked back and forth on the gooey moving highway in ever deeper and jerkier arcs, about to lose his own balance. But Grimfir caught Charley's elbow with his claw and firmly yanked him from the traveling gel, pulling him rapidly off onto solid ground. This pulling of Charley made him jump and pitch like a marionette in a windstorm, but the solidity and purpose of Grimfir and his grasp was enough to give Charley a chance to let the awkwardness blow through him and regain his steadiness.

Grimfir let go of him and said, "You'd better get used to traveling around here, as this is the only way we get anywhere."

This of course reminded Charley of a T-shirt of Irish Bull that he had once seen on an older kid at an amusement park, but as he couldn't remember any of the quotes, he dismissed it from his mind.

"Where are we going?" he asked Grimfir, who was already marching off.

"The same place as before—home," replied the lizard, a little annoyed at the obviousness of it all.

"I don't suppose you mean my home, by any far, far chance, do you?" muttered Charley, looking at his feet, surprised to see how cleanly they had emerged from what he later learned was called, in a fit of civic utilitarian imaginativeness, the Slimeway.

"Stop muttering."

They walked on a bit, and then a bit farther, down wide streets of low houses. Charley, in thinking of going home, realized that these were not tree-lined streets, and that a street without trees can try but never succeed at having genuine character. No trees somehow removes any sense of age and identity. Trees take time to grow; a street without them has no history.

A good twenty-minute walk later, Grimfir turned toward a dwelling on what Charley supposed was the east side of the street. He had no reason to suppose it was the east side other than intuition, and, had he thought about it, it might have defeated him to think about how arbitrary and useless this sort of assumption was. The house looked almost like a city barn, if such an image may be conjured. It was at once dilapidated and urban, fitting in with the landscape. It was narrower than your typical barn, and it appeared to be constructed not out of sagging wood but some similar, albeit fancier material that also sagged brownly, without indication of money or durability having been a consideration. Grimfir walked directly up to the house, removed a medium-sized metal key from a front pocket, and unlocked the heavy wooden door. He swung it inward and strode over to the wall, knocking sharply at about chest level. A second later, light flickered on where he knocked, and then spread out in both ways from the starting point, extending along a rectangle about a foot wide all throughout the house.

Charley, following Grimfir inside, went to examine

the slightly fluttering light. He saw that the source was a fish tank set in the wall that ran the length of the residence, including up and over doorways, and inside of it were thousands of tiny white and yellow fish swimming furiously to and fro, emitting light from their stomachs that, cumulatively, provided decent light to all of the rooms.

"What are these?" exclaimed Charley.

"Lightfish—what other kind of fish would they be?" replied Grimfir so matter-of-factly that Charley felt it was so obvious even to a stranger that these light-emitting fish would of course be lightfish.

"How do they work?"

"What do you mean, 'How do they work?' How do you work? How does anything work? You feed them, they make light. You knock on the glass and they know what you want. Don't waste my time, and go to bed."

Charley followed Grimfir down a hallway, and he couldn't help but think that this house smelled like a barn, a wet barn, or some combination of vaguely familiar smells that Charley associated with a farm, wood, and the smell of under a sink. The walls, apart from the lightfish tank, were mostly bare, as the fish were situated at about the perfect height for normal wall decorations. Charley found the fish rather mesmerizing as he followed the gruff lizard. Grimfir opened a door on the left and said, "This is you."

Charley walked into what would be considered the master bedroom anywhere else—a large, square space with reasonably high ceilings. The room was soft. Quite literally. All of it. The floor was like one large cushion, or, as the case was for its design, a mattress. It was dark in here, and Grimfir walked to the wall and tapped on the glass. There were a few sparkles of light at his touch, and then a few more, but just weak flickering overall. He tapped again and got a slightly better result, but it was still far from enough to light the room properly.

"I don't use this room a whole lot. The lightfish need to be changed," Grimfir said, tapping repeatedly on the tank and getting a repeatedly disappointing sputter of light. "The separate rooms all have their own tanks," he continued, "off of the main channel." Grimfir left the room as Charley moved toward its center, no longer as interested in the lightfish as he now was in the floor-to-floor mattress, or mattress-to-mattress floor, as the case appeared to be.

Grimfir returned shortly with a large bowl of light-fish, some fish food, and a net. He slid a panel above the tank open and dumped in the new batch of light-fish, and the room immediately brightened.

"See, the glass of the tank also magnifies the light," he said as the new fish scurried about, evening out the dispersion of illumination. With the net he scooped out about a bowlful of dead lightfish. Then he sprinkled some fish food into the tank and closed the panel. He turned and began munching on the bowl of fish. "So, you're all set. I'll wake you first thing in the morning. I'll show you around the house then."

"Where do you sleep?" Charley asked, certain that Grimfir would not give Charley a better room than himself, making him wonder what the actual master bedroom must be like.

"I sleep in the room just off the gathering room. We passed it on the way in, off to the right of the front door."

"And where's the bathroom?" Charley asked.

"Out the hall, go left, second door on the right."

"And how do I turn the fish off?"

"Smack the tank with your palm, flat and hard—without knocking. I've got them well trained. Just like we'll get you—responding to knocks and smacks!" Grimfir chuckled and left, shutting the door behind him.

Charley padded over to the wall and peered closely at the little fish. They paid no attention to his looming face, and he saw that the blue-white creatures appeared to have no eyes, though they did have tiny whiskers. He tried to follow one lightfish on its crazy meanderings, but he couldn't keep track of them as individuals. He slapped the tank with his palm, and within a few seconds, the light all but flickered out. He lay down. A few seconds more, and he was in complete darkness—the one window in the room had a heavy curtain pulled across it.

Charley lay motionless in the deep darkness in the strange bedroom in the strange house that belonged to the strange talking lizard man in this strange town in this strange world. It was very quiet. Charley closed his eyes for maybe a minute. He opened them again and strained to see the slightest detail to the room, but he could discern nothing. He thought, "I am in my own home, in my own bed. I just woke up, and I am in the safe, warm darkness of where I live and belong. I can't see where I am, but I know that my bed lies against the north wall, and the night table is just out of reach this way, and it's six steps to my dresser, and just to the left is Grandfather's chair, and next to that the window that looks onto the yard, and then the Bernsteins' house, and then more trees, and then the water, and then the stars. I know that all I have to do is swing left to get out of this bed, my bed, and then I will feel the thick, coarse, green carpet under my feet and in my toes, and then a few steps toward the foot of the bed I will feel the refreshing coolness of the wood floor on the soles of my feet, and then the door, and then the rest of my house."

The comfort felt so delicious, so luxuriant, so easy, that Charley almost felt pampered.

"I will this. I *will* it. All I have to do is get out of bed to confirm that I am home. That's all."

He lay there for several more moments. Charley knew that he could confirm that he was home by getting out of bed and finding his room as it always was, as it always had been. But he remained where he was, knowing that he was doubly safe at home if he *didn't* confirm his surroundings and went on trusting that, just beyond the edges of what he was able to sense in the darkness, everything was in place as it should be, including himself. The darkness continued. Charley decided to risk it. He had to know. He rolled over, feeling for the end of the bed. Maybe it was just a little bit farther. He rolled over again. And one more time. And once again. All the while, the soft, comforting mattress supported him, valiantly serving its purpose. Charley rolled desperately to the wall. No doubt about it: He was not at home.

Charley sat up with his back against the wall. He felt a little sick, and then he laughed quickly and sharply. He felt his face smiling away, in the dark. He stood up and turned to the wall and knocked on the glass with his knuckles, and the light flitted back on. He slapped, and the fish went out. Knocked again, and back the light came. He tried slapping and knocking different parts of the tank to see the light begin to diminish or reappear from various sections of the room. He tried knocking and slapping in rapid clack-smack-clack-smack succession, achieving a dull strobe effect. He tried knocking very quietly and observed how the light very slowly came on or went out in different pockets. He knocked with his left hand at the same time that he slapped with his right, sending the fish into a bit of an uncertain frenzy. He tempered it a bit, doing both softly, at exactly the same time, with his hands right next to each other. He did it again, this time with his arms spread wide, which made it more difficult to hit with the same force, hand to hand. He could tell that he almost had what he was going for, but, despite his arm span (which was not too shabby for a boy of his age), couldn't quite cover the distance to provide the right balance of stimuli to produce the desired result.

Charley leaned full against the wall, feeling the warmness of the tank across his shoulders. He reached as far as he could. Then he reached a little farther. Then even a little farther. He stretched as though he were on a medieval rack, and suddenly, once again, he felt his very fingers, his fingerprints, extending beyond their natural boundaries. He felt the queasy pooling of liquid in the bottom of his stomach as he did when fingering the lock of Onnser's carriage. He felt the fleshy part of the back of his legs begin to suck in, as though in a whirlpool, as though they were ever so slowly imploding. Like water undermining a sandcastle that slowly suffers from a foundation built upon sand. His fingers continued to reach, to elongate. His palms followed. It felt gross but exciting. It felt unnatural but he didn't want to stop it. He felt the tightness at his elbows relax, and he felt ripples in his forearms, as though they flowed like water, lapping at the shores of his wrists. He began to panic, as he had thought all night that perhaps what had happened with Onnser's carriage had been a fluke, a trick of his exhausted mind, the aftereffect of alien canapés.

With immense focus, he decided to ignore the strange shape his body was taking and continue with his fish tank experiment, and with his extraordinarily extended hands, he smacked with his left and knocked with his right at the exact same time, with the exact same amount of force, and then Charley promptly fell back from the tank, feeling his body snap back to normal and fall onto the mattress floor. The light in the room altered. Charley's test paid off: The simultaneous knock and slap, beginning equidistantly from the sides of the tank, sent messages back and forth throughout the lightfish, so that some were lighting up while others were dimming down, and then the fish fed off the signals of those around them, and the result was a wave of muted light, shimmering slowly back and forth through the tank, making for the cozy atmosphere he'd sought. Our exhausted Charley barely had time to recognize his success, as he very quickly was very asleep.

Chapter Six

"Get up, boy! Time to get up! Work to be done! Up!"

Charley opened his eyes to the harsh sight and sounds of Grimfir standing in the doorway, dressed as sharply as he was the night before. Charley lay there, blinking up at the reptilian Grimfir Boldrock, while Grimfir stood there, blinking back at the human Charley Tooth. It took Charley a few seconds to place Grimfir, to re-accept where he was and what this creature was that stood in the door, and what his new situation was. He wondered if Grimfir was going through the same resignation.

Charley sat up, and Grimfir continued.

"Come on, now. Lots of chores to get through, and Onnser wants to see you this morning, so let's get to work."

"Good morning, Grimfir."

"Yes, it's remarkably terrific," growled the lizard. "Now get up and get to work. Come on."

Charley got up and followed Grimfir down the hall to the kitchen. The room was cool and dark, the floor made of smooth cobblestones. There was a wooden counter and a fireplace with a heavy iron pot and skillet, though they looked to be in some disuse. There was a sink and a large metal cabinet that served as the refrigerator. On a thick table by the window there were stacked plates, bowls, and silverware of various designs and states of cleanliness.

"You need to clean this place. The house, I mean." Grimfir handed Charley two buckets. One had rags, a coarse sponge, and a heavy brush in it. "You know how to clean, I take it?"

"Is there soap?"

"No soap—I don't like it. Too fruity and allergy-causing and overkill. Water is in the sink. Scrub hard. Anything else?"

At that moment, Charley's stomach rumbled audibly, and Charley realized he was extremely, extremely hungry. "Is there a way I could have breakfast before getting to work?"

Grimfir grumbled as though he had been hoping to avoid having to feed this teenager, but being a slave to his own stomach, he understood Charley's need for some food. "I generally only eat eggs, fish, and roots at home. I'm out of fish."

Grimfir opened the fridge and brought out a large basket of large eggs. They clearly weren't chicken eggs, as Charley had been hoping, but he thought maybe it would be for the best if he didn't ask as to their origin. The eggs were dun-colored, about the size of warped tennis balls, and their shells looked thick. Charley figured that two or three would probably set him just fine for the morning, even if they were just cold-hardboiled. Surely Grimfir had salt.

Grimfir picked up an egg and handed it to Charley. Charley felt its comforting weight and found that the shell was indeed quite thick. Grimfir was looking at the eggs and Charley's fingers.

"Here," he said. Taking the egg back, he held up a dark claw and tapped firmly in two places opposite each other at the top. He returned the egg to Charley. Charley began to pry at the holes.

"What the hell are you doing?"

"Trying to get the egg out of the shell."

"You just drink it right out. Quit wasting time."

"Hum. . . . You mean these aren't hardboiled?"

"No."

"Can I cook them?"

"And just when would you do that? Are you going to start a fire, get the eggs cooked, eat them, and get all of your chores done before Onnser appears? I doubt it. If it's something you actually think you can do, then go ahead and be my guest." Grimfir took up another egg, holed it, and sucked out its contents. Paying Charley no obvious attention, he took another egg. Charley watched Grimfir eat the first; then he looked at the fireplace, his own egg, and the bucket. He peered into his egg and sniffed it, and his stomach gurgled again. Charley lifted the egg to his mouth and poured. Given its mucousy consistency, it didn't pour easily, and Charley found that he had to suck the raw egg out. It wasn't bad, but it certainly wasn't easy to ingest. Still, hunger won out, and Charley finished. Grimfir chortled.

"That's a good lad. Put scales on your back."

"But I don't want scales on my back."

"It's just an expression. Where are you from,

anyway!"

Charley and Grimfir both paused at this question, and both felt uncomfortable. "Have another egg, Tooth."

After breakfast, which lasted another eight minutes or so and consisted of an additional egg and a glass of water, Charley got to work scrubbing. Grimfir had advised him to end with the kitchen and bathroom, so Charley headed off to the gathering room, which was the principal space in the dwelling. The room did not have a lot to it other than stumpy places to sit and smaller stumpier places for smaller people to sit (or more probably for food and drink and the like). The floor was a solid piece of slatish stone, dark gray to the point of almost being dark purple. An enamel-like covering somewhat softened it. The walls in the room, apart from the lightfish tanks and four windows, had on them framed and unframed parchments of writing and drawings of groups of people. There was a small fireplace along the wall to the left of the entrance.

Charley decided to begin with the structures in the room, but he was surprised to see how clean they already were. Sure, there was a regular bit of dirt and dust, and a ring from a drink on the table in the corner, but it was certainly cleaner than Charley's room back home, and he had considered himself to be an above-average clean teenager. Still, he was diligent yet expeditious in cleaning all the protruding surfaces, and then he moved on to the floor.

The floor appeared to have been swept in the recent past—apart from some dust bunnies (or whatever parallel creature they might be called here), it was in good shape. Still, Charley went over it with a wet rag.

He had the strange feeling as though he was mistakenly repeating a task he had completed not long ago but forgotten as being already completed. Like going to lock the door to find he'd already locked it, or getting out of bed suddenly to open his algebra book and finding that he had already done the homework, hours earlier. Still, he cleaned. Grimfir came to the doorway.

"How is the cleaning?"

"Fine, I guess. I'm nearly finished in here. It's a clean house, I mean."

"Oh, well, you know, don't rush through anything. Take your time and *make sure* it's clean. Plenty of work to keep you busy, I should think." Grimfir nodded slightly and disappeared back down the hallway toward the kitchen.

Charley paid extra attention to the front door area, as it was understandably a bit grimier than the rest of the room, and then he moved on to the next room, which turned out to be Grimfir's private quarters (or quarter, actually, thought Charley, as it was only one room. And more of a nickel than a quarter, at that, he added to himself).

The room, in addition to being small, was dark. There was an armoire, a low set of drawers, and a mirror on one side. On the other side of the room, extending into the middle, was a pile of rocks. Some were smooth, some rough, and they varied in size from that of a shoe to that of a watermelon. There was a dampness to them, and Charley was struck by how much cooler and moist the air was in here than in the gathering or guest rooms. It took Charley a moment to realize that Grimfir slept on, or in, or under these cool, damp stones. They were his bed.

Despite Grimfir's obvious lizard background, there was something about seeing him in his fancy clothes, hearing him speak, seeing him mingle, that had made Charley forget that, when you get right down to it, reptiles are perfectly at home on a pile of rocks. Or under one. He wondered, again, what Grimfir thought of him, and others like him, who preferred the softness of cushions and mattresses. To be sure, Charley liked a rigid support for his sleep. He was suddenly reminded of a time in seventh grade when he spent the night at Clint Ryder's house (yes, Clint from the Grace falling down stairs and the broken wrist poker night).

Clint and Charley had stayed up late, eating as much sugar as possible and trying to outwrestle Clint's older brother Curtis. At two in the morning, Clint and Charley went on a self-evolving scavenger-hunt-cum-swap-meet, returning to Clint's house a little after four, having redistributed nearly a hundred articles from neighbors' yards and porches to other neighbors' yards and porches. As they went to bed, Charley began to feel a bit ill. He was sleeping in the basement, in the spare room on an old, overly soft bed. By six o'clock, Charley was still unable to sleep and his throat was nearly unbearably sore. He got out and sat on the floor with his back to the wall. The carpet underneath his feet was short and bristly and beige. He lay flat on the floor, appreciating its solidity, and fell deeply asleep. He awoke nearly five hours later completely refreshed, though his throat was so sore he couldn't speak. He had dreamed that he was flying a small airplane but was having trouble getting altitude. He kept trying to climb, but found himself not going to clear the treetops. As he approached the first batch of trees, just before reaching them, he closed his eyes and braced for the awful impact. It never came. He opened his eyes to find the plane flying through watery branches, unsteady but unharmed. He flew through them and kept trying to climb, only to keep flying into the liquid trees, and to scrape up and down sandy hillocks. It made him queasy but not unhappy. Ever since then, on nights of insomnia or discomfort, Charley could get a good night's sleep with unsettling dreams by sacking out on the floor. He wondered how that must be for Grimfir every night, or if when he couldn't sleep, Grimfir did the opposite and sought refuge in the sponginess of the mattressed room.

At this point Grimfir came in.

"Clean this room like the other, but don't bother cleaning the bedstones. Just pour some water over them and that will be fine. Take your time and make sure the job is done properly."

It occurred to Charley that Grimfir wanted Charley to be busy at this squire work when Onnser the semi-Magnificent arrived. As Onnser inspired respect in Charley, he was okay playing the role that Grimfir his host requested of him. He would have preferred that Grimfir had just been open about it with him, as it would have made the role-playing a bit less embarrassing, but perhaps this tacit way was the best way to preserve the class structure as it was between the three of them. In fact, Charley decided to play it to the hilt.

He went to the kitchen to find Grimfir, but it was empty. Charley went to the back door, which was opened, and looked out into the yard. "Yard" turned out to be a generous appellation, as it was more of a walled-in mud pen. Windowless buildings rose past the fence on all three sides. In the far left corner of the enclosure were four large, nearly birdlike creatures picking at an odd strand of yellow grass, and behind them was what must have been their pen. To the right was a hut made of carefully mashed together corrugated metal, mud, and stone. It was about eight feet high, twenty feet long, and eight feet deep. The door to it was cast open, and from within Charley heard rummaging sounds. He went.

Grimfir was tidying up, apparently. The space was packed with vials and jars and books and tubes and papers and the like, and Grimfir was working at putting some of it back onto the shelves that lined the walls. Charley coughed, and Grimfir turned to him.

"You can't already be finished cleaning. If so, clean again."

"Oh, no, I'm not finished cleaning at all. I just wanted to know if you would like me to answer the door when Onnser arrives, or if that's something you wanted to do yourself."

Grimfir thought this over, visibly.

"Yes. That would be fine for you to answer the door. But keep quiet, be respectful, and come get me *immediately*. Got it?"

"Yup. What is this place?"

"The lab. Get back to work."

Charley could feel Grimfir watch him go, hear him walk back through the mud, back into the house. Charley went back to Grimfir's room and finished scrubbing around. As he was pouring water over what he smiling called to himself the "bedrock," a knock came at the door.

Charley had a flash of inspiration in which he pictured himself as a nouveau Cinderella. He would bring the bucket and rags to the door, as props, and everybody roots for the downtrodden. So he quickly gathered up his stuff and made for the door. As he pulled the door open, he prepared to cast his eyes toward the ground in humility. But, on the other side of the portal, there was a conspicuous lack of the personage of Onnser the semi-Magnificent. Instead, there stood a most amazingly cute girl. She was thin but unmistakably strong, with straight dark, dark gray hair and a clear face. Her eyes were sharp gray and gold, and she was, at the moment, not smiling.

Suddenly, Charley wished he were home in Connecticut. Suddenly, there was nothing more gut-wrenchingly needed than for him to be home, where his family and his friends were; where in the yard he had eleven trees whose rough bark he loved to run his palms over; where there were streetlights whose refracted halos in the windshield made him feel as though he was the only person alive; where his school, where he had gone for all his life, was like a little brother in that it was annoying, familiar, hated, and loved; where he would ride the bus and sit right behind Grace O'Malley; where Clint Ryder would bring out the more adventurous side of his life; where he could bike down to the creek and do nothing the whole afternoon; where, in the immense and unassailable solitude of his own room, there was no one and nothing that could unsettle him. And here he was, wherever he was, facing this beautiful girl, and he realized that what he wanted above all else was to be home. Certainly, he wouldn't object to being home with her, where he would be in the know and she might feel like he did at this current moment, which was lost, stupid, teetering, and nauseated.

Regardless, in the presence of this striking female, Charley suddenly felt like home. At the same time, he felt like an idiot, standing there with the bucket and rags and a half-fixed expression of half-fixed deference on his face.

"Hi, um, hello," Charley stammered impressively, "I . . . was just, um . . ."

"Cleaning up Grimfir's house?" the girl finished for him.

"Yes! Well, that is, I mean, no, not like that. . . ." Charley hastily put the bucket down.

"Not like what?" she asked, looking at the bucket.

Charley picked the bucket up. "Yes. Hum. Um, I was just finishing up here and there, that is."

The girl looked at Charley. Charley put the bucket back down.

"I'll go get Grimfir."

He turned and made it about six steps before turning and quickly coming back. "Um, would you care to come in?"

The girl stepped into the house and to the side. Charley picked up the bucket again and skedaddled off toward the kitchen, feeling even the back of his neck turn hot red. Once in the kitchen, he hurriedly rid himself of the bucket, castigating himself for his performance the past few minutes. He trotted out to the yard and called for Grimfir, who presently stuck his head out and said, "So he's here, is he?"

"No. It's someone else."

"Someone else? Who else? Who is it?"

"Um . . . I don't know."

"What? What do you mean you don't know? How do you not know? Didn't you ask for a name?"

"Um, no. No, I didn't. I didn't ask."

"Good lord. Brilliant, Charley, really brilliant."

Grimfir came out, wiping his hands on a rag, which he pitched behind him back into the shed without looking. Charley followed him back through the house to the gathering room, where, next to the door, the girl stood exactly where Charley left her.

"Hello, Grimfir," she said politely but not deferentially.

"I take it Onnser is not coming, then?" Grimfir asked her with a slight bow.

"No, he sent me over to ask you to bring Charley Tooth over to him. . . ." and she looked at the still-red-faced Charley with some measurable skepticism.

"Then we had better go. Charley, are you ready to go?"

Charley nodded. Grimfir looked down at himself, brushed his front off, and turned to the girl. "Off we go."

They left the house and silently headed back toward the slimeway. They maneuvered into the interior fast lane that carried them along in the same direction Charley and Grimfir had traveled the night before. Grimfir stood in front, and then the girl, and Charley was just off her left shoulder and behind her a step or two. After riding for a few minutes, Charley got up the nerve to speak.

"How far is it?"

But instead of the girl responding, Grimfir turned his head and said, "What? What's that?"

"How far—I was asking how far was it—is it, to Onnser's?"

"What? Speak up, boy!"

"I was just asking! How far!" Charley now felt like even more of a dolt, and it occurred to him that

Grimfir might just be pretending not to hear him to embarrass him on purpose in front of this girl. Nobody said anything for a minute.

"About ten minutes," the girl said, without turning around.

Encouraged, Charley then leaned forward a bit and said, "I am Charley. Charley Tooth."

"Yes," said the girl, still not turning around.

"What's your name?"

From behind, it looked as though she kind of sighed, kind of slumped her shoulders, as though giving in to the inevitable. "I am Wednesday O'Friday."

What a wonderful name, Charley thought to himself. Wednesday O'Friday. He decided to press the issue.

"Wednesday O'Friday. Really? It's funny, Wednesday and Friday are days of the week where I come from."

"I can see that is tremendously amusing. Charley doesn't mean anything here. Tooth means tooth."

"Yes." That was all Charley could say in response. He waited a few more minutes, allowing that awkwardness to sort of pass before he tried again.

"So, Wednesday, do you work for Onnser?"

At this, Wednesday turned her head slightly back to Charley. "Onnser is my uncle."

"OnnserismyuncleOnnserismyuncleOnnserismyuncle," chattered in his brain, like some furiously repetitive Tourrettian disease. Her uncle! What did this mean? Was she also a wizard, but a young female one? Did that make her a witch? Had Onnser told her about how Charley had freed him from the locked carriage? What magic could she do? Why wasn't she there last night? Was she Onnser's apprentice? His heiress? Would she someday be the semi-Magnificent one? Wasn't she already magnificent in her own way? Would she be hard to impress because she already knew magic?

Exhilarated, Charley decided this merited further questioning, even if she had so far not been the most receptive being Charley had ever encountered (and made Grimfir seem downright chatty). He moved to stand next to her, forgetting that the gel of the slimeway held his feet fast and that this wasn't your average earthly airport moving sidewalk. As he tried to step, his body lurched, and his hips and torso continued forward without benefit of the support of his legs and feet. He flailed, pitched forward even more precipitously, and said, "Nuts."

He fell forward, and instinctively reached out to Wednesday to keep him from falling. Unluckily, she was just a tad bit out of reach for him to be able to use her to right himself, and all he did was knock her well off balance as he himself fell down completely. Before he hit the ground, though, he found himself thinking about a trip that his family took to New York City several summers earlier.

In addition to hitting the normal sights for tourists—the Statue of Liberty, Empire State Building, Central Park—the Tooth parents (Teeth?) had also decided to provide the family with a more thorough experience, so they ate at places like Katz's Deli and Zabar's, said no-thank-you to the pot pushers in Washington Square Park, and rode the subway. Charley remembered the smell as they descended the stairs underground. Wet, acrid garbage and urine mixed with the heat of the tunnel.

They'd got on a crowded 6 train, wedging themselves in among the commuters and the students.
After two stops, a soft-looking man with a portfolio
under his arm came on to the train, and as he was
switching the portfolio from one arm to the other, the
train lurched forward. Charley watched as the man
made a frantic lunge for a handhold, but it was a
futile attempt. He fell sidelong into a middle-aged
woman with very short hair and very black frames on
her glasses and a very pinched face. The two of them
fell into a solid man with a mustache who was the only
one of the three to remain standing.

The woman wailed, "Ow! Ow! Watch out! Ow! My
ankle!" Most people backed away, suddenly and
miraculously finding room in the car to give the scene
some space. Three people helped the two people up.
The woman was bent over, holding her ankle and still
yelling, "Ow! You jerk! You shit! You twisted my
ankle!"

The man who'd fallen was gathering up the pieces
from his portfolio that had come loose. He looked
apologetic, frustrated, and embarrassed. "I'm sorry,
I'm terribly sorry," he said to the woman, and to the
people around.

"Sorry doesn't help anything, you idiot!" crowed the
woman. The man went to her and tried to help her
up. "Ow, get off of me, you've done enough!" The
train lurched again, and the man stepped on her toe.
"Ow, goddammit, what's wrong with you! Get away
from me!" she screamed. He looked to the man with
the mustache and said, "I didn't mean to—" but the
mustache said, "Learn how to ride the subway, jerk."

The first man looked around, but nobody met his
gaze. "It was an accident," he said, to nobody in particular

but for the benefit of the silent witnesses who feigned interest in the middle distance. At the next stop, the man with the portfolio got off the train. As he did, the woman with the ankle said, "Jerk," one last time. The man paused in the doors, hearing this insult at his back, but he didn't turn around before he continued on his way. Though Charley had sensed a general feeling of distaste toward the man from the people in the car, at his departure and the final gripe from the woman, Charley felt the people's attitude shift to one of being annoyed with the woman, especially as now her ankle seemed not to be bothering her anymore. All in all, it was a pretty vile incident for everyone, and Charley felt nauseated at the way all the people interacted or had avoided interacting, himself included.

It was a similar feeling of nausea that seized him now as he fell on the slimeway. It seemed like everyone was always falling down. He was conscious of hoping that he would not hurt Wednesday O'Friday's beautiful ankle, and then he was conscious of being full-out on his stomach in the goop. Wednesday O'Friday was conscious of the same feeling, as Charley's feeble attempt to use her to brace himself had only succeeded in knocking her down, as well.

Given that the goo on the slimeway served the purpose of holding a traveler's feet relatively firmly in place, it should have come as no surprise to Charley that now, with much more of his surface area sprawled out in the gel, he was being held even all the more firmly in place as the thoroughfare moved him along. The same could be said for Wednesday, though she was in a state of higher surprise than Charley, making her much more vocal as she fell than he was. Grimfir turned to see what the commotion was, and he was perhaps most surprised of all, beholding the two of them completely stuck, lying at all angles, as the slimeway continued on. It took several inelegant minutes of unwieldy maneuvering for Grimfir to get the tangled duo back to their feet, and by that time they were well past their turnoff to get to Onnser's place. After extracting themselves from the situation, Charley was certain that Wednesday O'Friday would prefer to walk the rest of the trip, but he underestimated her (or, rather, the distance to Onnser's, as that was the real reason), for she made no bones about getting back on the slimeway, with the single caveat that she ride a good ten feet behind Charley.

Charley, at last being completely embarrassed into complete silence, spent the rest of the short journey imagining that a mugger of some sort, or a handful of muggers, would suddenly appear and threaten them, and somehow Charley's quick thinking and amateur athleticism would carry him to vanquish them and into Wednesday's heart. He was playing out these various scenarios when they arrived, and it was only then that he realized that a mugger or muggers would probably best be fought by Grimfir, and though this certainly wasn't Grimfir's fault, the result was Charley felt even worse about himself, and about Grimfir for besting him, and about Wednesday, because why should she go for Grimfir just for being able to fend off a couple of jerks, when what it really should take is personality, and sure, maybe Charley hadn't had a chance yet to show her that he wasn't a bumbling oaf with nothing to say, and maybe he showed her that that was exactly what he was, but she should be able to see deeper than that, and certainly his personality should be more appealing to her than, say, Grimfir's, and wasn't Grimfir more than twice her age, anyway, and if that was considered normal on this planet, or world, or dimension, or whatever the hell this place was, then maybe she wasn't the right girl for him, because someone like that isn't worth the effort, after all, and why should all the effort be left to him, man, this whole thing was so unfair!

And there they were, at the front door to Onnser's abode. The house stood alone, with yard all around it populated by bizarre trees of varying colors, many of which appeared to look rather unnatural. There were also trees that, upon second look, were made of bunches of smaller trees that were growing on top of and out of each other. Parts of the lawn had bands of grass that were actually just one, thick long blade. Before Charley had time to come out of his reverie and pay closer attention to the exterior of Onnser's home, Wednesday led them directly inside.

Inside was a smallish foyer, and then a long, straight, dark hallway with closed doors lining it all the way down toward a solitary bright window at the end. They walked all the way down to the window and took a left into a large, airy room of honey-colored wood. It was Onnser's lab, and it was easily six times the size of Grimfir's. There was a book fluttering its pages like bird's wings, but other than that, the room was still. Then Charley noticed the room wasn't still at all, but that nearly everything, live or inanimate, was somehow squirming, shifting, pulsing, or turning, so very, very slowly. Charley blinked, and everything looked still again.

Wednesday moved some papers off a stool. "Uncle

Onnser? Uncle Onnser! We're back!"

There was a puff of smoke from the far right corner of the room. All three of them looked at it. Charley squinted, trying to pick out Onnser as he material- ized. As it happened, Onnser was actually standing behind them, having just come to the doorway.

"Ah! Hello, Grimfir, hello, Charley, hello, Wednesday. I trust you all had no problem in getting here?"

Though the question was innocent enough, Charley again flushed red as both Grimfir and Wednesday shifted uncomfortably. A sudden thought struck him: They had all engineered his falling down—it was some sort of magical conspiracy. A second later, he was able to dismiss this thought almost completely from his mind as almost completely ridiculous. Onnser had already moved on.

"I hope that I might see some magic today, young Tooth. Hm? A few of your tricks? Perhaps, if time is not an issue, the extent of your repertoire?" Grimfir opened his mouth to speak, but Onnser held up a hand. "Not to worry, Charley. Grimfir knows that I would certainly never steal a trick or divulge a secret. I was impressed by your performance last night—not even my trusted attendant Vang could get the lock open. And I hear you are a wiz with coin tricks?" Again Grimfir tried to interject, this time by stepping forward. "Of course, Grimfir, I would not disparage the boy's tutor by not asking you if you would like first to give an exhibition of your own selection of magic. I defer to your discretion. . . ."

Onnser settled back comfortably, waiting for Charley, or Grimfir, or both to make a move. It was the exact same thing that Charley and Grimfir were also awaiting, though Charley with more reluctance than Grimfir. Grimfir, especially unhappy at now being responsible for the decision, was about to indicate that Charley should go ahead when Wednesday suddenly piped up.

"Uncle, maybe you should show them around? Charley has never been to our house before."

There was visible relief on Grimfir and Charley's faces as Onnser said, "Oh, my, of course! How abhorrent a host I must seem!"

At first, Charley thought that Wednesday had done him a favor, and just as he was beginning to picture them canoeing together across a quiet lake to a picnic, he realized that, so far, he had only performed well under sudden pressure, and here he had not only time to think of something that would sink him, but he also had an audience whose expectation would be building for some sort of formal, thought-out presentation.

Onnser led them through the house, but Charley was paying so little attention that none of it made an impression on him, even when Wednesday chipped in a comment here and there. Charley felt himself sweating more and more. And more. He could feel it on the backs of his thighs. He felt it running down his ankles. He felt actual drops falling from his armpits, like rain, or more aptly, like from an air conditioner.

Soon enough, the four of them were back in Onnser's lab. Vang entered, bearing tall, cool drinks. He just as unassumingly left, after smiling at Charley, indicating that he remembered him from the night before. After Vang withdrew, there was a heavy quiet in the room, loaded with expectation. Everybody politely looked at everything in particular, as though it were a summer day at the swimming pool and everything was unremarkably fine. Charley himself felt the tension so compounded that he himself was ready to break the contrived ignorance and say it was time for him to prove (or, more likely, disprove) his mettle. However, as is often the case, it was someone else who stepped forward in order to exacerbate Charley's uncomfortable situation. In this case, it was Wednesday.

"Okay, Charley. I guess we are ready for your show. If that's okay with you, Uncle?"

It was. Onnser nodded his assent and indicated for Charley to take the center of the floor. He followed the gesture with, "Yes. Charley, I can't tell you how keenly I have looked forward to this since seeing—or at least experiencing from behind a locked door— you in action last night."

Charley looked to Grimfir, who looked back at him with a blanched blankness that Charley felt a sailor must have experienced upon looking at his mates seconds before being keelhauled.

Charley cleared his throat, stepped forward, and ran his hands up and down his forearms in a vague nod to the old "Nothing up my sleeves" maneuver. A hundred thoughts came to his head. Among them:

Run for the window—and just keep running.

Wake up. Just wake up. Do it. Do it now.

This is a big joke. Nobody expects anything. It's just a joke.

They are going to kill you because you are a fraud.

Wednesday is really beautiful. Undeniably so.

My mother is frantic right now, calling all the local hospitals.

I haven't even begun the research on my history term paper that's due in less than a month.

What do I do now?

What do I do now?

Do something.

What do I do now?

And, just then, there was a solid knock at the door. Charley looked inquisitively at Grimfir, who looked deferentially at Onnser, who looked blankly at Wednesday, who looked skeptically at Charley.

"I'd be glad to answer that," said Charley.

"No, no, of course not," replied Onnser, "I'll be right back. Please, do wait for me."

Onnser glided purposefully out of the room. The remaining three people were silent for a moment or two. Wednesday looked from Charley to her fingernails.

"Looks like you caught a moment's break, eh, Charley," she said without any emotion or hint of tone.

Charley looked at Grimfir and tried telepathically to implore the lizard to do something to save him from the situation, even if it meant Grimfir biting his arm off. Better that than Grimfir biting Wednesday's arm off. It was a beautiful arm. But Grimfir didn't hear Charley, or ignored him, or Charley was not telepathic, or any combination of those factors was true, for Grimfir remained unblinkingly inscrutable.

Charley thought about what the next ten minutes or so would bring, as he knew full well that he had no magical capabilities, and he was pretty sure that Grimfir knew he had, at best, very little. And now he was being asked to perform not only in front of a legitimate wizard, but also his legitimately stunning niece. And possibly in front of whoever was at the door. That would be, in a word, awful. And where would that leave him? The people in this room were the only people on this world that he knew, and to disappoint them, to try to trick them, to present himself untruthfully and be caught so blatantly would mean that he would be alienating the only people he had. And if he were to find his way home, what better team could he assemble than a man versed in sorcery, a large, stubborn lizard, and an attractive girl?

"I have no magic," he said quickly.

Grimfir looked up sharply. Wednesday looked up only slightly less quickly.

"I have nothing to show Onnser," Charley continued.

Grimfir stood up and sputtered, "Why, you—" and then caught his own indignation and quickly shifted almost to a cooing—"certainly do, though you might feel a bit anxious. Quite understandable, Boy, but when Onnser the semi-Magnificent invites you to his home to see what you can do, you must show him *something*."

Charley turned to Wednesday, wondering if she understood. She was looking at him in a blank, quizzical way. Just then, Onnser came back, and behind him was Tandor Ovenheat. Tandor was dressed sharply, in black with starched white showing at the collar and cuffs. In the light of day, Charley noticed how dark black Tandor's eyes were. He had with him an unpleasant briefcase.

"Tandor Ovenheat," said Onnser to the room.

Tandor nodded to Grimfir and looked at Wednesday.

"Hello, Ms. O'Friday." He bowed.

"Hello, Mr. Ovenheat."

"Please, you know you can call me Tandor."

"And you have been able to call me Wednesday since I met you when I was a child."

"I tend to stand on formality."

"I tend to ask you not to."

Charley thought this conversation had gone on long enough, as it was more than he himself and Wednesday had ever bantered, even if this exchange was contentious.

"Hello, Tandor," he said, interrupting.

Tandor faced Charley and regarded him carefully. "Hello, Charley. I understand we are about to see you impress us with your prodigious array of amateur and perhaps not-so-amateur tricks?"

Charley stumbled through saying: "Yes, well, I was just talking about it with everyone, with Wednesday and Grimfir, that is, and I was thinking that maybe the time to do this would not be now, but not now but at another time that isn't now, with and for all of you. . . ."

"Clearly the boy is nervous about performing in front of such an impressive and honored audience, and perhaps the illustrious company is too stimulating for the lad to begin just at this moment, for an assemblage of unexpected luminaries," buttered Grimfir expertly but a little thickly considering the sharpness of the company.

Onnser looked at Charley and said, "I really must insist on seeing what Charley here is capable of, for reasons that might not be clear to the rest of you at this point. However, however, perhaps the immediate setting is not the most beneficial for this particular interview. Therefore, Charley and I will meet alone, so that there are no distractions and he will be most at ease. If you all would please wait somewhere, we shall be through in presumably half an hour."

Tandor stepped forward. "But Onnser, I don't think . . ."

"Tandor, we will discuss your interests and requirements later on. I am resolute about meeting alone with Charley in this initial examination. Now, please, gentlemen, Wednesday—excuse yourselves."

Grimfir stood and left, followed by Wednesday, who coughed as she passed Tandor, indicating that he should also leave, rather than to continue to stand looking quizzically and discontentedly at Onnser. Once the three ancillaries had left, Onnser shut and locked the door. He turned back to Charley, who looked as though he were either going to puke a lot or had just finished puking twenty minutes ago.

"Well?" said Onnser.

"I don't have anything to show you."

"Sure you do. Don't worry about making mistakes. I don't expect you've had much training."

"I haven't had any training. There is no training because there is no magic. I mean, there's no magic where I am from, so there's not really anything to train, and I am not the guy who would be trained in something like that even if it did exist and there were training for it."

"Hm. No magic?"

"No. I don't have any. I really would rather just go home. What do I have to do about that?"

"Charley, listen. You are here for a reason, I am sure, and that reason is not just to go home. I asked Grimfir to bring you over to determine what potential might be within you for the craft."

"But that's the thing. I don't have any potential."

"You opened the lock on my carriage last night. It had been locked with a spell, and so it could only be unlocked with a spell."

"There was no spell. I just managed to pick it, really."

"But I distinctly recall Grimfir requesting that you use the unlocking spell he had taught you that you'd been practicing. What about that?"

"It wasn't a spell, so much as it was . . . well, Grimfir covering. The rest was just luck. He's never . . . uh, we haven't exactly gotten to the unlocking spells yet."

"There had to be some magic there. I could feel in the air a quiet crackle. And you opened the lock."

"It was just my finger. I was able to pick the lock. That's really it. It would be cool to be able to say that I said something and waved my hand and the thing opened, but really, it was just luck."

"Let me see your hand, then."

Charley extended his right hand to Onnser, who examined it and then the left.

"Remarkable. These hands are completely unremarkable. Hm. Hm, indeed. Still, though, I am convinced in your magic. That lock could not have been picked."

Charley felt a pang in which he thought maybe he should mention to Onnser the weirdness that he'd felt when his finger drained into the lock, or when he stretched out past his span to smack the lightfish tank, but he felt that these were easily explained away by his tiredness, the strangeness of the world, and the malleability of memory and perception. So instead he looked at Onnser blankly.

"I can't force you to show me any of your abilities,

Charley. Not fairly, anyhow. But I know you have it in you."

"I am terrifically sorry, but I really don't think I do. I'm pretty normal."

"Well, let's at least see if you can do some run-of-the-mill easy-to-teach-easy-to-learn tricks. These are spells from long ago, and most have forgotten them. Wave your hands thusly," and Onnser made an interesting motion with his two hands, "point at that candle and say, 'Roolay kahm fresno ferwit.'" Awkwardly, Charley did so.

The candle burst into flame at the wick—a bright, greedy flame that began as green and quickly shifted into brilliant white. Charley sat down hard on the floor.

"Ah! How wonderful! Well done, Charley! Let's try another!"

"How the hell did I do that?" Charley asked aloud.

"See? You surprise even yourself, but the magic is there. Not just anybody can do that trick. Very few, actually. Few indeed. So, why don't you get on up, and we'll try another one. We'll see what you can do."

Charley got up and looked at the candle, and then at his hands. He felt his fingertips for—for what? Singeing? He didn't even know. Neither do we, nor is it important. He looked at Onnser palely.

"Okay, Charley. This next one is slightly more complicated. Clap twice, say, 'Tofty fosty foo, cardmium flah, vlint vlint gorky,' clap thrice, do this with your fingers, this with your elbows, and then, as though playing the pianoforte, gesture at the candlestick and summon it to you."

He talked Charley through the spell again, and sure enough, when Charley gestured toward the candle, it wobbled a bit, rose from the table, teetered, and shakily floated toward the wide-eyed, unbelieving Charley. He kept waving his fingers, bringing the candle close, to the point where he didn't know what to do, how to react, how to stop it. Onnser watched, amused, until Charley suddenly batted at the candle, which dropped to the ground, extinguished. Charley regarded the candle, lying on the floor with a trail of wax seeping from it like translucent blood.

"How can I do this?"

"It's complicated. Actually, it's not really complicated. Some people can do magic. Just like some people are double-jointed, some beings can write their names in the snow, or some creatures are allergic to water."

"Allergic to water?"

"Yes, very sad. Very thirsty people."

"How come I've never been able to do this before?"

"Did you know how?"

"No."

"Well, there you have it. Simple. Now, shall we try a few more?"

Onnser led Charley through some other straightforward tricks: manipulating liquids, making a pencil write, levitating heavier objects, and stunts of that ilk. Charley grew slightly more confident in repeating Onnser's words and motions, but the blank fact that these inanimate objects were responding to his rough beckoning continued to bewilder and delight him. Onnser seemed to be having almost as much fun as Charley, basking in doing these simple acts that, Charley guessed, Onnser probably had not gone through in quite some time. Charley, as he often was, was wrong. Onnser made Charley practice some of the tricks four or five times until he had the motions and words down, and then he suggested they bring in the others to watch.

"You see," said Onnser, "Tandor is an officious, excuse me, *official* investigator, and it would be nice to show him that you are a genuine apprentice rather than one of the many frauds."

"But I never said I was a magician or anything," Charley protested.

"No? Well, you did in a manner present yourself last night as one."

"I'd be glad to take it all back. I'll even sign something. Gladly. In fact, can I request it? Should I ask Tandor for some paper to sign? There has to be a form. I'll sign it. We can do that right now."

"No, there's no need to do that, Charley. We now know that you do have magic. The question is how much, isn't it?"

"Um. I don't know. Is that the question?"

"I'm going to call the rest of them in, and we will show them these last few tricks. Grimfir will be relieved, no doubt."

"I really don't think—"

"And Wednesday so loves a nice display of magic. I'm sorry, what were you about to say?"

Charley sat quiet. Was Onnser baiting him with the casual mention of Wednesday? Impossible. Impossible? Yes, surely. After all, Charley had just met her, and Onnser had only been witness to them together for a few minutes, and their interactions were nonexistent since entering the house. Onnser had no time and no evidence that Charley had any interest in Wednesday. In fact, if anything, the only observable dynamic was perhaps a faint disdain on

Wednesday's part, directed at Charley. Was it worth trying to show off in front of her? Onnser shifted noisily and spoke up again.

"If you'd really rather not, though, I am sure I could convince Tandor to tell some of his stories of investigations. The detective work, the arrests, the high drama of a fleeing suspect—all of it makes for a fascinating listen. Why, Wednesday practically grew up on the stories of Tandor bringing down such nefarious villains and frauds as Ell Elton, Horace the Menace, Bliver Redthumb, and Carl Frowner. When he really gets into a story, it's an amazing—"

"Maybe I might as well show them some of my tricks. You know, to pacify them, and then maybe I can move on and figure out how to get back to my home."

"I'll ask them to come in," Onnser said as he made for the door. As he opened it, he turned back to Charley and said nonchalantly, "And maybe we can still get Tandor to tell a story or two, after you are finished with your magic." And with that he turned and left the room, apparently missing Charley's semi-successful attempt to suppress a heartfelt glower cast after him.

CHAPTER SEVEN

Charley went through the basic tricks for the full critical audience, and in order of those impressed, most to least, were Grimfir, Tandor, and then Wednesday. Now, you might be thinking to yourself, "Oh, of course. Grimfir had no faith in him and the most exposure to him, and therefore was most surprised and impressed. Tandor was skeptical to begin with, being a magic fraud investigator, but that didn't make him an unbeliever—he just needed to see some evidence of magic, and so he was impressed. And Wednesday, well, she was still sore about being knocked down in the slimeway, and she hadn't been impressed by Charley from the get-go, so it stands to reason that she had the furthest to go to be impressed, and it just didn't happen."

Now, having just thought that to yourself, sitting there with a smug smile on your face, or perhaps ready to skip ahead, what would you think if I told you that, of those witnesses present, not including

Onnser, the range of skepticism, from greatest to least, was Tandor, Grimfir, and then Wednesday? Perhaps this fact is not what you thought? Perhaps you didn't bother to think about it at all, but that does not mean it's not an interesting idea to consider. To begin with, the fact that Wednesday was somewhat less than swept away by Charley so far had no bearing on her opinion of his ability to perform magic. She was rather like those fortunate sons and daughters who grow up in families of intelligentsia, literati, and the like, surrounded all their young lives with the vibrancy of the sharpest of minds and talents who come to visit and hang out with their similarly smart and capable parents. They are never particularly surprised to encounter someone else capable of greatness; it has become de rigueur that those they mix with should be eminently capable of just about anything, and that goes for those who have contrary personalities or are otherwise unlikable. So, here was Charley, one of any number of fledgling magicians, performing basic acts of enchantment, like so many others, but nothing that was especially dazzling, remarkable, or noteworthy. Therefore, Wednesday had no default of suspicion.

Grimfir was in the middle, which is the spot that tends to draw the least amount of initial attention, the spot that allows its holder to slide one way or the other as necessary, as prevailing winds establish themselves. In times when a majority is needed, these folk who sit in the middle are generally courted quite nicely by the extremes, though not without some measure of suspicion. Not to say that Grimfir knew how much Wednesday and Tandor believed, but his disposition tended toward a middle opinion when his blood wasn't up. His middling skepticism in regard to Charley's magic was a blend, of the oil-and-vinegar variety, of what he thought he believed in his heart and what he thought he knew in his heart. A fine distinction, to be sure.

It went like this: Having spent the past evening, night, and morning as Charley's ward, Grimfir had a pretty good idea that Charley was not all that much of a magician, all that much of a performer, and not all that much of a conversationalist. Had Grimfir known Ms. Formfal, Charley's math teacher, he probably would have agreed with her that "bobulous" was as accurate a word as any to describe the young Tooth. However, he also knew that Charley had shown flashes of promise, and that he had actually been able to free Onnser from the locked carriage, somehow. On top of that, Grimfir desperately wanted to believe that Charley could do magic, as everybody at Hololo's party who made up the bulk of the entertaining circuit now had it in their minds that Charley was Grimfir's apprentice. Grimfir's skepticism was held in check by his desire to believe, and his desire to believe was kept in check by his skepticism. This dichotomy would mean that Grimfir would throughout his life be somewhat grumpy.

And why was Tandor the most skeptical? Over the years, Tandor had investigated many magicians and so-called magicians of various degrees of talent, fraudulence, flatulence, goodness, and darkness. Those investigated had responded with violence, tears, murder and revenge, suicide, mockery, and good-natured laughter, and the responses seldom seemed to reflect the magician's legitimacy. To see Charley perform these tricks was certainly not a mind-blowing, awe-inspiring experience. On the whole, what Charley had done was relatively mundane. And while the performance had left Tandor of the mind-set that Charley was not to be considered an outright phony, there were certain elements to the presentation that raised flags in Tandor's intuition. Some of the spells sounded a mite archaic, and it was surprising to see someone as young and unknown as Charley Tooth muttering them to make a candle come alight and travel. These were spells that one would most likely learn only after reaching a certain skill level and choosing a course of study that demonstrated a keen interest in the historical aspects of magic, more than the practice of magic itself. In other words, overall these were smart, useless spells.

Now, Tandor was no expert magician (after all, he was leagues less able than Onnser, who himself was only semi-magnificent), but he had a keen instinct about this kind of thing, and the antediluvian spells made him wonder. Charley displayed none of the other characteristics of a magician of such education. Also, though he couldn't be entirely certain, it sounded to Tandor as though Charley had actually made a mistake or two in his recitation of the spells. There is a certain flow to an effective glamor, especially those of yore when magic was a much more graceful and erudite endeavor, and Charley had hit some hard spots that just didn't sound right. And mispronouncing a spell means, of course, that the spell won't work. But Charley's spells all carried themselves out smoothly. It didn't add up. However, since the spells were old and unknown, Tandor couldn't quite be sure of his conclusions.

When Charley performed the spell that made the

candle bend and flop like a piece of cooked spaghetti, Tandor was struck by Charley's use of the word "Bobdylan," which was something Tandor had never heard before. He suspected the actual word that Charley should have said was "bodlinian," whose etymology actually had to do with a certain eel-like fish, and therefore would have made more sense in the spell. These factors made Tandor suspicious, and he wondered if perhaps Onnser himself were doing something to help the boy out. But why would he be protecting Charley? Or even secretly aiding him? Onnser was a respected magician, and he had always advocated the exposure of fakes, the defrocking of corrupts, and the pursuit of purity. In many ways, Tandor felt that Onnser was even more zealous in the pursuit of maintaining authenticity in the field of sorcery. Onnser and Tandor were, generally, kindred spirits, acting as hunters who maintain the integrity of the flock. They might have differed in opinion and temperament, but their missions were similar.

Facing all of these questions, Tandor decided the best plan was to remain quiet on his objections and see what would unfold after further investigation. He felt an embracing, upwardly cascading feeling of excitement and familiarity wash over him—this was his element. The temperature of the day, the angle of the washed-out white light coming through the old windows in Onnser's lab, the smell of a lingering magic trick, and the thought that there was a puzzle to solve—all these thrilled Tandor, and he recognized that most comforting and exhilarating pang of a hunt that had just begun.

Had he and Charley been good friends, and had he mentioned this feeling to him, he would have found

Charley knew the exact feeling. It was akin to the feeling Charley got in the late fall, when soccer season began. Damp yellow and brown leaves on the sidewalks, a slight bite in the crispness of the air, stiff short grass, clear blue skies, and an impending soccer game combined to give Charley goose bumps every year.

But Tandor and Charley were not friends, and so the conversation did not come up. In fact, Tandor and Charley were practically the opposite of friends, as Charley was the prey Tandor was hoping to flush out. Charley did not necessarily view Tandor as an enemy or adversary, though he certainly felt ill at ease in his presence. But at this moment, he wasn't giving him much thought, as he was quite busy mooning inside about Wednesday O'Friday. He was thinking in particular of a scenario in which it was terribly dark out and Wednesday was terribly scared, and by making a candle light and float about, he would win her love. But he had a feeling that Wednesday was really very unafraid of the dark, and she didn't like showboating. Onnser brought him back to reality by standing and taking the attention of the room into his outstretched arms.

"There we have it! Bravo for Charley!"

The others gave a smattering of applause, and Onnser continued.

"Grimfir, we are to congratulate you on bringing us a young magician full of such promise and potential. I, of course, am honored to take him in as my apprentice. We will make a great magician of him yet. Serve him well, Grimfir. I have a feeling there's a lot in store for this boy here."

And, with that, Onnser quickly and forever changed

the relationships between the people in the room and Charley. Grimfir was no longer Charley's master, but rather more or less his valet. It was sort of an awkward occurrence for Grimfir, as he couldn't complain too much, despite the slight he must have felt at the role reversal between himself and his guest. After all, Grimfir looked up to Onnser, and still being associated with Charley would be good for his career, as well as stabilizing his social standing, which heretofore had often fluctuated. And now that Charley was the apprentice to Onnser the semi-Magnificent, Grimfir too would be vaulted echelons in prestige, akin to a minor-leaguer being brought up to the majors. Onnser, as a semi-Magnificent, was at the top level of magicians practicing in the land at that time. The Historic Ganka was much higher, but as he had been exiled, he was not officially recognized by the official officials. The Ruling Powers had decided at this point that no magician would be higher than semi-Magnificent, with the singular (well, double, actually) exception of Dix and Dax, the Orphan Lords. Perhaps not surprisingly, Dix and Dax were the Ruling Powers. So Onnser, and about two dozen other magicians who were semi-Magnificent, operated under the auspices of the government, so long as they didn't stir up trouble. It was, in effect, as high as you could go without being brought into the actual administration of the Ruling Powers. And Onnser, like many of his ilk, had zero desire to be a part of that system, so he was quite content to be where he was and not draw huge amounts of attention to himself.

Dix and Dax, the Orphan Lords, were joint rulers of Nivalg. They often claimed to represent all sides of the populace (well, both sides), with Dix often claiming to support the regulatory commissions that controlled how much a farmer could produce, how much magic a wizard could engage in, and why a raise in taxes would benefit the social services that were sort of in place. Dix pushed government intervention to initiate progress and radical change in order to ensure the status quo of the world. Dax, on the other hand, advocated allowing groups to regulate themselves, believing that free enterprise would keep everyone from farmers to magicians in check. Dax claimed that radical change was bad for progress, and that the natural disposition of the people in continuing their traditional values and institutions was the correct way to ensure the status quo of the world. He backed government intervention to guarantee that government agencies did not intervene too much in the lives of the populace. Dix and Dax, the Orphan Lords, often switched philosophies, depending on the issue at hand and the way the media reported the majority of opinion seemed to be leaning.

Wednesday explained all of this to Charley as they headed into town to collect supplies and groceries that Onnser had sent them to fetch, while Grimfir stayed behind to discuss Charley's training with Onnser. Tandor had excused himself at the natural conclusion of the meeting in which Onnser took over responsibility for Charley. Tandor suddenly had another element to his job of investigating Charley. That Charley was now a legitimate apprentice to a recognized semi-Magnificent wizard meant that investigations into Charley's authenticity would have to be more covert than before, but also more important. Charley had just unwittingly taken his first step into the politics not only of wizardry but also of Nivalgian government. Wednesday did not explain this part to Charley, as she knew nothing of it.

Charley was elated that Onnser had sent just the two of them on errands. And although Wednesday did not appear to share his enthusiasm in their sojourn, she had gone into a thorough explanation of the workings of the government, practically unbidden. Charley had hoped to engage her in personal discussion in order for them to get to know each other better, but he found the politics interesting and bizarre. In fact, he was so engaged by the topic of discussion that he continued it, rather than trying to divert things back to Wednesday herself.

"If Dix and Dax rule jointly, are they always fighting?" he asked.

"They often argue in public, to show that each represents a portion of the constituents, but then they retire in private together to make their decision. Invariably, each will end up portraying whatever ruling comes out of their meeting as advancing the interests of their own party so that everyone feels satisfied."

"What's the point, then?"

"Most of the masses, I guess, feel comforted by it. There's not a lot of thought on the part of the average person. Everyone pretty much struggles to stay out of the way of the government."

"So which one did you vote for? Dix or Dax?"

"You have to vote for both of them."

"Why?"

"Why? Because there is nobody else to vote for. And Dix and Dax insist that we appoint both of them."

"And nobody else runs? Nobody else complains?"

"Well, there certainly have been agitators and independent people who push for change, or some sort of meaning to the whole thing, but they usually find themselves destroyed."

"Destroyed? Financially? Politically?"

"Physically. The Orphan Lords' policy on dissension is notoriously aggressive."

"That's terrible. How long have things been like this?"

"Dix and Dax have been in power for generations. Generations."

"So . . . they must be getting on in years then?"

"Actually, no. They manage to move around in the time zones on the planet, allowing them to remain much younger than you would think. I must admit it's a pretty brilliant tactic."

"The time zones?"

"Yeah. You aren't familiar with time zones? They don't have time zones where my name is a day of the week? What kind of place are you from, anyway?"

"No, we do have time zones. But all that means is that different parts of the world are at different hours at the same time. And then sometimes that changes with Daylight Savings, except in those places where people choose not to observe it."

"That sounds really efficient there, Charley. What good are they, then?"

It was the first time she had called him by his name. Charley was instantly blushing, but encouraged.

"Well, Wednesday, I suppose it helps make sure that people are all watching the right television programs after dinner. I think that's the big thing. How are time zones here any different?"

"Time zones here don't vary by mere hours. Everything varies, and by magnitudes. You'll see a spaceship in one time zone, a horse and carriage in the next."

Wednesday and Charley were now well into the shopping trip. Wednesday did all of the selecting, and she gave Charley the bags to carry. He didn't pay too much attention to anything other than Wednesday and what she was saying. He assumed what they were buying were the standard magic and witchery items such as eye of newt, bat wings, and spider hearts. He was more or less right.

"But how do these things exist together in one time zone—like Onnser's carriage and the silver-air-speeder thing that I saw Duke Riebald vomit on at Hololo's party?"

"Simple. It all depends on where you started. If you began with a bicycle in one of the mid-era time zones, and then take it into a later time zone, it updates itself into something more advanced, such as a rocketbike. But if you start with something like a spaceship and then go into a time zone of less-advanced technology, you'll probably find yourself driving a horse and buggy. If you are clever and have the money, you can keep moving around and improving your stuff, playing the markets well, and do all right for yourself. Dix and Dax, the Orphan Lords, are great at it, manipulating the zones to their advantage. It helps to have the most powerful magic in the world."

"Does it affect anything else? The time zones, I mean?"

"Oh, sure, just about everything. Building structures, fire codes, health care. I won't lie to you—it can be annoying."

"Thank you for not lying to me. It does sound inordinately frustrating."

"It certainly keeps things interesting."

In the meantime, Tandor had returned to the Ministry of Investigation. He needed to figure out for himself what it was that Onnser was doing, if he was protecting and even covering for Charley. What did Onnser know that Tandor did not? Tandor and Onnser had worked together in the past on this sort of thing, and Onnser had never tried to deceive Tandor as he just had. It didn't make sense. Tandor had a professional duty and Onnser a moral obligation to remove fakes from the industry. Tandor worked for the government, and though it could be argued, quietly, by some, that the methods the government used to censure the frauds were often severe, bloody, and extreme, it was the law of the land. It was the law of Dix and Dax, the Orphan Lords. And as long as they were in power, Tandor worked for their bureau. He knew well what Onnser's sympathies were, and that Onnser's primary interest was in doing right by the society of magic, not by the decree of the Orphan Lords. So, what was it that was making Onnser behave this way about Charley? Tandor was back at his desk looking through his files to see if there was anything to dig up on Charley Tooth when there was a sharp knock at his door.

"Come in," he called, looking up.

In strode Gwenowit Husk, Tandor's boss's boss. Head of the division. Gwenowit was large, solid, and hatchet-faced. He had been a knight of single purpose and singular strength, and now that he had joined the administrative side of the government, he found that his doggedness translated well into good results that pleased Dix and Dax, which therefore meant that Gwenowit made a decent living for his family. He still wore his sword every day, and it was with great gusto that he would take himself into the field to mete out justice, which was quite unlike others of his position and standing, who remained more office-bound. What he lacked for in cunning he made up for in devotion and perseverance. He was a tough man, a fair boss, and dutiful provider for his family. He was, by most accounts, in the prime of his life, and he knew it. It was a great surprise to Tandor that Gwenowit should make an appearance in his office. He had only done so once before, and that was when Tandor had first started with the agency. Since then, it had been customary for Tandor Ovenheat to be summoned to the Office of Gwenowit Husk if Gwenowit wanted to see him. Tandor stood up briskly.

"Good afternoon, Sir Gwenowit!"

"Please, please, Ovenheat, sit, sit. And the 'sir' bit is unnecessary, though flattering. I do miss the days of being an out-and-out knight, and it's nice when the younger generation recognizes the effort and sacrifice knights have put in over the years. Now, sit, please, I insist."

Tandor sat down at Gwenowit's bidding. Gwenowit then looked about for a place to sit, as well. But, as Tandor certainly was not a higher-up in the agency, he had the standard government issue of a single chair, a single desk, a single bookshelf, and a single filing cabinet. The rest of his floorspace was a labyrinth of stacks of papers. Upon seeing Gwenowit look for a seat, Tandor stood back up to offer his chair. Gwenowit waved him back down and leaned impressively against the shabby filing cabinet, his great hand resting on the hilt of his sword.

"No, no, sit. I don't need to sit. I was just popping in to say hello."

"Hello, sir."

"You were at the gala at Dame Summersweat's last night, yes?"

"Yes, I was, sir."

"Lovely woman, she. Completely charming, if I do say so myself, eh, Ovenheat?"

"A treasure, sir."

"A treasure! Yes! I like that! How was the party?"

"Excellent as usual, sir. She's a most accomplished hostess. I am sorry you were not able to attend."

Tandor had never known Gwenowit Husk to be so chatty. This man was affable with his workers, but it never treaded into sociability. Ever keen, Tandor was immediately suspicious that something was up. Rather than quickly negotiate his way out of this unfamiliar and somewhat uncomfortable conversation by pressing Gwenowit to the point of his visit, he figured he would keep things going, glean what he could, and leave any pointed remarks up to his boss's boss.

"Ah, well. My youngest, Mopslin, had his first public tilting and jousting, and I certainly wasn't going to miss that. Now, at this party, was there anything unusual?"

"No, sir. Nothing in particular, I don't think."

"Really? It was my understanding that Onnser the semi-Magnificent introduced his new apprentice."

Tandor had made something of a name for himself in the agency due to his ability to assess things quickly, and he felt immediately the danger of the situation at present. He could go either way with his answer, and it was in a matter of seconds that he went with his instinct.

"No, sir. I suppose you mean the boy who performed. He was actually there as the squire, I believe, to Grimfir Boldrock."

"Boldrock?"

"A minor showman, really. An entertainer more than anything. He often performs at the Summersweat parties."

"Scaly fellow? Dark green? Kind of gruff?"

"Yes, sir."

"Hmph. Well, I have good information that Onnser was interested in this squire. What do you think?"

"Well, sir. As you know, Onnser actively pursues the trials of young practitioners, in the interest of keeping his profession pure. He seemed to show the same interest in this boy's abilities as he has in the past with any number of like persons who have exhibited some magical leaning."

"Yes, of course. Onnser's record stands for itself. But let's not forget that he has refused, time after time, an invitation from the Ruling Powers to join them in full-fledged investigation. In no small way has this limited his rise as a wizard. While we as the government seek to control those who practice magic for the good of the population and in the interest of progress, he seems more interested solely in the purity, and therefore the strength, of those who practice magic. Understand?"

"Yes, sir. I am very familiar with Onnser's file."

"Of course you are, of course you are. You are close with him, yes? I believe you are rather social with him?"

"Yes sir, I—"

"Comparatively, yes, of course, I know. Good work. Had you not been, I would be telling you to become so in this very conversation. Now what do you think of that? I recognize the tactical advantage of having one of our own close with Onnser. I am not saying I don't trust the man. No. But we do need to keep an eye on him. And not to worry, I am not asking you to jeopardize your established relationship with him. On the contrary, keep it up. I am going to get personally involved with this case, you see. Onnser will be expecting us to investigate any claims of legitimacy if he takes on a new apprentice. My presence will show how serious we are taking the case, and it will distract any suspicion toward you. You are already the inside man. I am not asking you to do anything unsavory or unethical; I just need you to keep your eyes open. If this boy turns out to be a fraud, your job is to turn him in. If this boy turns out to be what Onnser might present him as, then that's fine. Fine, of course. And if he turns out to be stronger, more powerful, more magical than we think, then your duty is of course to alert us at once, so that we may move to constrain him."

"More powerful, sir? I have never seen anything in my—"

"Yes, of course, of course. Just a normal precaution we have to take, you see. You see?"

Tandor very much wanted to ask a question, but he didn't know the best way to raise it. Gwenowit noticed the pause.

"Question, Ovenheat? You can ask me anything."

"Well, sir, it's just that I have worked here for many years, and never has this sort of interest or directive been given to a situation such as this one. And yesterday was the first time the boy ever made the scene. On top of that, allow me to say that he did nothing in particular at the Summersweat party that was particularly impressive. So. Why the special attention?"

Gwenowit straightened up amiably and powerfully. He smiled, and headed for the door.

"That, my boy, is classified. Keep up the good work."

Tandor watched as the door shut behind Gwenowit. His heart was pounding. The hunt was on. Something far more extensive than he had imagined was afoot, and it was clear that his role was going to be a most difficult one to carry out. It was imperative that he see Onnser again as soon as he possibly could, for a private conversation. If Charley were to be formally announced as Onnser's new apprentice, it would draw such scrutiny that it would be near impossible for Tandor to carry out his job as he hoped. The best thing for all concerned parties would be for Charley to remain at Grimfir's longer, and train at Onnser's as a visiting student rather than an apprentice. This appealed doubly to Tandor. It was clear to him that Charley had a crush on Wednesday, and it wouldn't be healthy for him to be around her all of the time, as he would be as an apprentice. "Yes," Tandor said to himself, "it is better for Wednesday, as well. He's not right for her."

Tandor was cheered up just thinking of the plan. He enjoyed visiting with Onnser, regardless. And it was undeniable that Wednesday had blossomed into quite the devastating young woman.

Chapter Eight

After Wednesday and Charley returned from picking up the sundry items that Onnser had requested, Onnser suggested to Charley that he bring his stuff over from Grimfir's. He again sent Wednesday with Charley, as he wasn't convinced Charley would be able to find his way back and forth through town yet. About halfway to Grimfir's, Charley remembered that he actually didn't have any stuff.

"No stuff? No stuff at all?" Wednesday asked incredulously, and not a little impatiently.

"No. I'm sorry. I completely forgot. No stuff."

"How is that possible? How do you travel?"

"I really don't know how I travel."

"You can be really exasperating," she said, exasperated, as she stickily made her way to the edge of the slimeway.

Charley followed her as they got on the other direction and headed back to Onnser's. When they returned, Onnser and Grimfir were wrapping up their discussion, which really was not all that interesting a discussion, so we won't go into it here. Wednesday explained the situation to them, which made Onnser laugh and Grimfir roll his eyes and look almost imploringly at Onnser. Onnser stood up and they followed him into his office, which was down the hall from his lab. In his office, which was remarkably clean, organized, and well-lit, Onnser went to a desk drawer. He removed a large wallet and looked through it.

"Let's see what we can do for you." He flipped through the billfold and brought out a stack of paper money. He handed it to Wednesday. "Will you help Charley find a clothier and some suitable clothes? I am sure that this one outfit will not be comfortable day in, day out."

Wednesday took the money and turned to Charley. "Okay, let's go."

"Wait. I don't want to be ungrateful or anything, but I really don't think I need you guys to buy me any clothes."

"What are you going to do? Wear your only set of clothes into tatters?"

"No. Hum. Well. See, the thing is, I have to get home. I mean, I don't plan on staying. It's very generous of you all to offer me the chance to be an apprentice of some sort, and to buy me clothes, and all that sort of thing, but I really have to be going. I want to go home."

There was an empty silence for a few moments as Grimfir, Onnser, and Wednesday looked at him. Wednesday spoke first.

"How will you get home, Charley?"

Charley looked at them for a few moments in

silence.

"You don't know?" he finally asked. "I thought you would know. I need to get home. I really do. There has to be a way. Nobody else in my family ever thinks to throw out expired medicine, which reminds me that it's probably well past my turn to take out the trash."

Onnser replied, "That's beyond any of our powers, Charley. I don't think even Dix and Dax have that kind of oomph."

"But there has to be a portal? Clearly, logically, there was a way here, so it stands to reason there is a way back."

"Not to be a killjoy, Boy," said Grimfir, "but you can't put a lot of stock in clarity, logic, and reason. It doesn't usually pan out. That's the way the life works. I don't mean to discourage you, but there you have it."

"But I can't stay here. I don't belong here. I need to find a way home."

Onnser sat down. "Charley, we will help you in any way we can, but we can't control how, when, or why it happens. There's really not a whole lot you can do, so you might as well get comfortable. Does this make sense?"

It sort of made sense to Charley. But he still didn't like it.

"But I really need to find my way home. Excuse me."

Charley walked out of the room and left Onnser's house. He got outside and looked up at the sky. There had to be a way home, somewhere. Charley felt melancholy, and then he thought to himself, "Wow, I am actually feeling melancholy. Is this how

Hamlet felt? Isn't that what Mr. Vaughan said? Or was that Macbeth? No I think it was Hamlet." Then he got to thinking about Mr. Vaughan, his English teacher. Mr. Vaughan was a creative, respected, but somewhat ridiculous teacher who often levied outlandish challenges upon his students. In Charley's case, he challenged him to use the word "maleficent" legitimately in every single composition he turned in that year.

As Charley continued walking, he realized he was actually thinking about classes at school, and he didn't feel quite as melancholy, oddly enough. He began walking slowly, thinking that he would scour the town, the countryside, the world, until he found the way home. Shortly, he realized that he was engaging in behavior similar to characters in eighties movies, in which the protagonists would go out late at night and ride the bus or the subway or walk around or drive around, all alone, with some maudlin song playing, while they Thought About Things and did their best To Come to Grips with Sadness, Conflict, or Loss. As soon as Charley realized this, he felt ridiculous, so he turned around and went back into Onnser's house.

The other three had remained where they had been. They looked at Charley. Charley looked at them. Wednesday moved toward him.

"We should get going if we're going to get you some new clothing before the shops close."

Charley followed her back out of the house, back to the slimeway, and they rode to town in silence. The first store Wednesday led him to specialized in men's suits, nearly identical to ones he might have worn on Earth. An extraordinarily thin, pale thing came over to assist them. It was slender and lithe, with its entire body having the dimensions of a shelf in a bookcase, though it was easily six feet tall and smoothly flexible. Its face was on the narrow edge of the body, and it wore goggles over its delicate eyes.

"We would like to buy some suits," Wednesday said.

Charley looked at her. "Actually, I'm not much of a suit wearer."

"You have to get some suits."

"I'd rather not. I don't really wear suits."

The suit clerk, sensing the disagreement, quickly and quietly shimmied out of earshot. Its ears were large and on the broad side of its body. Thinking about it later, Charley realized the clerk would not have been out of earshot had it been in Namibia, and Charley wasn't even sure where Namibia was, as he was only slightly above the average American high school student in terms of knowing geography. Wednesday turned to Charley.

"Look, apprentices wear suits. That's what they do. They wear them. You are an apprentice now. You wear suits now. That's why we are getting you suits. Got it?"

"What, this is like a uniform? Apprentices have to wear uniforms? Like in a school? Like in one of those schools that teach geography really well?"

"Whatever." Wednesday turned back to wave the clerk over.

When she said, "Whatever," it immediately remind-ed Charley of Samantha Mallory, a transfer student at Charley's high school. Whenever she recounted a conversation or similar interaction, she always used the "She was all, 'I didn't say that,' and he was all, 'You did last Saturday at the putt-putt course,'" structure. It annoyed Charley, but getting to know Samantha in drivers' ed. class, he found her to be really funny, and her language charmed him. She was from California. She was lanky, with blond hair dyed black. They would usually hang out after class, to go to the diner or to a movie with the other classmates. Charley would usually ask her as class was winding down if she planned on going to the postclass thing, and she invariably would reply, "Whatever." And, invariably, she would go. Sometimes it would be just the two of them. And, as always, when he asked what she wanted to do, she would say, "Whatever," and he would tease her about it.

In the summer, she called him up once and asked him if he wanted to go bike riding at the abandoned carnival that evening. He did want to, but it was his aunt's birthday, and he was required to go to that. Samantha's response was, "Oh, that's too bad. It really is. But, you know, whatever." Charley never heard from Samantha again—when school started up and she didn't show, he found out her family had moved again, this time to Kansas City. It was with great regret that he realized much later that she liked him, and that he had let the opportunity slide. He knew it was ridiculous, but now whenever he heard a girl use "whatever" so liberally, he thought it might mean that whoever it was liked him.

Except Wednesday, who had made it pretty clear that she didn't. Knocking her into the slime probably hindered things, Charley knew. He sighed aloud. The suit clerk had finished measuring him and had suits for Charley to try on. Charley went into the changing room six times, for six different suits, thinking about

Samantha, his drivers' ed. teacher warning against overdriving one's headlights, and how old his aunt was. When he emerged wearing the final suit, Wednesday said, "We'll take them all." They moved on from that store to a few regular clothing stores, where Charley picked up pants, shirts, socks, a hat, a coat, and even a tunic. He and Wednesday talked very little until finally Charley said, "Okay, I think that'll probably do me just fine."

Wednesday turned to him with a slight smile on her face and said, "Are you sure? Are you sure that's everything?"

Charley, seeing the hint of a smile, felt his throat clutch itself and all the moisture in his mouth suddenly go vacationing off the face of the planet, perhaps back to Earth. "I—I think so. Is there something else you think I should get?"

"Well, I was wondering if you maybe wore underwear."

The sun in the solar system that contains Charley's home planet, Earth, has a surface temperature of about 10,000 degrees Fahrenheit. Charley remembered this from Mr. Blanchette's science class, because Mr. Blanchette was crazy, scared all the students, and made learning fun. At this moment, in front of Wednesday, Charley's face felt approximately as hot as the surface of the sun.

"Oh! Ah. Hum. Yes, I do. I mean, I do wear underwear. I do."

"Well, then maybe you should get some more. Unless you want to wear the same dirty pair day in, day out. What kind of underwear do you wear?" And she held up several options, including a very skimpy one on which she tested the waistband.

Due to the tremendous amount of pressure bearing down on its core, the center of the sun is made all the hotter, approaching, it is thought, 30,000,000 degrees Fahrenheit, making it the hottest naturally occurring object in the solar system. Now, Charley was no man of physics, but he was reasonably certain that his face was running a close second. Wednesday was still holding the underwear, looking at him with a raised eyebrow, her gray-and-gold eyes flashing with amusement. Charley was no stranger to being embarrassed. He was, after all, bobulous. There were a number of responses that he had given in embarrassing situations, all of them standard—pouting, hiding, pretending nothing happened, turning on someone weaker, and so on. This time, looking at this strange, beautiful girl holding up this pair of strange, ugly underpants, here in this strange, strange world, with him still stumbling through things not knowing what the hell to do, all he could do was grin. And then smile. And then he said:

"How terribly embarrassing for me."

And then, proving the existence of a higher power, Wednesday laughed. She laughed loudly, and sweetly, and strongly.

The first time you make a girl laugh is the most golden moment imaginable. A laugh that defies her ability to stop it. Something that overtakes her, something that reveals to you what her happiness looks like. Charley, seeing Wednesday laugh like this, felt radiant, as though he were as bright as the sun. But he didn't remember how bright that was, so he couldn't really back it up. Incidentally, the sun's brightness is said to be 328.6 trillion trillion watts.

Wednesday put the underwear down, and Charley

grabbed a couple of packs of a standard boxer-type of undergarments, and after Wednesday made an obvious deal of having the clerk do a price check over the P.A. system and then paid, the two of them headed back to Onnser's. Evening was descending as they rode the slimeway (which Wednesday referred to as "The Way") back out of town. The two of them remarked on casual things, such as the prettiness of the sunset, the pleasantness of the weather, and the man they passed on the way, sleeping peacefully in the slow-moving slime. Charley had figured he might as well not push anything with Wednesday, as it was enough for now that he'd got her to laugh, and seemingly not at him as much as at his ability to handle his embarrassment. He'd chalk that up as a success and see what followed from it.

When they returned to Onnser's, the door to his office was locked, and there were muffled voices from the inside. Wednesday and Charley stood outside the door, unable to make out who it was. Wednesday brought Charley back into the living room, and from there she called out, "Uncle Onnser, we're ho-oome!"

A few seconds later, they heard the office door unlock and open, and then Onnser call out, "O-okay! Be there in a minute!" and then the door shut and locked again.

Wednesday led Charley upstairs, where a hallway branched off in each direction. She led him down the one on the left, to the door on the right. She opened it, said, "Light," and the room brightened up immediately, as though from everywhere.

"This will be your room," she said to Charley. "Bed, dresser, closet. Window." All of these existed in the room, as she indicated. "Drop your stuff, make yourself comfortable, and then we'll meet back downstairs with my uncle to go over the plan."

The room was spare. Apart from the low, single bed and the high, plain dresser, there wasn't much to it. There was a single wall decoration, which turned out to be kind of marvelous. It was a planet with three moons, rotating and orbiting around the entirety of the room, traversing the walls. Other heavenly bodies, such as comets and meteors, occasionally swung into view. It orbited slowly, deliberately. Charley watched it for a few moments, and then he was drawn to the window by a sound outside. The single window in his room looked over the back of Onnser's house, and there was apparently some sort of back door, for a figure was stealing away into the darkness of the trees, looking as though it came from the house. Just before the darkness completely obscured the figure, Charley was able to make out who it was. Tandor Ovenheat. Charley shivered. He gazed out of the window for a few more minutes until he heard Wednesday's voice call him from downstairs.

The living room of Onnser the semi-Magnificent was a striking place. The furniture had a lot of character—couches, chairs, bookshelves, and tables all had intricate carvings of beings and animals. There were ornate lamps that instead of shades and bulbs or candles had floating clouds of color. There was a large, dark-leafed plant in one corner that seemed to seethe ominously. A large fireplace in the image of an open-mouthed lion took up the center of the far wall. There was a carpet that looked like a garden-variety-oriental rug, but wherever your feet touched it, the colors would rush and scatter, like minnows in a shallow pool. When Charley came downstairs, Wednesday was curled up in a large comfortable chair, and Onnser was reshuffling some books in one of the bookcases. Charley sat down.

"You'd better not get too comfortable," Onnser said.

Charley immediately hopped back up again. Onnser turned, smiling.

"No, I mean upstairs. I've been rethinking things."

"Oh?"

"Yes. Please, sit, I really didn't mean for you not to be comfortable right here and now."

Charley sat in another less comfortable chair. Wednesday shifted where she was, and the cat came rolling in. This cat looked in many respects like a cat you or I would be familiar with, but with one startling, glaring difference that Charley would never really get used to. Rather than four legs, it had twelve legs, and they stuck out from its body on all sides. To move, the cat barely had to exert any leg muscle power at all, other than to pitch itself one way or the other in a roll, where the next set of legs would take the ground and continue. It made for a very agile cat, one that could switch directions at the speed of thought. Something about it vaguely upset Charley, and always would. Maybe it was that a creature with more than four legs, in Charley's experience, never had fur. Charley continued to look at the cat warily.

"Charley, I think it might be better for you if you stayed at Grimfir's for a while."

Wednesday looked at Onnser quizzically. Charley noted to himself that she looked at her uncle that way, without any sort of disappointment or other emotion.

"But I just moved in here. I am a little confused.

Actually, I am a lot confused."

Onnser sat forward and rested his forearms on his knees. "Well, Charley. Perhaps we were a bit hasty in moving you over here. After all, Grimfir is your attendant, and he already has a place to live, with room to spare. If I took you in now, then how would Grimfir be able to assist you effectively? Until such time that you are an official apprentice to me—and there is still a ways to go on that—it just makes more sense for you to stay with Grimfir. I don't have the room or the need for both of you to be living here, so until you are somewhat established, we'll just keep you over there. I apologize for this inconvenience, but I'm afraid it really is the wisest move given the circumstances."

There was not a whole lot more for anyone to say at that point, so, appropriately, nobody said anything for a minute or two. The fire continued to crackle. Charley continued to process what was going on. He thought about Tandor, and decided to speak.

"I have a question, actually."

"Yes, my boy?"

"I saw Tandor sneaking off into the trees just before I came downstairs."

Wednesday looked sharply at Onnser, this time with a pointed edge to her face. Onnser remained quiet, but a thoughtful look was in his eye.

"That's not a question."

"Why not?"

"I mean, what you said to me was not a question. It was a declarative statement. You began by saying you have a question."

"Oh. I guess it's more of a concern. I guess."

"I see. What is your concern?"

"Why was Tandor sneaking off like that?"

"Why is that a concern of yours?"

"I figured it had something to do with me."

"Why did you figure that?"

"Because you said he investigates magician-types."

"But I thought you professed not to be a magician-type."

"I'm not. But if he thinks I am, then he's probably around to investigate me, right?

Wednesday spoke up. "But you are a magician-type. We all saw you do some tricks."

Charley blushed again. "I mean, yes, I am, maybe, but not. . . ." He didn't know how to finish.

"Charley," Onnser broke in, "there is a difference between being a magician-type, wanting to be a magician-type but not being a magician-type, not being a magician-type, and being a magician-type but not wanting to be a magician-type. You've had a long couple of days—you're tired; you're confused. Don't worry about Tandor—we will be able to deal with him just fine. Vang will take you and your stuff back to Grimfir's tonight. Tomorrow you and Grimfir both will come here, and your training will begin. At some point down the line, you probably will move here, but I do not know when that time will come. But it's getting late, so you best be off."

It was not the first time Charley knew an adult was lying to him or otherwise masking the truth, but it was the first time that adult was someone like Onnser, rather than being a relative or a schoolteacher. Charley's respect for Onnser was different than it was for family members and teachers, so it troubled him to find this deceit. He'd come to appreciate Onnser's reasons in later years, though he would never fully agree with it.

Onnser waved his hand in the air, and a soft chiming was heard. In short order, the tall and quiet Vang appeared, dressed in black tails, black shirt, black hat. He stopped just inside the doorway and nodded his head to Onnser.

"Vang, Charley will be staying at Grimfir's. Please help him with his luggage and take him to Grimfir's as soon as he is ready. Perhaps we should have dinner first—you must be quite hungry, Charley."

Vang nodded and disappeared, and Onnser, Wednesday, and Grimfir adjourned to the dining room, which was a classy blue space with a mid-sized black table in the middle, six black chairs, and a band of lightfish around the walls.

"I find the lightfish add a pleasant atmosphere to this room. It's the only room I have that still has them," said Onnser as he waved his hand and muttered a quick word, bringing the fish to an appropriate brightness. Vang almost immediately returned downstairs with all of Charley's new clothing packed neatly into two suitcases. Charley marveled at how quickly Vang had taken care of it. Vang disappeared into the kitchen, reappearing a few minutes later in three trips, first with a substance not unlike mashed potatoes, then with a kind of leafy salad, and finally with a main platter with a delicious slab of some sort of meat on it. Charley did not even ask what any of it was, allowing himself to pretend that there would be nothing revolting in it. The food was delicious, the conversation sparse, and soon enough Charley found himself in the loaded carriage as Vang took a long step up to get into the driver's seat. And off they rode into the black, black night.

Charley gazed out the windows at the stars, wishing that he knew more constellations than Orion, Cassiopeia, the Seven Sisters, and the Big Dipper. He wondered if any of the stars out there might at least confirm in his mind that he was in the same galaxy in which he'd grown up.

It seemed to Charley that they were taking the back roads. They were not near The Way, and the roads they followed were dark enough for Charley to believe they were far from the main drag. The only light was from two moons, the larger of which was about twice the size of the one Charley was used to. At one point along the journey, the carriage slowed considerably, and Charley saw, or maybe felt, a shadow from above left come gliding swiftly down toward the front of the carriage. He heard a slight rustling of papers, and then nothing. As the horses regained their pace, he cautiously poked his head out of the window to sneak a look at the driver's seat, half afraid he would see nothing but the bloody lower half of the chauffeur; but there was the inscrutable Vang, sitting silently and looking dead ahead down the quiet road before them. Somewhat chilled, Charley brought his head back in and closed the small window.

As Charley sat back against the bench, it occurred to him that maybe he had in fact died, and this was the afterlife—a bizarre mix of creatures in a somewhat recognizable world. Not heaven, hell, or purgatory, but just another life, this time with an odder assortment of characters (though, to be fair, Charley's cousin Millie was still, all things considered, the oddest being Charley had ever encountered. But she lived in Kentucky). After about half an hour of thinking about it, Charley decided that he was in fact still alive, and that this was in fact not any sort of afterlife or new life. After all, he was still Charley Tooth. No one seemed to doubt that.

He began thinking of what it meant to be Charley Tooth. He thought about his parents, and about his sisters Cynthia and Tabitha, and his good dog Shiny. He thought about his friends at school, his teachers. He thought about the work he had done at school, and he thought about his after-school job working at the deli. He thought about his free time, watching TV, playing soccer (which he loved) and basketball (which he didn't), and about whole days in which he did nothing at all. He began to wonder what it was about himself that made him himself. He wondered what it was that allowed him to be the same person when he woke up in the morning.

He remembered Mr. Blanchette teaching him that the body, every seven years, has generated a whole new set of cells. When someone in his class asked how, then, could someone know he was the same person as he was seven years ago, Mr. Blanchette had laughed almost balefully and said, "I teach science, not psychology." Mr. Blanchette went on to tell the class that blood completely circulates the body every twenty-three seconds, and ever after Charley often found himself counting to twenty-three without even thinking about it as he walked, or sat on a bus, or waited for sleep to overtake him.

He now thought again of the workings of his body, and he keenly sensed the weight in his feet, even as he sat, that indicated the mass of his body, and how that mass and that body had changed and grown—out of nothing, so to speak—over that past decade and a half. He tried to debate with himself whether the personality, the self, the ego finds its identity in what work it has accomplished, in its physical existence, or in its in relation to other selves. Or if it was some delicate combination of those factors. He was nowhere near a satisfying resolution to this question as he dozed off, and as soon as he dozed off the carriage pulled up to Grimfir's.

Vang had him quickly unloaded, and Grimfir had been expecting him. Charley went down to his room, felt the soft mattress of the floor under his feet, and shut the door, again exhausted. He went over to the wall and looked at the lightfish tank. This time, he spread his hands out wide and felt something in him a little more under control as he stretched and stretched, and his hand went out and out, and he slapped both at once, getting the desired dimness after only a couple of tries. Satisfied, he pushed his suitcases against the wall and went to sleep.

Chapter Nine

The next day, Charley and Grimfir again ate breakfast, but this time Grimfir did more preparation, and even had juice already poured for Charley. And they both cleaned the house, rather than just Charley. Late morning, they set out for Onnser's place, for a full day of training and tutoring for Charley, with Grimfir attending. To Charley, the whole day felt like the first day of any school—learning where things were, certain protocols, getting a feel for the flow of the hours, the uncertainty and the too-much introductory work right up front. Wednesday was there, picking up some of the lessons as well, but doing more administrative work for Onnser. Just after lunch, Charley and Grimfir were working with Onnser on copying down some spells in their notebooks, and Wednesday was upstairs looking for a missing text, when there was a knock at the door. Shortly, Vang appeared at the door to the lab and simply looked at Onnser. Onnser nodded to him, and Vang disappeared again. Onnser turned to Charley.

"There is someone here that wants to meet you. He works for the government. His name is Gwenowit Husk. This much is important—you are not yet my official apprentice. Once you are, he will be a regular, snooping figure in your life."

Grimfir's scales bristled and the lizard showed his teeth. "Everybody snooping, everybody snooping. We can handle this Husk person. Let's go."

The three of them headed into the hallway. As they approached the living room, Grimfir decided to begin his offensive, and said just loud enough that someone waiting to be received would be able to hear:

"And Gwenowit? What kind of name is that? Isn't Gwenowit a girl's name?"

Just then they came into the room and encountered Gwenowit, who stood fully and majestically just inside the door. His large hand was, as usual, on the large hilt of his large sword. Grimfir looked at him with wide eyes. As did Charley. Gwenowit looked levelly at Grimfir and adjusted his sword hand ever so slightly.

"Do you want to fight to the death?"

"Not in the slightest."

"Then it looks like both our questions are answered." Gwenowit gave a powerful and patient smile to Grimfir, displaying his superiority. While the two of them looked at each other, Charley felt Onnser touch his shoulder firmly but quickly. Suddenly, Charley felt ill. Extremely ill. He felt wobbly. Onnser stepped forward.

"Good afternoon, Gwenowit Husk. I am honored

that an official of your stature should pay me a visit. It's been many years since our paths have crossed thusly. I trust all is well?"

"Allow me to pay my respects to you, Onnser the semi-Magnificent. All is indeed well. The ministry is busy as ever, but it gives a man energy to have this kind of work to do, wouldn't you agree?"

"Undoubtedly. There is certainly impressive energy in your ministry."

"Quite right, quite right. And now, may I presume to be introduced to your guests?"

"By all means, of course. This is Grimfir Boldrock, the entertainer, and this is Charley Tooth."

"And may I ask you, Mr. Tooth, who you are?" inquired Gwenowit benignly.

"I am not feeling so well," said Charley. He looked awful, actually, with his skin a pale green and nausea visibly churning inside. Grimfir was startled to behold it. And Gwenowit too, as he looked closely at him, was taken slightly aback at how ill Charley looked.

"Excuse my rudeness; wouldn't you please have a seat?" said Onnser solicitously to Gwenowit as he helped Charley sit down on the couch. Onnser gestured to a chair just to Gwenowit's left.

Gwenowit, still somewhat distracted by Charley's pallor, began to sit uncertainly. The chair was a shallow one, not built to seat a large man with a sword on his hip, and there was an embarrassing minute as Gwenowit was stymied in his attempts to sit. He elected to stand instead of removing his sword. He tried to recover by directing the conversation back to his advantage.

"Your young apprentice looks very ill."

"Ah, you are slightly misled. Charley is not my apprentice. He currently works with Grimfir. Sadly, the boy's constitution has not been taking the weather so well, so I have agreed to treat him as best I can. With his condition, I imagine Grimfir will be bringing him here rather regularly."

"Curing him with magic?"

"Not at all, really. I'm afraid my semi-magnificence is unable to overcome even the common cold. I am just trying to make him more comfortable, and hopefully much less contagious, as he learns his magic with Grimfir."

"O-ho! So the lad is a magician? A magician, are you, Tooth?"

Charley, feeling feeble and febrile, managed to say, "Not really yet, sir. Not much of one," before visibly breaking out in a foul-smelling sweat.

Onnser himself looked somewhat repulsed, but managed to say, "It's remarkable what an improvement he's made."

Gwenowit watched Charley intently for a few seconds, and then something registered in his face.

"Much less contagious, what?"

"Yes," said Grimfir, "much."

"I see. And just how contagious?"

"Not as much as he was before."

A look of nearly genuine concern crossed Onnser's face as he said, "You of course came inoculated, Sir Husk?"

"Inoculated? No, I . . . how was I to have known?"

"Oh, dear. I assumed that your office had looked into this more. I am surprised they didn't already know that he is so sick."

"Yes, well, my understanding is that the boy only

arrived on the scene the day before yesterday and certainly isn't all that important, so I think you can understand that we might not have that kind of information."

"True enough. Not much to go on when someone's only come into the public eye a day or two. I mean, what really can you be expected to know about him? All we can be sure of is that he performed some minor magic tricks under the auspices of Grimfir Boldrock at the party of Dame Hololo Summersweat. I trust you already know that Charley is not my apprentice. But wait, it seemed you were unclear on the matter. What is it that you do know about this poor, sick boy, and what is it you wish to know that we might be able to help you out with?"

Gwenowit seemed flustered. "No, of course. Of course we don't know much about the boy. I mean, we do, we do know what we need to know. No harm in knowing. I was asked to stop by, introduce myself, and the like. We are always interested when someone new pops up—as you are, Onnser."

"Oh, yes, of course. And to have someone of your esteem so interested in our mundane concerns is a great privilege. Would you care to stay for dinner, and we can address any and all concerns or questions you might have? We could even arrange for you to spend some time in an unrestricted interview with young Tooth here." As he said this, Onnser moved over to Gwenowit and touched him lightly on the shoulder.

As if on cue, Charley let forth a particularly wet and productive cough.

Gwenowit looked somewhat agitated. "If the boy is sick, and I actually have not taken any preventative inoculation, it would probably be best if I didn't stay too long. You know, it wouldn't do me or the ministry any good to come down with something, and I certainly don't want to do anything that gets in the way of the boy's recovery. Perhaps we should meet again at some point in the future."

"The boy is on the mend, comparatively, and I do believe you have a famously strong constitution, so if it would be easier to take care of things now . . ."

"Oh, no, no, that's quite all right, quite all right. My famous health may in fact be due to avoiding instances of disease such as this! I am no stranger to blood and death, but disease is something else entirely." Gwenowit cleared his throat somewhat scratchily, and felt within him a paranoia that he was suddenly feeling a bit nauseated himself.

"Well, then, shall we send Charley to meet with you as soon as it appears that he is well enough not to pass on whatever this awful thing is? Tomorrow or the next day, perhaps?"

"There's really no hurry now, is there? Let the boy mend, and as he is such a novice of a magician at this point, with an entertainer rather than a productive practitioner—no offense, Boldrock, I actually have seen you perform and enjoyed it immensely. I recall a trick in which you made eleven white doves appear from within a lily, and then you consumed all eleven doves as well as the flower—I suppose that there's no call for an official inquiry. At this point. However, as soon as the matter approaches a more meaningful level, we really must meet. My superiors insist upon it. But for now, in the interest of all things good and fair and just, I should be going. The Orphan Lords send you their good wishes."

"And please return to them fully their same sentiments from us."

Gwenowit shot Onnser a sly look at this comment, but Onnser maintained a look of innocence and genuineness, so there was nothing for Gwenowit to do but head out of the door.

"Good evening to you all, and may you feel better soon, Tooth."

"You should indeed feel better soon," said Onnser to Charley a few moments after Gwenowit headed down the path. "But you probably won't be one hundred percent for another day or two." He again laid a hand on Charley's shoulder, and when he withdrew it, Charley did indeed feel better. A modicum better. He suddenly bolted up, lunged into the bathroom, and vomited. After that, he felt a tad bit better than before. He vomited a few more times, and felt better still. When he was through voiding the contents of his stomach, he returned to the living room, where Onnser and Grimfir remained. He collapsed exhaustedly on the couch, and just then Wednesday came stomping downstairs. She looked provoked.

"Uncle Onnser! May I ask why it is the past twenty minutes or so I have been unable to get out of your upstairs den? The door mysteriously swung shut and locked, and no matter what kind of unlocking spell I tried, the door wouldn't budge!"

"My dear niece, you are not a magician, remember?"

"But I can work simple unlocking spells, and I certainly know a triple-hex lock application when I see one. So who was here and why did it require you locking me upstairs?"

"Your studies do you credit, Wednesday. Gwenowit

Husk, Tandor's boss, was here. He wanted to meet Charley."

"I vaguely remember meeting Sir Husk many years ago. Why did you not want me to meet him now?"

"I assure you, it is not through any fault of your own. I am generally most pleased to be able to introduce you to anyone, but I feel that it is not in your or my best interests for Gwenowit to meet you, truth be told. Even Tandor would agree with me on this point."

"It sounds fishy to me. But really, Uncle, next time you could just ask me to remain out of sight, rather than using magic against me. That's just mean."

"I am sorry. It seemed at the time to be the most expedient way to handle the situation."

Wednesday looked at the pale and trembling Charley on the couch. "What's wrong with him?"

"Onnser made me sick," said Charley ruefully.

Onnser stood up quickly enough to startle the other three occupants of the room. He held his hands out, bringing everyone's attention to focus on him. The light created starkness in his face. "Under no circumstances are you ever to tell anyone at all outside of this room anything about any indication that I might have had some hand in making Charley sick for the meeting. It could compromise everything."

Visibly agitated, Onnser strode from the room. The other three all looked at each other. Grimfir absently picked at the threads in the couch with a dark claw. Charley got up again, went to the bathroom again, and vomited again.

Lessons resumed that afternoon, but there was a certain tension running between everybody, and Charley could not really see why. And, as he was pretty certain that much of it centered on his role, his appearance, his magic, on him, he grew perturbed that he seemed to know least of all what was going on. Even Onnser was still being snippy and short. Finally, at a point in which Charley was drawing off a dram of coniine for a sleeping potion, he stopped. He had an open bottle in one hand, a spoonful in the other, and Onnser was holding out a test tube expectantly. Charley just stopped. Onnser leaned forward with the test tube, without looking at Charley's face. Charley took a step back, and Grimfir sucked in his breath. Wednesday looked up, Onnser looked up. Charley looked back.

"I need to know some things. Some important things."

"Put the coniine in the tube, Charley."

"I need some questions answered."

"Fine, but that is a very volatile poison you have there, and having it out in the open, breathable air like this is not the best of situations."

"It seems like there are a lot of not the best of situations, and this current one is the only one that I actually have a grasp of. So I need some questions answered."

Charley looked over at Grimfir and Wednesday, and in the second that he did, Onnser flashed forward at him, emitting from his fingertips a sudden thick misty spray that froze Charley momentarily. In that moment of no movement, Onnser swept a heavy, sheer dishtowel-sized fabric over Charley's hands and then whipped it off of them, putting the now-writhing cloth into a large mason jar, which he immediately capped. The spoon and the bottle in Charley's hands were now completely empty. As soon as Charley felt he was able to move his arms again, he found them pinned behind him by the capable claws of Grimfir. Wednesday was still wide-eyed, which is quite understandable, as the whole scene took less time than it did to read about it.

"Never do that again," growled Grimfir. "There are some things you just don't take chances with, and as a learning magician, you must follow instructions."

"That could have gone grievously wrong, Charley," added Onnser.

"I need you to tell me what is going on."

"You need to learn how to act properly in a laboratory, or we'll stop teaching you magic."

"Then stop teaching me magic. Keep trying to teach me, and I suppose I'll go on behaving the same."

This silenced Onnser and Grimfir. Onnser motioned for Grimfir to release Charley from his scaly grasp. He did so. Charley remained where he was, and Onnser sat down. Grimfir picked up the mason jar with the fabric in it and gave it a shake. Then he, too, sat down. Charley remained where he was, in the middle of the room. Onnser looked him over with old, tired eyes.

"If you stop learning from me, how will you find your way home?" Onnser asked, pointedly twisting a barb in Charley's psyche.

"You've said that you have no idea how I can get home, and that it's not within your magic."

"But being recalcitrant here in the lab certainly isn't going to help you get any closer."

"But it might get me some answers. Answers about me and what the hell I'm doing here, what you people want, and what these other people I don't even know want with me, as I seem to be of great interest to them. So I did what I had to do."

"Did what you had to do?"

"Yes."

"So you realized that your actions could have caused serious harm?"

"I—"

"And not just to yourself, but also to me, also to Grimfir, and also to Wednesday. And that was okay with you? You felt it acceptable to take that chance with other people's health? What has Wednesday done to you that you feel you could endanger her like that?"

Here Onnser had Charley. Charley broke his eye contact with the semi-magnificent man and looked down.

"No. Of course not." He turned and looked at Wednesday, who was still wide-eyed.

"I'm sorry, Wednesday."

Wednesday nodded at him, for lack of anything better to do.

Charley turned back to Onnser and said, "But I still deserve to know what I need to know." With that, he got up and left the room. Onnser and Grimfir looked at each other, and Wednesday looked back and forth between the two of them.

"What is it that he needs to know?" she asked, but neither Onnser nor Grimfir even looked her way. Grimfir got up, went over to the mason jar, and pulled out the cloth. The jar was now half-full of water.

"The digesting cloth is finished," he said, folding it and putting it on the table next to Onnser.

Wednesday got up and followed after Charley. She had heard the front door shut already, so she trotted to it and opened it, expecting that Charley might be right there on the front step. But no, he was already down the path, on his way to the slimeway. She ran after him, and just as he was about to step on, she called his name. He turned to look at her, waited a few seconds, and then got on the slower moving bluish channel, which allowed Wednesday to catch up with him by taking the fast brown channel. She pulled up next to him and stepped into his lane of goo.

"Charley."

"Yes."

"Come back. You should come back."

"No. No, I really shouldn't. I don't know what's going on, but it seems that everything gets more and more complicated and sinister and full of import, and it all has to do with me. I don't know what I'm doing here, and I don't want to be here at all, but if I am going to be here, and if everybody is going to pay particular attention to me and take a special interest in what I am doing, the least they can do is tell me why."

"I admire you for standing up to Grimfir and my uncle, Charley. I really do. I've never seen anyone in your position do that before. But I don't understand what you think you're standing up for. What is it that you want to know?"

"Why is everybody so interested in me here? Grimfir, Onnser, Tandor, Gwenowit. Why all the secrecy? What is so special about me?"

Wednesday looked genuinely confused and concerned. "Would it make you feel any better if I assured you that, to the best of my knowledge, there is nothing special about you?" And she meant it.

"That means a lot to me," said Charley, also meaning it. "But I need to hear that from Onnser, and I won't believe him if he tells me."

"Then what can I do? To help?"

"You've been helpful already, with the shopping and stuff. Thank you. But please, excuse me. I'm going back to Grimfir's."

And with that, Charley firmly stuck one foot into the speedier flow of brown slime, and turned to say good-bye to Wednesday. But he turned, forgetting that he now had one foot in faster-moving gunk, and one in slower moving gunk, and before he could say "good-bye," or anything more than "erp," the slime forced him almost into the splits, and he fell squarely on his backside into the brown goo, which swiftly carried him off, facing backward at the slower-traveling, bewildered Wednesday.

Charley went back to Grimfir's. He let himself in and went to his room and lay on the floor. Wednesday hopped across the avenues of slime and caught the fast one heading back home. When she arrived, Grimfir and Onnser were sitting in the living room, each having a drink. She stood just inside the door and looked at them.

"No Charley?" asked Grimfir.

"No, he seemed pretty single-minded about all of it. What is it that he wants to know?"

"I'm not sure it's anything that you should hear too much about," asked Onnser.

"Is it something that he should hear about?"

"Grimfir and I were just discussing that. I don't know. There's so much about Charley that we don't know, that he won't be able to answer. We have to move cautiously, with or without all the facts about him at hand."

"Well, you might consider that you will be moving without him at all if he doesn't get any answers. I think he's exhibited strong enough mettle to show that he's perfectly willing to forgo this whole apprentice thing."

"But he needs us. He realizes that if he's going to find his way home, his best bet is *through* us. And if he's going to go through us, it will only be if he first goes *with* us."

"You said that you didn't know how to get him home."

"I don't. I sincerely don't. But what other chance does he have? As long as he thinks there's a possibility he'll find something out through our magic, then he'll end up having to cooperate."

"That's terrible! You're just going to let him go on thinking that he might find a way home through you? Just so you can get what you need out of him, despite whatever dangers there are with Tandor's crowd?"

"You have to use what you've got, my dear Wednesday. And there are some struggles that are bigger than their players, more important than their dangers."

"Ridiculous. The ends don't necessarily justify the means, Uncle."

"I don't know about that."

"Then the least you can do is let Charley know what you might be getting him into. The very least. Because if you don't, then I'll be forced to do my best to protect him."

"Wednesday, I am only interested in justice and the greater good. You know that."

"I do know that. I am also interested in justice, and

the greater good, but for each person on his own."

"Some battles cannot be fought one at a time. It's simply impractical."

"Well, Uncle. You also taught me that the most important thing is, 'Pick your battles.' I know you thought my parents made a mistake in their decision to move against the Orphan Lords, but weren't they also interested in justice and the greater good, just the same as you? Weren't you working with them, as a matter of fact?"

As soon as Wednesday mentioned the Orphan Lords, Onnser threw out his hands and cast a quick spell that bound the room in an oppressive air. He stood up and crossed to Wednesday, causing the rug to ripple brilliantly with each step. He put his hand on her shoulder.

"Your parents picked a very noble battle to fight, and I do not argue with that. Yes, I was helping them, but I disagreed with their timing. I told them so. I gave them all the support that I felt I could give, but I told them and I told them that the time was not right. They went in knowing full well what could happen, and you should be very proud of that. We all are. And we will find them. We will."

"As you say, they knew what they were getting into. That's more than we can say about Charley, isn't it." And Wednesday quickly went upstairs into her room.

Onnser sat down on the chair nearby, the one that Gwenowit had found unaccommodating. He let out a deep exhalation. He looked over at Grimfir, who was nonchalantly pretending to pick his claws clean. Onnser kept looking at him, but Grimfir allowed himself to be completely engrossed in his nail-cleaning. In fact, Grimfir pretended so well that he actually *did* become completely engrossed in his nail-cleaning, pretending so well not to be interested in what had just transpired that he indeed forgot where he was until Onnser spoke up again.

"Well, my old friend. Sometimes I forget how quickly Wednesday is growing up, and how smart she has become."

"She certainly takes after her mother."

"Yes, she does. I just hope that she shows more patience."

"How much patience, Onnser? The longer we wait, the more consolidated our enemies' power becomes. Now, I am ready to stop talking about it if you will dispel this gloom you've cast on the room."

Onnser did so, and the living room immediately felt brighter, easier to breathe in. Grimfir stood up to leave.

"I will bring Charley back tomorrow. And though I might not usually agree with Wednesday on these things, as I don't like to agree with people in general, I think the girl has a point. I don't know just what you have in store for Charley, or if he will in fact turn out to be the one that you want, but if you're sending him into what I think you might be sending him into, he should at least have an idea of what he's up against. I think. It is up to you, though—I won't go behind your back, and I won't tell him anything important without your instruction. I remain your humble servant. Good night."

Grimfir was standing by the end of his speech, and he tipped his head to Onnser as he left. When the door shut behind the lizard, Onnser remained in the chair, brooding. He clasped his hands, intertwined his fingers, pressed them tightly together, and then slowly drew them apart. Thin strands of light connected fingertip to fingertip, weblike, like a cat's cradle. He brought his hands apart about the width of his chest. The ropy bands of light shimmered and twisted between his hands, forming a boxlike frame. Within the box appeared an image, out of focus, but slowly drawing itself sharper. As Onnser gazed at it, the picture became clear. It was an image of a woman with Onnser's eyes and noble bearing; a man of thick gray hair, angular features, and dark passionate eyes; and a little girl who was unmistakably a young Wednesday O' Friday, but with light blue hair and blue eyes. The vision dissipated as another one took its place. This one was of a younger Onnser and the woman from the previous image, his sister. They had their arms around each other's shoulders and were smiling directly out at Onnser. The pictures began changing regularly, every minute or so, and Onnser looked at old images of his entire family, of his sister's wedding, of the new addition of Wednesday. The family pictures stopped once Wednesday was about six years old, and then there were just images of her, and some of her with Onnser, and in these her hair and eyes were the gray that they still were today. He gazed intently at these memories until he fell asleep.

Chapter Ten

When Wednesday came down in the morning, she found Onnser asleep in the chair. His hands lay in his lap, still emitting slight sparks. Wednesday shook him lightly, and he awoke. She went on into the kitchen, and he followed once he fully woke up. The two of them ate a silent breakfast in the kitchen, the sunlight streaming in a little too brightly.

Just as they finished, Grimfir and Charley arrived. Charley was looking a bit sullen, Grimfir a bit agitated, but that was nothing too extraordinary for either of them. Wednesday and Grimfir cleaned up as Onnser motioned for Charley to follow him into his office. Onnser closed the door behind them and gestured for Charley to take a seat. Onnser pulled down the shade over the window, and then he too took a seat and looked at Charley. He raised his hands, and again cast the enclosing gloom over the room, but much tighter, much thicker, so that he and Charley in their seats were enveloped in the muffling mist. Even still, Onnser the semi-Magnificent leaned in somewhat conspiratorially.

"All right, Charley. You and I are going to go over everything, get everything clear, get you all caught up on all we can help you with. Okay? So, do you have any questions so far?"

"Yes. Could you tell me why, at Hololo Summersweat's party, Ulmuth Wagonspack was so snobby about—"

"Any *important* questions?"

"Oh. Well. How is it I am to know they are important?"

"I see. Let's start this way: Charley, do you know what's wrong with this world?"

"Well . . . "

"You see—"

"I could start by talking about the weird creatures who pass in and out of my day as though it's normal, or maybe the fact that there's all this so-called magic, and everyone not only believes it but relies on it, or maybe I could talk about the logical discrepancies of the whole planet, the anachronisms, the inconsistencies, or I could go into what I perceive to be the economic incongruities—"

"I am talking about Dix and Dax, the Orphan Lords and the grip they have on this world and how it is up to you to defeat them."

"Hum. What about the fact that different time zones use different bases for math?"

"Charley, yesterday—"

"I know, I know. There's just so much, and I don't know who I can really trust, and what people are really telling me."

"That's fair. That is fair. And I don't think there's

anything I can really do or say that will indicate to you who you feel you can trust. That is something that only you can decide, and only after you've accumulated all the information you can. So, what I am going to do now is provide you with the information I have. There's a lot of it, and I'll try not to go on too long, and you'll have to choose for yourself what you believe, what you think, and what you will do."

"This sounds like it's going to be awful."

"Dix and Dax. The Orphan Lords. Do you know anything about them?"

"Yes, some—Wednesday gave me an introductory . . . introduction . . . a talk . . . on them. Briefly."

"Dix and Dax are the Ruling Powers. They run the world. The way they've been able to maintain their power is through fear and force. They've managed to regulate the practice of magic to the point that nobody's power can even approach theirs. The Ministry of Magic Investigation, Regulation, and Accountability—the very division that Tandor Ovenheat and Gwenowit Husk work for—is the bureaucratic arm that Dix and Dax employ to make things look nice and above-board. It is, of course, a ministry of terror."

"But Tandor? And Gwenowit? Neither are my favorite people, but neither seemed to me to be, well, evil."

"There are certainly good people throughout the ministry. In fact, Dix and Dax have many good people throughout their government. Something is rarely entirely evil or entirely good. Even Dix and Dax have their positive characteristics, I suppose. I suppose. And the people who work for them are often just people like you and me—people who need jobs, people who believe in the role of government, people who genuinely believe that they are helping out society. People make the wrong choices all the time, align themselves with the wrong entities, compromise their own principles in the name of a paycheck or a promise for something better. The beautiful thing about a big bureaucracy, in terms of the agenda of Dix and Dax, is that it is so wide, unwieldy, and cumbersome that most of the employees don't have a sense of what is going on overall. Not even all of the populace does, though you will find there is a general feeling of discontent, and nobody seems completely enthralled with being under the twin thumbs of the Orphan Lords. For my money, the busiest ministry is Public Information, which is at it around the clock trying to spin the latest brutalities and injustices in a positive light regardless of the obvious facts, and sometimes in blatant disregard of them. Not surprisingly, the turnover rate in that division is pretty high, though many who leave their jobs are not heard from again."

"This is pretty depressing."

"Try living here all your life."

"The whole reason I am here right now is to figure out a way to avoid that scenario."

"Yes, I know. I was merely being illustrative."

"Oh. I see."

"Now, there is of course a Resistance. It's fragmented but somewhat effective. There are agents throughout the Ruling Powers' camp that help the Resistance out—even within The Ministry of Magic Investigation, Regulation, and Accountability, which I shall refer to simply as the Ministry from now on, for sake of case. The Ruling Powers have found it more difficult to infiltrate the Resistance than for the Resistance to infiltrate them, which I think speaks rather nicely for the ideals and actions of the Resistance. Are you following me?"

"I think so. How does all this work with you?"

"Well, you see . . . as I said, the Resistance is fragmented. It's always been clandestine, of course, because that's how a resistance has to be, but it certainly used to be more powerful and more organized. As you know, Wednesday is my niece. . . ."

Onnser fell silent, thinking. Charley coughed lightly, and Onnser looked up and continued.

"The Ministry as we know it know came into being a little over ten years ago. It used to be simply the Ministry of Magic, and it was more of a union than anything. Issues of enforcement and the like were distributed among the more military-concerned divisions, and there had even been a special committee designed to deal with the Resistance. About a decade ago, the leaders of the Resistance thought the time was right to strike. And strike they did—they took on a hundred years of tyranny, and they nearly succeeded. Nearly. But they weren't strong enough, and their failure only made the Ruling Powers stronger. The rebel leaders were caught and are being held somewhere, somewhere in the government compound. We haven't been able to find them yet. The two people who led the Resistance were Sholto and Clarus, who were husband and wife. His last name is Friday, and Clarus is my sister. Wednesday's parents."

"Oh! Oh. Man. Wow. But then you? I mean, how is it that you are here, and still semi-Magnificent, and with Wednesday, and everything?"

"Yes. Very complicated. I was investigated.

Severely. To a point that I think no one should ever have to endure. As it was, I had been a Magnificent magician. Superlative. Clarus, Sholto, and I agreed early on—not long before Wednesday was born—that I would distance myself from the Resistance as much as possible and try to remain a disinterested party. After they were captured in the uprising, I was, as I said, investigated, and my magician's status reduced. Every major practicioner of magic had his or her status similarly reduced or license revoked—they used me as the public example. It was all I could do to keep out of jail, or worse, I suppose. I did what I had to do to ensure that they would let me go, allow me custody of Wednesday, and continue to practice magic. Before the uprising, I was rather well-known to the public. I did and still do prosecute false magicians, often in conjunction with the Ministry. They are interested in keeping tabs on just who can actually perform real, and therefore to them dangerous, magic, and I am interested in keeping out the fakes in order to find those who can help the Resistance. After my interrogation, the Ministry of Public Information realized it would be good PR to show that I was set free, in an example of blind justice not laying waste to the thousands that it secretly did. But, as you can guess, I must be most careful about what I do and with whom I interact. I have cultivated a measure of goodwill with the Ministry, though they are right not to trust me too much. And there are those in the Ministry on our side who make it known to me when a particularly interested eye is being cast my way from somewhere within Dix and Dax's cadre of black crows."

"Tandor? Is Tandor part of all of this?"

"Tandor is a mystery. He was a student of mine, actually. I used to teach a class to government investigator recruits. I didn't really know him then, but he was a bright young one. He joined the Ministry's select crowd just as the Resistance was making noise. He's a good person, and we have developed a good relationship, but I don't know how to trust him. It is hard for me, and I suspect it always will be, especially as long as my sister and Sholto are in prison."

"I don't know what to say."

"I don't expect you to have to say anything on most of this. You had no control over any of it when it happened."

They both sat still for a few moments. Charley's heart was beating fast with the story—this kind of political intrigue was exciting, especially when it involved the people Charley was most closely associated with. Onnser's heart was pumping quickly as well—perhaps even more quickly than Charley's. Onnser never had occasion to relate this whole history before, and in doing so, he was reliving those days over ten years ago. He could clearly see the secret meetings he'd had with Clarus and Sholto, in damp basements and in murky woods, wrinkled papers hurriedly passed around, read, and destroyed. He saw the eager, unfortunate ones who went on missions to help the Resistance only to meet with horrible martyrdom. He could reconstruct the mood but not the exact words of the arguments he had with Clarus and Sholto about the most prudent plan of action, and the merits of holding off on an all-out attack. He could recall the overwhelming adrenaline and nausea he felt on the day when the Resistance took that huge, fateful step forward as he watched from the safety of the office he maintained at the government building. He felt the wrenching panic when he learned of the failure of the uprising and the slaughter, and the capture of the principals. He could smell vividly the sweat and the dankness and the hurting flesh of his two-week-long interrogation. And the years afterward appeared to him like an overcast day, all together. Charley leaned forward in his chair.

"But where do I fit in?"

Onnser sat back and looked at Charley, feeling suddenly very old and very tired.

"Charley. Where does Charley Tooth fit in? The most important question of all, perhaps. Or, more accurately, the most important answer? I get so that I don't know anymore, sometimes. Charley Tooth. Well, you see, Charley, it's like this: Dix and Dax must be defeated. It has long been thought that a magician of singular capabilities would arrive on the scene and engender this change of rule. Even from within Dix and Dax's inner circle are reports that this mysterious stranger will wield the Talking Sword of Flassto in bringing about their defeat."

"The Talking Sword of Flassto? What is the Talking Sword of Flassto?"

"Nobody knows, actually. Part of me hoped that you would know."

"Me? Why would I know anything about some chatty weapon?"

"Because there is a very good chance you are that magician sent to deliver us."

"Oh. Oh-ho. No. No. I am not."

"Don't be so sure, Charley."

"No disrespect, but I can't be. I have no magic abilities—despite the nice parlor tricks you taught me the other day, I have no desire to become mixed up in whatever political upheaval is afoot, and I have never heard of nor do I ever plan on hearing of or from firsthand the Talking Sword of Flassto."

"My how grown-up you can sound when on the defense!"

"I'm serious. I just want to find my way home. Without getting involved in any wars."

"Charley, has it occurred to you that perhaps you were not brought to us by accident? That is, the reason you are here among us is to accomplish something, and the reason that we don't know how to send you home is that we have no control over it. Maybe the only way for you to return home is to accomplish some sort of a mission here. Not to deceive you—it's possible that somewhere in the instruction of magic in this house you might discover some way to get back to your loved ones, but I promise you that I have never seen anything to indicate it. So, barring some surprising unearthing of a long-forgotten spell, the idea that you are here to accomplish something specific is the most optimistic and logical scenario I can come up with. Unless it is all pure, unmitigated, and immitigable chance that brought you to where you are right now, with no hope for the future or a reward, and that's practically too depressing to contemplate, so I wouldn't recommend it. Does this make sense so far?"

"I have seen some . . . shows . . . that are based in this kind of thought."

"Good. I hope that might make your acceptance of it easier."

"I don't think I'm ready to accept anything quite yet."

"What is sad and unfair, perhaps, is that you might find that you don't have a choice. Now wait, don't get upset at me; I am not the one forcing you to take up this burden. Gwenowit Husk came over to meet you, through no bidding of my own, and Tandor swore to me through no internal report of his own. This is very unusual—someone of Gwenowit's stature does not get involved in run-of-the-mill inquiries about boys who show up as apprentices to low-level entertainment magicians. It is no coincidence that Gwenowit and the upper echelon of the Ruling Powers are aware of your presence here, and let us hope that it is no coincidence that you were put immediately into our custody. They will pursue their interest in you until they are completely and unequivocally satisfied with their findings, and I can guarantee that their findings will insist upon neutralizing whatever sort of threat you might possibly in a million years be able to pose. If you follow."

"You're right, that is really unfair."

"But that's the way it is. There is some good news, though."

"What?"

"I think you, more than anyone I have encountered, might actually be the wizard we have long been awaiting."

"That doesn't strike me as particularly good news."

"Don't you see, my dear boy? If they're going to come after you because you might be the one to deliver us from the domination of the Orphan Lords, and if you just turn out to be the one with the power to deliver us, then it stands to reason that you have a fighting chance!"

"But I don't want to fight. I don't want the chance.

I'd still be more than willing to sign something saying so."

"Look, Charley. I know this is all terribly confusing for you, overwhelming. I can't imagine the things that you have been dealing with, and I must say that I don't at all envy what you might find yourself going through. But you can't run from it. I can't hide you from it. Part of me, a small part of me, really wishes that I could, but overall I know it is unavoidable, and that it is something you must undergo. And ultimately you will find yourself going it alone, and I am sorry for that. But what I can do, if you are willing, is teach you all that I can, so that you have a strong foundation you can rely upon and build upon. Again, there's a chance that you won't need any of it, and that you aren't the one we've been waiting for, and that you might come across some way to get yourself home without ever having to get into the thick of things here. I don't want to discourage you from hoping, but I want to prepare you just in case. We are here to help you. I am here, Grimfir is here, and Wednesday is here. There are others here you don't know about—many of whom you will never know, and some who might never know specifically of you—but they are all also working to help you, or the idea they have of who you might be for them."

Charley slumped back in his chair and put his hands to his face.

"Man, this sucks."

"Yes, it totally sucks."

Charley rubbed his face.

"Why me?"

"There is no real answer to that, I don't think."

"Then how come you think it is me? How come you

thought it was me?"

"There certainly were a number of factors. There was a certain energy in the air that night, and there was a certain crackle, almost of electricity, when I got to Hololo's mansion. Magic is a very physical thing, Charley. Most people think it's about mental prowess and recitation and that's it, but the true fact of the matter is that every bit of it involves the body, and how the body changes and reacts. Whether it means scrunching up your toes until they cramp, compressing your pancreas, twisting your warfle—"

"I don't think I have a warfle, whatever that is."

"No matter. Regardless, when the party came out to my carriage, I could detect a definite vibe in the air. And as for the carriage, Charley—I had cast a locking spell on it of my own devising, one that had no known counter-hex. I had Vang try his best to unlock it, and when he couldn't, I knew that it would be a valid test that only an accomplished wizard—or one of great and natural potential—would be able to pass. You were able to unlock it, Charley. And I can't figure out how you did it. I was listening, feeling, waiting to see what you would do, but whatever you did was new to me. Can you tell me how you did it? How you got the door open?"

Charley felt himself both blush and go pale.

"I . . . really don't know. I was . . . just able to open it. It opened. It just kind of happened."

Onnser looked at Charley with a slight smile and a lot of patience.

"I hope it's something you rediscover, then. The better practiced you are, the more understanding you have of your abilities, the better chance you have in facing down your obstacles."

"I know. I know."

"So what happens next for you is in your hands. Will you accept my teaching? If so, I need you to be willing to devote yourself to learning. There's a lot of ground to cover, and it won't be easy."

"I would be your apprentice, then?"

"Yes and no. Yes, you will be my apprentice, but nobody outside of you, me, Grimfir, Wednesday, and Vang can know. Tandor, too, I suppose, though it is best not to ever get into a discussion with him on it— we should leave it a tacit understanding. Everybody else will go on thinking that you are Grimfir's squire, receiving some training and some health care from me. You understand it was necessary to deceive Gwenowit, and that is why I made you ill the other day. Once the government recognizes you as my official apprentice, it will be open season on investigating you. While you are still nominally with Grimfir, it doesn't attract as much attention, and it might send a message to them that I haven't discovered anything particularly interesting about you. Might. So you will continue to live with Grimfir until such time that I think you will be able to handle yourself sufficiently to be named my apprentice. And who knows what happens after that."

"Is Wednesday also your apprentice?"

Onnser paused and ran a hand lightly over his brow.

"Not so much. Wednesday can no longer perform magic."

"No longer?"

"No. She is a most adept assistant, though, and she knows far more about magic than many who practice the stuff do. She is a girl of amazing intellect, but she can't perform any acts of wizardry."

"That seems odd. Were both her parents able to?"

"Yes, they were. Yes. In the aftermath of the insurrection that her parents led . . . certain concessions had to be made, certain measures taken to guarantee that Wednesday would be allowed to continue . . . to live in my protection. I don't think she remembers most of what went on in the year after her parents were captured, and I don't think it's something you should bring up with her. There is a chance, though, that one day, when we are able to free Clarus and Sholto, and reunite them with Wednesday, perhaps we will be able to reverse some of the past. Perhaps. I don't know. I suppose a lot of that might depend on you, and what you and we are able to accomplish. One thing you will have to confront is the very real possibility that death will be an integral part of this process. It's easy enough to say in advance, but it's hard to recognize fully until you are actually face-to-face with it."

"What am I supposed to say to that?" asked Charley, refusing to think about the possibility of being killed.

"I don't know, Charley. And this may sound callous, but you are more important than any of the rest of us, in terms of accomplishing our mission. More important than me, more important than anyone from the Resistance you might work with. More important even than Wednesday. Let us hope any death you do encounter is not your own."

"Man," said Charley, sitting back in his chair, tilting his head all the way back. "Wouldn't it be great if all I had to do was deliver a letter somewhere or help someone build a go-cart or something, and then I could go home and avoid all of this?"

"I am sure it would be great for you. But it would

not be great for all of the populace who have been waiting for so long for deliverance."

"I wish you would stop talking like that."

"Do you accept? Will you join us?"

"I really don't see much else I can do. But please stop talking about it as though I am some sort of Chosen One."

"Good, good. Charley, I can't tell you how pleased I am to hear it."

"So. If all goes well, I take on Dix and Dax, the Orphan Lords, with the Talking Sword of Flassto, and it's happy ever after?"

"More or less."

"More or less?"

"Well, it will be difficult, of course. And you'll have to deal with Dix and Dax's minions."

"Right. And the whole Talking Sword of Flassto? There's no lead on this? Nothing?"

"It is my understanding that there is only one man who knows a thing about it, and he is harder to get to than Dix and Dax. His name is Mr. Hiram Poison."

"My, what a lovely name."

"I have never met him, never seen him. I don't personally know of anyone who has. He keeps close counsel with the Orphan Lords, I understand. Searching him out is most likely a dead end. So to speak."

"Har, har."

"Grimfir and Wednesday will be glad to know that I have brought you into all this knowledge. They requested that I disclose the information to you, especially Wednesday, against what was initially my better judgment. Now. Let us join them and begin training. If you have no more questions about all of

this . . . intrigue, I will dispel this cloud of privacy.
It prevents anyone from seeing us, overhearing us,
eavesdropping on us, and sometimes smelling us. If
you ever again want to discuss the topics we've just
covered, especially if it concerns Clarus and Sholto,
let me know. We should come up with a code phrase
to indicate it. Hmmm. Any suggestions?"

"Okay, what about 'How about those Red Sox'?"

"What on Nivalg does that mean?"

"Well, where I come from—"

"Good enough, good enough. How about those
Red Sacks."

"Sox. S-o-x. They're a baseball team."

"Sox it is. How about those Red Sox. Good. Now,
let's get to work."

Onnser snapped his fingers and the murkiness
around them evaporated. The room grew bright
again, and Charley was surprised to find himself in
need of blinking his eyes, as though he had just woken
up, or come out of a matinee movie, or both. The two
of them went back into the kitchen only to find that it
was already cleaned up and nobody was in there.
They went back down the long hallway to the living
room, and there was Grimfir, dozing on the couch.
Wednesday was reading in the chair by the window,
and she was taking notes in a simple leather-bound
notebook on the table next to her. She looked up
when Onnser and Charley came in.

"Did you guys get everything straight?" she asked
Onnser, and then looked at Charley.

"I believe so," said Onnser, who then also turned to
look at Charley.

"Yes, yes I think we did," said Charley, and
Wednesday broke into a big smile. It was the first

genuine, nothing-held-back smile that Charley had seen her give, and it made him dizzy with joy. He felt as though his stomach had left its dull placement in his belly and was rising up, floating freely and happily up his body. He wondered if this was what it meant to swoon. It did. Onnser noticed it, and spoke loudly.

"Grimfir! No time for napping! Charley is ready to get to work!"

Grimfir lazily opened one eye, the first set of eyelids flipping back, and the second set of eyelids sliding back. The eye on the other side of his head opened. He leaned his head forward, and then followed slowly with his shoulders. He turned his body to get a clear look at Charley. He looked at Charley and blinked all four eyelids. He blinked them again. Lazily, he lurched his body forward and off the couch.

"Okay, Charley. You finally ready to let this all begin?"

Chapter Eleven

And so it was that Charley formally entered his unofficial training with Onnser the semi-Magnificent, under the aegis of Grimfir Boldrock, with the assistance of Wednesday O'Friday, with the attendant interest of Tandor Ovenheat and the frustrated oversight of Sir Gwenowit Husk and unnamed emissaries of Dix and Dax, the Orphan Lords. It was a pretty good setup for Charley. He had his own room at Grimfir's place, and he got a little time outside every day as he traveled to and from Onnser's. Sometimes Onnser came to Grimfir's, and oftentimes, when the weather was pleasant, they would all arrange to meet in a secluded town park or even out in the countryside. Grimfir usually accompanied Charley to his instruction, but not always. Grimfir still had to earn his own way as an entertainer, so he had small soirees to attend to ply his trade, generally of the birthday or society variety. Charley went to some of these, and as time went on, he even performed here and there for the delight of the crowds and to establish more firmly for quiet observers that he was still working for Grimfir.

Charley found in himself a surprising natural aptitude for much of the average magic that Onnser taught him. He also developed the private hobby of collecting any and all locks and doorknobs he could get his hands on, practicing in quiet moments on the picking abilities he had discovered his first night on Nivalg. In his spare time, Charley would pore over the books that Onnser provided, and he would scour his bookshelves for texts and manuals that might have some sort of indication on interworld travel. Over the course of a few months, Charley picked up a lot. He was naturally a curious boy, and he found that trying to track down what he sought in the manuscripts of wizardry reminded him a lot of his fondness for dictionaries and encyclopedias.

When Charley was a young child, he would come across a word he didn't understand in something he was reading, and he would bring the book into the living room, where his parents would be in the evenings after dinner. If they were talking, they would not interrupt themselves upon his arrival. Nor would they look up from whatever activity they were engaged in simply because he came into the room. Charley would at first just stand there and wait for them to give him attention, but when he figured out that they wouldn't do this until they reached a natural stopping point in whatever they were doing, and sometimes not even then, he learned that he had to speak up for himself. If he didn't, he could just stand there with the book in his hand indefinitely, reading and rereading the sentence that he was stuck on. Eventually, either as a result of patience to wait or confidence to speak, Charley would go over to whichever parent appeared more receptive and ask them what the word meant, showing them in the book.

Invariably, his mom or his dad would suggest he sound it out aloud, syllable by syllable. He would do so. He would look at them; they would look at him. They would ask if he now knew the word. No, he would say. Then they would ask him to read the sentence aloud. He would do so, and then look at them expectantly. They would ask if thinking of the word in context of the sentence and the surrounding sentences aided in his discovering the meaning of the word. Sometimes it did, but not always. Then they would ask Charley if he recognized any parts of the word that might be found in other words, and how that might lead him to the correct meaning. Sometimes that was also helpful, but not always. After what could often turn into an exhausting and exhaustive back-and-forth with his parents, Charley would find himself completely unable to solve a word's meaning on his own with the tools at hand. Expecting his parents to admit there was no reasonable way he could then decipher the mysterious word, he was surprised (only the first few dozen times, and then he grew to expect it) to find that Mom and Dad Tooth would turn back to the activity that had previously engaged them and say to him, "Go look it up in a dictionary, then."

Left with no other recourse, Charley would do just that. He did get to the point where he would no longer bother asking his parents, instead heading straight for the old family dictionary. He grew to love that book. Charley got into the habit of being distracted by guide words and other entries on the page, being drawn into the bizarre and the familiar yet unknown, the fascinating etymologies, the homonyms, even the pronunciation keys at the bottoms of the pages. He could go to the dictionary to look up the word "eleemosynary," be distracted by "enchiridion," and an hour later put down the dictionary without ever having gotten back to "eleemosynary."

It was the same with encyclopedias. One of Charley's regular chance encounters in the encyclopedia was the entry for Mithridates VI, King of Pontus—perhaps there was a crease in the page, or a break in the binding, but Charley came across Mithridates VI every time he opened the "M" volume, reading about his tolerance for poison, his wars against the Roman state, and his self-ordered execution. It was a day of nearly unparalleled happiness when Charley chanced upon "mithridate" in the dictionary, and saw that it connected to his old Pontic friend; something coming together like that for him made him believe in a higher power.

And so it was with the books of magic in Onnser's library. He would sit down with some oversized, leather-bound, cracked, and disintegrating dark book of spells and lore with the intention of looking into transporting spells, portal-opening charms, cursed creatures who might serve as gateways, and the like, but he found himself quickly distracted by information and tricks he encountered on the way. He would come across an interesting paragraph on how to manage three magically airborne objects at once, his original mission would be forgotten, and he would while away the afternoon doing his best to master the trick, or at least gain a basic working knowledge of it.

For the first couple of months, Wednesday was for the most part around each day, but once what was apparently summer vacation ended, she was back in school three to five days a week. Charley missed having her around, of course, especially on the days that instruction with Onnser and Grimfir ended early, before Wednesday came home for the day, and he could go for a stretch of two or three days without encountering her at all. And some days when both he and she were around in the afternoons or evenings, she was at times so busy with her homework, or he with one of the technical skills Onnser was teaching him, such as metallurgy, weather reading, or animal identification, that they didn't manage more than "Hey, hi, hello, can you believe how busy all this work can be" kinds of exchanges.

There had even been a bit of awkwardness between them, a direct result of an exchange Charley had had with her and Grimfir about a month after he had had the big talk with Onnser. On this particular occasion, Charley, Grimfir, and Wednesday were out back in the garden, collecting shoots and leaves. Charley was sifting through the tangled roots of something called Liar's Smile, thinking about Dix and Dax, the Orphan Lords. Without straightening up, he asked a question to both Grimfir and Wednesday, though mostly to Wednesday.

"Why are Dix and Dax called the Orphan Lords?"

Wednesday stopped putting long stems into a cotton pouch and looked up, saying, "Because they are orphans, or were."

Grimfir straightened up and contributed, "Or have been. Maybe they have been."

"I heard they will be, or we all will be because of them," Wednesday countered.

"Maybe they would have been orphans had they not been. . . . Hm."

"I thought it was that, by the end of their reign, they shall have been," she replied.

Charley looked at her and said, "This all sounds like mere conjugation."

The gold in Wednesday's gray eyes flashed as she remarked, "There's nothing mere about it. Are you hitting on me? How protozoan."

"No, I mean . . . conjugation as in . . . verbish. . . ."

Charley was immediately as red as the Liar's Smile roots, which were very red indeed. He felt oddly guilty, even though he had not meant anything sleazy by it. He tried to speak again, but there was nothing he could say. Grimfir, meanwhile, was chortling quietly among the potatoes. Later that evening, Wednesday explained that she had just been kidding, and Charley did his best to laugh it off suavely, but he could not deny that relations between himself and Wednesday after that had to them a slight hint of uncomfortableness. Charley could never bring it up, and there had been no similar instances in which he felt either the opportunity or the inclination to address or defuse supposed issues of attractedness or non-attractedness between them, and so it festered ever so quietly, like a small stone in a shoe, or an unclipped toenail getting slightly snagged in the sheets. At one point, he even grew a bit upset with Wednesday, privately, for why shouldn't she take his comment as innuendo? Was he so laughable that she would never look at him as anything more than an oaf? Is that what was so funny to her? He got over this particular feeling, but he still felt there was a slight disconnect between the two of them, and he regretted it greatly.

One evening, after he had Wednesday actually laughing from his recounted tribulations of trying to acquire a fresh batch of gort blood, he felt good and thought of home. He was in the kitchen with Grimfir, tidying up, as they had spent the last couple of days getting lazy about housework.

"Grimfir, I never asked how it was that I came to be with you at Hololo's party, that first night that I met you and met Onnser."

"What do you mean?"

"How did you know who I was?"

"I guess I must have asked you."

"Well, where did I come from? How did I appear? Why did I join you at the party?"

"Who can say? You might as well ask what's for dinner."

"What is for dinner?"

"Hruckney, if you would prepare the sauce."

Charley loved hruckney. And, thus distracted, the argument was forgotten.

There came a point when it became useless to keep up the pretense that Charley was Grimfir's apprentice and not Onnser's. The three of them, with Wednesday, spent much time discussing how to handle the transition with the least amount of attention. Tandor was sometimes consulted on this decision, and he kept trying to encourage them to wait. But, after several months, they finally did make Charley Onnser's official apprentice. There was a small party, and the only major change was that Charley spent most of his nights in the room at Onnser's, rather than at Grimfir's. But Grimfir showed up every day, as now he was attendant upon Charley. Gwenowit made many appearances early on, but he was smart enough to sense that the household got very formal when he came by, so eventually he left all direct contact up to Tandor, as it had been before. Still, Charley was required to make appearances in Gwenowit's office every now and again in order to demonstrate his magical development and go through the regular registration and licensing procedures.

As far as the public was concerned, people did not take a whole lot of notice of the change. However, there was an engagement party at Lady Footslip's to celebrate the impending nuptials of Yorgad and Slusie Crinfaber at which the topic did come up. Glubdort Minxer was there, and he hadn't seen Grimfir or Charley since Charley's first appearance at Hololo Summersweat's. Grimfir was introducing himself around, now in the habit of saying that he was Charley's squire. He said as much to Glubdort, who recalled from long ago that it was the other way around. Not thinking anything much of it, he put his hand on Grimfir's arm.

"But Grimfir, I distinctly recall you saying that *he* was *your* squire."

"And I distinctly recall saying just a sentence ago that *I* am *his* squire. Do you disagree?"

Glubdort wisely removed his hand and shrank away. Sometimes, on occasion, might *is* right, even when it's wrong. Word spread quickly enough that nobody else ever asked or questioned Grimfir—or Charley—this change of titles. Charley felt good about it, too, as being the apprentice to a minor showman is not quite as challenging or rewarding, overall, as being the apprentice to a semi-Magnificent wizard—nor is it as appealing to the ladies.

Chapter Twelve

Part of being Onnser's apprentice seemed to be that Charley had to take on a greater role in the activities of the Resistance. And, as this became a regular if surreptitious part of Charley's day, so did training on things such as military movements and theory, hiding and sneaking, and basic hand-to-hand combat including with weaponry. Charley began attending secret meetings with Onnser, and sometimes without him. He met several key planners from the Resistance, and he became familiar with the bits of intelligence and stolen information that they had acquired over the years.

As Charley learned more and more, he noticed that Grimfir was more and more optimistic about the Resistance and its capabilities in terms of overthrowing Dix and Dax, the Orphan Lords. His squire's growing confidence made Charley uncomfortable. After all, it was one thing to agree to learn magic that he didn't believe in, and it was quite another thing entirely to join up with an increasingly militant group of insurrectionists ready to take on the oppressive government regime that controlled the world. One night, Onnser unveiled the plan to which the active members of the Resistance Planning Team would devote most of their time over the coming weeks: the rescue of Clarus and Sholto from the Ministry Prison. It would be the largest, most audacious and complicated undertaking the Resistance had planned since the initial uprising that Clarus and Sholto led all those years ago.

The Planning Team created a Rescue Team, and at Onnser's initiative, Charley was made reluctant captain. Four additional members were to join him: Deviz, a thin, scrappy asexual creature of bland appearance but obvious endurance; Orflung Oxlock, whom Charley had known as the local fishmonger; Hamar Creedle, a stocky, loud, energetic bird-man; and Bellanca Yippie, confident cousin to The Sisters Yippie that Charley had met at Hololo Summersweat's party. Charley wasn't sure what qualified each of these people for the Rescue Team other than that they were willing, which made them, in his mind, more qualified than he was. Still, he approached the task with a desire to learn, as he figured helping to free Wednesday's parents would take care of a number of problems for him—everything from letting them take over the Resistance and helping him get home to impressing Wednesday with his resourcefulness and bravery. So, he and his teammates spent hours upon hours discussing strategy and memorizing the blueprints of the prison, obtained courtesy of an unnamed inside agent. It was agreed that Tandor Ovenheat would know no part of their attempt to spring Clarus and Sholto, as it could compromise him too much. A date was set for the rescue, and soon enough, years before Charley felt ready, it was time to act.

Accessing a secure government prison building proved to be surprisingly easy. The Resistance had long been working on a tunnel, and redoubled efforts had pushed the tunnel far enough that they could walk underneath the prison. The prison, built before the time of Dix and Dax, was typical of the old government-issue style and funding you might see in any place where the government builds in times of financial crises. There was talk among more zealous members of the Resistance of simply filling the end of the tunnel with explosives and doing as much structural damage as possible. They were slowly dissuaded from this plan when they begrudgingly accepted that such a move might cause harm to prisoners, including the very two they hoped to rescue. Nobody knew the exact whereabouts of the cells that held the two most important prisoners, but oral histories told of certain floors and certain layouts, and that's what they had to go on.

Not even Tandor, who had been approached on this subject many times over the years, ever had any specific information on specifically where Clarus and Sholto had resided since their imprisonment. Charley and his four companions, working with the prison's original blueprints, a set of updated blueprints, and with the stories and legends at hand, came up with three or four spots that seemed likely candidates for where Wednesday's parents might be held. The tunnel was turned to head under a particularly unused section of hallway in the area where laundry was done.

Breaking through gradually and quietly, the terminus of the tunnel was a ventilation shaft that led to a metal grate in the floor by the laundry room itself. Using the ventilation shaft was Charley's idea, something he had picked up from just about every movie, book, or story involving the infiltration of a building. The other choice, of course, was to have some of the rescue party pretend to be guards delivering "prisoners," but that seemed too risky a gambit.

On the day of the strike, Charley and the team headed down the long, dark way, covering the whole distance in silence. They took off their shoes when they got to the shaft, traveling it one at a time to reduce noise and the unpleasantness of getting caught. At the metal grate, they encountered a slight difficulty in that it was securely locked. Charley, up front, put his finger through a hole in the grate, and then he willed his finger to stretch and patted around the edges of the grate. On the third side that he searched, he found in the floor next to the grate a keyhole, and after a minute or two of wrangling his finger, he beat the lock. The five were now inside the prison.

An hour later, they had made good progress, picking locks and timing their quiet sprints down corridors. At one point, they did come upon a lone guard who proved to be both a blessing and a curse. They surprised him, and just as he stood and drew his sword, Orflung and Bellanca slew him. Charley had never seen anyone dead before, and seeing someone go through the sudden process by which they become dead at the hands of another was startling. Still, he recognized that the situation was serious enough that he couldn't dwell on it now—there would hopefully be time for him later to think about it. The trick, of course, was not ending up dead himself. Luckily, the dead guard was extraordinarily handsome, which somehow made it easier—it was almost cinematic, and Charley had that unrecognized primal feeling that pretty-boys deserved to be knocked down a peg or two. Sure, death was many pegs down, but had the guard not looked like a movie corpse, Charley would have been caught up in feeling of remorse about whether the guard had a family, whether he was a likable sort, whether he knew the evilness that was his employer.

On the guard they found passkeys to corridor doors that would make their movements much quicker. However, there was the slight matter of the body. Not wanting to spend too much time hiding him, they ended up putting him in a chair and pulling the old "make him look like he's sleeping" trick. They then went on with the mission.

The first place they thought one or both of Clarus and Sholto's cells might be turned out to be a shower room. Somewhat frustrated, the team quickly moved on. As they approached the second destination, Charley felt that they had to be in the right area. The halls became more austere, the light more institutional. It seemed to be the kind of place that was unpleasant enough to deserve the criminals that the state most feared or loathed. The air itself seemed colder. Eventually, they came to a huge, heavy door that had locks on the far left and right. After some trial and error, the team deduced that to open the door they needed to unlock both sides at once. It was a time-consuming endeavor, but after a bit, it worked that Bellanca would use the dead guard's key and Charley would pick the other lock. Getting the timing down was hard, but successful in the end. They quickly opened the door, letting Orflung, Deviz, and Hamar rush through, prepared to forcibly overcome what they presumed to be a legion of soldiers just on the other side. There was nobody there. They made their way down the long hallway and paused at the corner.

Charley turned the corner and saw a cell with a triple outer lock. This must be the cell where Clarus is held, Charley surmised, thinking instinctively that she was the more powerful of Wednesday's parents. He stole quickly and quietly along the brightly lit corridor. The other four followed him. Once at the cell, Charley examined each lock and tried the handle. It was secured. There was no window to look in to see who was in there. Charley put his right hand on one lock and his left on another. Staring intently at his hands, he felt the center of his palms pinch outward and snake their way into the keyholes. A slight depression appeared on the back of each hand, but he could feel most of the flowing coming from his triceps and his stomach. His flesh wended its way around inside the lock, almost with a mind of its own as it felt out the pins and tumblers and inner workings. In less than a minute, Charley felt that he had them. His hands grew rigid, and he turned both clockwise. There was a clacking as the bolts slid back. To his companions, it looked as though he had merely placed his hands over the locks, maybe said some spell under his breath, and thrown the locks open.

He quickly dispatched with the third lock in the same way. They then all stood silently, making sure there were no footsteps approaching, alarms sounding, or other discouraging noises. Slowly, Charley swung the door out. The cell within was nearly pitch dark. Bellanca cast a glow from her fingers, and the glow floated quietly into the dimness. Charley entered the chamber.

"There's nobody in here. This place is empty."

The others followed him in to look at the cell. Suddenly, there was full light, startling the band of rescuers. Behind them came a voice.

"I arrest you under the authority of Dix and Dax, the Orphan Lords."

They turned around and saw three soldiers, weapons drawn. The speaker was none other than Sir Gwenowit Husk himself. His blazing eyes settled on Charley.

"Ah, Charley Tooth! I was hoping that it might be you that we would catch. I suspected that Onnser still had ties to the Resistance, and now here you are to prove it."

"I am acting under my own direction," Charley replied, hiding his fear. "I organized this group, and I alone am responsible."

"Very admirable, Tooth, but you know it won't hold up." Gwenowit put his hand on the cell door. Orflung jumped forward, blasting a light-and-wind spell at the soldiers, knocking all three of them back against the far wall.

"Run!" she yelled, but the rescuers, including Charley, were already in motion. They ducked left down the hall as Gwenowit and his crew picked themselves up in pursuit.

"Split up!" yelled Hamar, and at the next junction, Charley, Deviz, and Hamar went left, and Orflung and Bellanca went right. When their pursuers reached the same spot, two went right and Gwenowit came left, after Charley. Hamar turned to face the old warrior who charged toward them.

"Go! I'll stall him! Get out!" he yelled.

Charley turned to see Hamar raise his club, which was emitting thin bands of fire. As he raised it toward Gwenowit, though, the big knight leapt forward and brought his sword crashing down across Hamar, smashing through the club, and chopping neatly and bloodily into Hamar's body. Charley looked away, and he and Deviz ran left again, and then right down a hallway. At the end of the hallway was a heavy metal door. They reached it and found it locked, with no visible keyhole or handle on their side. They could hear Gwenowit thundering down the corridor. Charley frantically searched for any openings along the door while Deviz frantically cast several abrasive spells that only succeeded in slightly denting the portal's solid surface.

"Open the door, Charley! Open it!" yelled Deviz.

Gwenowit made the final right turn and approached them confidently, bloody sword in hand, the thrill of battle upon his face. Charley and Deviz turned to face him, stepping forward a few paces to keep themselves from being backed completely against the wall.

"There are two options for you," said Gwenowit. "Surrender, or battle to the death. While the Ruling Powers would prefer your capture, I myself am quite happy to battle. I wouldn't mind seeing what sort of magic you've got, Tooth."

Charley had no desire to fight, especially after seeing Hamar dispatched so gruesomely. He had never had to use his magic in combat, and he wasn't so certain he had anything that could slow the hulking Minister, let alone defeat him. On the other hand, were he to be caught, it would probably spell the final demise of all aspects of the Resistance. Onnser, Wednesday, Grimfir—everybody—would be apprehended. As much as he hated to admit it to himself, he was a prisoner whose capture would completely demoralize those people who had worked so hard and for so long to overthrow the oppression of Dix and Dax. He could not let that happen. As much as he did not at all want to be responsible for such a burden, he knew that the burden was there and only he could shoulder it.

Just then, the door behind them opened. Charley and Deviz immediately sprang away, to the side. Behind the doorway was a stairway, and in the stairway was Tandor Ovenheat. He moved the doorstop down with his foot and came into the hallway.

"The alarm has gone off. What is going on here? Charley, what are you doing?" He looked incredulously at Charley, and then at Gwenowit.

"Inspector Ovenheat!" said Gwenowit, smiling. "It seems your closeness with Onnser did not pay off as we had hoped. I discovered Tooth and four marauders in the cell that once held Clarus O'Friday. A capital crime, and we now have the most important catch we could imagine. Tooth is ours."

Tandor looked at Charley, looked at Deviz, then looked again at Gwenowit with his freshly bloodied sword. He stepped past Charley and Deviz and stood next to Gwenowit.

"In Clarus's cell?"

"Yes. No doubt to try and free her. And then, I presume, on to Sholto's cell? Hm? Or have you already been there and found it empty?" Gwenowit laughed. "Imagine their surprise, Tandor. Would you care to tell them where they might encounter their treasonous friends?"

Tandor smiled wanly. "A genuine surprise, certainly. Certainly."

"Or perhaps rather than tell them, we should just show them!"

Gwenowit raised his sword and stepped toward Charley. From behind him, Tandor spoke.

"Sir Gwenowit. I cannot let you do that."

Gwenowit turned to see that Tandor had drawn a sword of his own, which was short and stout.

"What's this, Tandor? Do you raise a blade against me?"

"Yes, sir. I cannot let you bring harm to Charley Tooth."

"That is treachery, Ovenheat, and I have no time for treachery."

"No."

"Apparently you got too close to the semi-Magnificent. Sorry to lose you, Ovenheat."

"Rokesy glim zoiner," muttered Tandor.

Gwenowit raised his sword. Tandor opened his hand, and his sword leapt into the air and found its mark, quick and true, just under the rib cage on the left side of Gwenowit's body. The force was enough to take Gwenowit back a step or two, as he looked in wild wonder at Tandor, and then at the blade. He fell back now, against the wall behind him, and blood darkened his shirt below the impalement. Charley and Deviz stood off to his left, frozen. Gwenowit turned to look at them. His eyes were still wide open, very wide open. Gwenowit looked to his sword, pushed himself off the wall, and tried to lunge at Charley. Charley and Deviz ducked out of the way, and Gwenowit's unsteadiness and momentum carried him crashing into the wall next to the door. This time, though, the wall was not enough to keep him upright, and he fell to the floor. Charley and Deviz still stood motionless, watching.

"Get out of here," said Tandor. "Take the stairs behind that door up two flights, and make a left. Down the hallway, on the right side, you'll pass three doors. After the third door, look along the wall where it meets the floor, and you will see a brick with three tiny grooves on it. Place your foot against it and say, 'Orlay vlinx,' and a corridor will appear. Keep following it straight, all the way. It will eventually lead you to a heavy door inside an old dockhouse down at the river. To open that door, put your foot against the bottom and say, 'Orlay trembum.' From there you are on your own. Got it? Remember that?"

"Orlay vlinx and orlay trembum," said Charley.

"Now go."

Charley and Deviz quickly disappeared up the stairway behind the door. Tandor turned to his boss. Gwenowit's breathing was rapid and shallow. His face was pale. His eyes, still filled with incredulity, were on Tandor, and his hand still held his sword, but he was now too weak to lift it. Tandor came over and knelt beside him. Gwenowit struggled to sit up somewhat.

"Traitor," he managed to say.

"No. I had to stop you, sir. Dix and Dax are traitors to this world, and in helping them we have been traitors to its citizens. I believe Tooth is the greatest hope for righting the wrongs. I really do, sir."

"Traitor . . . to me."

"I am so sorry. I am so sorry. I couldn't let you kill them. I couldn't let you to do them what we did to Clarus and Sholto. I couldn't do it, sir. I had to stop you, and it was the only way. I am so sorry."

"Lies. . . ."

"No, no. You never saw, you were never able to see that we were working for a greater evil. I know you did your job faithfully and honestly, but you never recognized what it all meant, what the ramifications were. I am sorry, I am so sorry. I know you don't believe me. I know."

"My family. My family."

"I give you my word that I will make sure they are taken care of, regardless of what happens. I never wanted to kill you. I never wanted to betray you. I didn't act out of hate. I did what I had to do to ensure the removal of the Orphan Lords."

With his left hand, Gwenowit grabbed Tandor's shirtfront.

"Your word . . . means nothing. Go to hell."

Tandor put his hand on Gwenowit's shoulder, but Gwenowit was already dead. Tandor released himself from Gwenowit's dead grip, and then he removed his sword from Gwenowit's body. He wiped the blade clean on the dead man's shirt and then placed it back inside the folds of his cloak. He checked Gwenowit's pulse one more time, and then he quickly absconded through the same door that Charley and Deviz had fled through several minutes earlier.

Meanwhile, Charley and Deviz had hurried through and were exiting the other end of the secret passage, coming out down by the river. Deviz led Charley along the banks for a while, and then through a small section of forest. They picked their way through, along and past a lake, uphill over some rockier terrain, until they reached a fairly sizable old brick building that looked to Charley to be of a religious nature. Deviz turned to him.

"This is a safehouse. We can stay here and get word to Onnser."

They had avoided the front of the building, approaching from the back, to a private entrance. Deviz knocked five times in an arrhythmic pattern, and in a moment the door opened and they were ushered in. Charley found himself in the company of the Abbot of St. Orson, whom he recognized from the party at Hololo Summersweat's all those months ago. The Abbot looked pale and nervous, and upon seeing Charley he went an even lighter shade of pale.

"I haven't heard that knock in a long time," he said to the two of them.

"Abbot, we need your help. We need you to hide us and get word to Onnser the semi-Magnificent. Tell him our mission failed spectacularly and that there were casualties. We are past the point of being able to turn back."

The Abbot took them through a few rooms into a small den. He rolled back the carpet in the room. He then went over to the wall and removed a framed painting of a short, heavy, clean-shaven man wearing a sort of long Nehru-jacket type of garment. The Abbot's hands were shaking as he brought it over.

"I haven't done this in a while. I hope it still works."

He placed the painting on the floor where the rug had been. He waited a few seconds, and then he gingerly lifted the painting from one end. As he did so, Charley saw that it had become a trapdoor. There were rough-hewn steps leading down into the darkness.

"Oh my, it worked!" exclaimed the Abbot, and he went over to a bookshelf and removed a small glass lamp containing lightfish. He knocked on the lamp and light sprung to life. He handed it to Deviz, and Deviz descended into the darkness, which was no longer so dark.

"I'll bring you some food and be right down," said the Abbot.

Charley was on the steps and turned to thank the Abbot, but, in turning, he lost his footing and promptly fell down the rest of the stairs, managing, it felt, to hit every single bone in his body on something sharp and unforgiving.

"Are you okay?" called the Abbot at the same time as Deviz.

"Yes, I'm fine," said Charley, who could immediately feel that he would have several king-size bruises in addition to the cut on his chin and on top of the embarrassment of falling down stairs.

Charley, once right-side-up again, took in the hiding space. It was of decent size. They were in a common area that had several simple chairs, a couch, and a desk. There was a small bathroom just off to the left, and a big room off to the right. The big room looked like a barracks, with bunk beds lining the walls, capable of sleeping about twenty people. Deviz had been knocking on the lightfish tanks in the walls, but they were all dead. Clearly, it had indeed been a while since the Abbot or anybody had been down. The Abbot came down shortly, bringing a basket of food and a jug of water.

"I hope this is all you will need for the time being, as I don't have much in the monastery right now. I will get word to Onnser at once, and bring back whatever news I can. Get some rest. I will be back as soon as possible."

"Thank you, Abbot," said Deviz, "and I am sorry we had to burden you with this emergency."

"Yes, well, I suppose we all have our troubles to bear," said the Abbot a little sadly, and he climbed back up the stairs, closing the trapdoor. Charley heard him rotate the painting and pick it back up.

Left in the relative darkness, Charley sat down on the couch. Deviz took a seat in one of the chairs. The lightfish lamp sat between them, on the floor. Charley looked at Deviz.

"I can't believe Hamar was killed."

"I can't believe that Tandor killed Gwenowit. I had no idea he had any leanings toward our side. This is big news. If Orflung and Bellanca managed to escape, and to slay those two soldiers, we might be able to sneak our way out of this disaster. With Tandor's help on the inside, things could be looking up. But if there is anyone who can name us as being there, then we are in some major trouble."

"Either way, I suppose it will be next to impossible to get Clarus and Sholto out, even with Tandor's help."

"True. Not finding them today is a major failure. The Resistance will have to act quickly, I think. Such interesting times." There was a heavy sadness to his voice.

They both sat in silence, and Charley actually fell soundly asleep, right there on the couch, dreaming of nothing.

When he awoke, Onnser and the Abbot were sitting in the room with him and Deviz. He rubbed his eyes and Onnser looked at him.

"You were quite asleep there, Charley. Deviz was telling us about the mission. Sounds like you were lucky that Tandor arrived when he did and did what he did."

"Yeah. What about Orflung and Bellanca? Are they all right? Did they make it out? Did you hear about Hamar?"

"Yes, I heard that Gwenowit killed Hamar. And, unfortunately, Orflung and Bellanca also perished. However, the two guards who pursued them were killed in the fight, so it seems that the only person who knows that you and Deviz were there is Tandor. However, I of course am to go in for questioning. As is Grimfir. As will you be, I suspect. And as will Wednesday. I am afraid these questioning sessions might . . . last for a long while. Indefinitely, so to speak. The Ruling Powers will do what they can to eradicate the rest of the Resistance. I don't think even Tandor can help us now, though he might be able to buy us some time. It is imperative that you not get caught, because without you, Charley, I think we are finished. If only we had been able to find my sister and her husband! If only Tandor knew. Maybe that could help us, though I am sure they've tightened security around them. At any rate, Charley, I plan to turn myself over to them tonight, and maybe buy some time for you. I will do what I can to give the Ministry the gentle impression that I led the rescue mission, and that will distract them from you for a little while, I hope. You'll have to be on the lam for a while, but if you can find out more about Clarus and Sholto, or even how to acquire the Talking Sword of Flassto, then we might stand a chance to turn the momentum back into our favor. If not, all is lost. How does that sound?"

"Awful."

The Abbot of St. Orson choked on his glass of water at this, and Onnser began laughing. Deviz and Charley began laughing as well, and soon they were all in hysterics, with tears streaming down Onnser's old face as he laughed.

"Yes, Charley," he said, when they calmed down and caught their breaths. "It does indeed sound awful. Awful for everyone involved, and probably with worse to come. However, let us hope that through the other side of this awfulness there might be some peace, some good that we can achieve, and make sure things never get this awful again."

"And what should I do about getting my end of things done?" asked Charley. "I mean, where do I begin?"

There was silence as Deviz, Onnser, and the Abbot all looked at each other. Onnser was the first to speak.

"I don't know what to tell you, Charley. There's not much more I can do for you. You'll have the resources of whoever in the Resistance is still active, free, and available. You have your training, and you have your common sense."

"I don't feel like any of this is much to go on."

"But that's all we've got. All you've got. At least, that I'm aware of. Have courage, Charley."

Onnser got up, as did the Abbot. He shook Deviz's hand, and then Charley's.

"I hope to see you both again sometime."

The Abbot followed him up the stairs, and the trap-door closed behind them.

Charley lay thinking. He was thinking about the people in his life that he had lost touch with—the ones that he wondered if he would see again, given that his life returned to the normal path it had once been on. He thought of Jonathan Baldwin, his best friend in pre-school and the person who taught him how to raise one eyebrow and how to wiggle his ears. He thought about Blaire Fry, also from pre-school, who was the first girl he knew who wore glasses and his first crush. He didn't know what became of either Jonathan or Blaire, but he thought it would be nice to reconnect with them one day, and how easy it would be if the two of them had married. He thought about Will Chang, a good friend in second grade who moved to California, and Jill Spenser, who was his best friend for two years in third and fourth grade before her parents divorced and her mom moved with her to Milwaukee.

There were hurried sounds from above as Charley and Deviz could make out the rug hastily being pulled back and the painting clattering to the floor. Fearing that they had been ratted out, Deviz and Charley put out the lightfish lamp and hid, as best they could, in the room. Charley ducked behind the couch, and Deviz behind a chair. The trap door opened, and a figure came hurrying down.

"Charley! Charley? It's me, Wednesday! Charley?"

Deviz put on the light again, and Charley stood up behind the couch to see Wednesday come running at him, smiling, but clearly after a bout of serious crying. She ran to the couch, hopped up on it, and hugged Charley to her so tightly and powerfully that it actually pulled him over the back of the couch, bringing them both falling to the floor. The Abbot came down nervously behind her. Charley quickly got up to make sure Wednesday was okay, which she was, and she hugged him again.

"Oh, Charley! I was so worried about you! I was so worried about you!"

"I'm okay, Wednesday. It's so great to see you. Are you all right?"

She released him. "I heard about the mission, and that you couldn't find my parents. And I heard that Hamar, Orflung, and Bellanca all were killed, along with some of the guards! And I heard you guys had to kill Gwenowit Husk to escape!"

"There were some unavoidable measures that had to be taken, I am sorry to say," chimed in Deviz, nodding at Charley. "And Tandor Ovenheat helped us in our getaway."

"Yes," Charley said, understanding that Wednesday did not and should not know about the particulars of Tandor's involvement in their escape. "The mission was a failure."

"But at least you got out safely," said Wednesday.

"But others died. People died, and we have nothing to show for it. I don't know what to do. I don't know how to feel."

"Feel lucky. Orflung, Hamar, and Bellanca knew what they were getting into, and they knew the price that they might have to pay. They died fighting. And at least—at last—you guys were trying. You were actively taking on Dix and Dax. It's really all we can do. I know you didn't find my parents. I know people died. I know that now the Orphan Lords are going to strike back. But we are doing all that we can, and just knowing that we are trying is encouraging. It gives people hope."

"Man," thought Charley to himself, "this girl is fantastic. Who else could make you feel that the disaster of a rescue mission you just headed up was as wonderful a thing as scoring the last-second, game-winning goal in the finals of the World Cup?" And this was a remarkable thought, as Charley had only ever played as a fullback in soccer.

"My uncle is gone," she said. "He went in for questioning. I didn't even get a chance to talk to him beforehand. Grimfir, too. Charley, I am scared. Uncle Onnser brought me up with this day in mind; it was something he taught me we would have to face someday, but I never really considered it as an actual . . . thing. An actuality. You think things will never change, you think life goes on in its same way forever, even though you know there will be times of pain, times of death. You just don't believe you'll ever have to face it. And then when you do, it can shut you down, you know? You think maybe you can just lie low, maybe you can just go to sleep, and everything will right itself by the time you pull yourself back into the day. But it doesn't. It can't."

Wednesday sat on the couch. Charley sat next to her. He didn't want to say anything; he wanted Wednesday to go on talking, to go on and on. She turned to him.

"Tandor contacted me. He said he needs to meet with you—tonight. I'm to take you to the dockhouse that you were in earlier today. We will leave as soon as it's dark."

"That will be in about an hour and a half," said the Abbot. "I'll get some things together for you and come down when it's time for you to go." He returned upstairs, and Deviz discreetly excused himself and went into the bunkroom.

"You talked to Tandor?"

"Yes. When I heard that Uncle Onnser had gone to turn himself in for questioning, I went after him. Tandor was actually on his way to our house, and we ran into each other. Tandor told me to find you as soon as I could and arrange for you two to meet. He said it was a matter of life and death."

"He actually said it was 'a matter of life and death'?"

"He did. He looked very worried. I've never seen him look quite like that."

"Did he say anything else? Anything helpful?"

"I don't think so—it was a very quick meeting. Like what?"

"I'm not sure. Maybe something about finding your parents, or even something about the Talking Sword of Flassto. When we meet with him, let's try to get as much info on what we should do next. Since he's inside the system, he might be the one who can best take up Onnser's planning, you know?"

"Maybe. But the thing is, he was explicit that it's just going to be the two of you meeting. Not with me. Just you and Tandor."

Charley suddenly felt nauseated, as though he were going to be called into the principal's office for cheating. Wednesday noticed the change in his demeanor.

"Are you okay? What's wrong?"

"I don't know. I just got this feeling that meeting with him alone doesn't bode well. I mean, why would he *not* want to meet with you? He's always been glad to have you there in the past, even more so than to have me there, sometimes, I think. So what does this mean? What if he is back with Dix and Dax now, and this is a trap to get me?"

"Hm. As much as I have not been a big fan of Tandor's, and even though he works for a pretty despicable group, I don't think he would do that. I think he genuinely likes Onnser, and I think that he genuinely likes me, so it would surprise me to think that he would do this to you, especially using me. Besides, it doesn't make any sense that he would've let you escape, because you would be able to use that against him in an inquiry, especially as you have Deviz as a witness, and whomever else. It doesn't add up. But I see your point about it being somewhat suspicious and maybe not as positive as we would hope."

Charley, though trying to focus on the discussion at hand, couldn't help but feel somewhat warmed that though Wednesday acknowledged Tandor's affection for her, she voiced her somewhat disdainful opinion of him overall. He begrudgingly moved his thoughts back into the territory of the fate of the world.

"Then I guess I have really no other choice. Yuck."

"I have faith in you, Charley."

"That means a lot to me, Wednesday. It really does. But what can I do? I tried to get your parents out, but I couldn't do it."

"It was beyond your control."

"It feels like everything is beyond my control."

Wednesday took his hand, and he looked at her. She raised her left hand to his face, placed it along his jaw under his ear, leaned in, and kissed him. She brought her head back slightly to look Charley in the eye, and then she leaned in to kiss him again. Charley put his arms around her and kissed back. He kissed her and kissed her and kissed her.

About an hour later, the Abbot of St. Orson rolled back the carpet, took the portrait down from the wall, and opened the trapdoor. He came down the steps with a small bag. Wednesday and Charley now were apart on the couch, with Charley feeling slightly guilty about the romantic interlude he had just had in the secret hiding room in a monastery. Deviz emerged from the bunkroom upon hearing the Abbot come down, so they were all together in the room. The Abbot gave the bag to Wednesday.

"It's about time for you to leave, I think. I wasn't sure what I had that would help you, so there is a little bit of food and some water in there. And a sweater. And a little bit of money. I don't know what else. Do you need anything? I also put in there my leather pouch. It will come in handy at Lake Fritz, as you can use it to cross directly and save yourself some time. Plus, nobody will be looking for you on a lake. I don't suppose anyone will be looking for anybody on a lake. You know? I've never showed it to anybody, but the pouch was a gift from The Historic Ganka. In it you will find waterwalking spread. Cover your bare feet up to your ankles with it, and you'll be able to cross on top of the water."

"Thank you, Abbot, that's very generous," said Wednesday.

"It's really something," replied the cleric, somewhat wistfully.

"Do you want me to come with you, Charley?" asked Deviz.

"No, Tandor wants me to meet him alone. Won't do you or anyone any good if you're caught hanging around."

"It might do the Orphan Lords some good."

This was true, and so Charley smiled. "I hope to be back before too long, anyway. With any luck, he'll hand me the Talking Sword of Flassto as well as the map and keys to wherever Clarus and Sholto are being held."

"Or the secret on how to get back to your home," said Wednesday, smiling.

Charley stopped and looked at her. In the excitement of the past few days, he had completely forgotten about getting home. It wasn't that he didn't want to go back, but he had suddenly become involved in very active, very important things, and he certainly felt as though he were needed here on Nivalg. Or, at least, as though other people felt he was needed here on Nivalg. But really, wasn't that what all this was about, anyway—finding a way to get back home? It made the most sense, just as Onnser had said, in the face of a lack of any other method to return to his family.

"You two really should be going, really," said the Abbot, nervous now that the time had come for these two to be off. Charley and Wednesday followed him upstairs through the trapdoor. They helped him in quickly disguising the entry to the hiding place again, and then he let them out the back door.

"You two know where you're going? I couldn't bear to have it on my conscience if you guys got lost from here."

"We'll be fine, Abbot," said Wednesday cheerily. Very cheerily, considering the day so far. Together, she and Charley headed down the steep slope behind the monastery, avoiding the path that led away from its front door. Not long after they were completely out of sight of the building, Charley stopped Wednesday, pulled her to him, and kissed her again. They kissed for a few seconds, but she stopped him and took a step back.

"We'll be late." With that, she took Charley's hand, and they began running through the woods toward Lake Fritz, as dusk was setting in. They ran, holding hands, until they reached the edge of the water, and there they paused to catch their breath as they took off their shoes and socks. Wednesday opened the bag and pulled out the pouch. She opened it and looked inside, sniffed. She handed it to Charley.

"Here, you do it. I don't like to handle magical things so much. I'd just as soon let someone who deals with this kind of stuff regularly manage it."

Charley took the pouch from her and scooped his fingers inside. He immediately felt the tingling of the magic, and he brought his hand out to look at it.

"Don't waste it; you never know how much we'll need, or how long it will last."

Charley took Wednesday's right foot in his hand and caringly spread the stuff all over it, up to the ankle. Then he did her other foot. Then he did his own. He slung the pouch around his neck and tucked it under his shirt. Wednesday put their shoes and socks into the bag, and again holding hands, they stepped gingerly onto the water, bobbing slightly. Taking a few more steps, they began to get a sense of their balance. It felt as though they were walking on a very thin water balloon, and both Charley and Wednesday were consciously walking as though they were afraid too much weight here or there would puncture the delicate surface tension and send them down into the cold lake. They also both were unconsciously holding their breaths, inhaling and exhaling as little as possible and only when their brains demanded oxygen.

They crossed the lake in quiet, in wonder, having never heard of this potion or ever even thought about it. They huddled close as they walked, feeling the ripples their footfalls caused go rolling out in all directions. At just about the midway point, Wednesday stopped Charley, and they momentarily had to struggle to maintain their balance. The sky was deep violet, and Wednesday kissed him again. They kissed, standing in the center of the lake, until a fish jumping jolted them back to the present, and they hurried to the other shore.

On the other side, they tried scuffing their feet on the grass, but that wasn't very productive. Wednesday took the blanket out of the bag, and they used that to rub their feet clean and dry. They quickly put their shoes back on and headed for the river. Charley recognized the general way he had come earlier that day with Deviz, but in the growing darkness he was all the happier to have Wednesday with him to make sure he got there. As they followed the river and neared the dockhouse, Charley began to feel very nervous all over again. After all, it was nighttime, he was on his way to a secret meeting with a man who worked for an evil government and who had killed his own boss, the meeting probably had something to do with Charley being the last hope for the world or something, and Charley still didn't entirely believe in his abilities. And his feet were cold from the lake crossing. He slowed his pace somewhat, a bit of him hoping this walk with Wednesday might last forever, even with its uncomfortable anticipation of the end. Wednesday must have sensed his growing reluctance, for when they drew in sight of the dockhouse, she stopped him again to kiss him, and she held him very, very tight to her. She looked up into his eyes.

"I want you to know that you are terrific, Charley. No matter what happens, I think you are terrific, and I am so grateful to have gotten to know you. I have so much faith in you, Charley." And she kissed him again.

Charley felt a burning where her arms were, and it spread throughout his body, up into his face, up into his head. It felt like a million fiery butterflies swelling out into every bit of his body. Like lightfish flashing on and off and on a trillion times in his bloodstream. He felt elated. He felt like he was floating.

"I'll wait for you here. I'll hide out in that clump of brush. Come find me when you finish." She kissed him again. Kissing Wednesday was a lot of fun. She had two tongues.

Charley practically ran the rest of the way to the dockhouse. The sooner he got through the meeting with Tandor, the sooner he could be back in Wednesday's arms. Reinvigorated with confidence, he prepared himself for the interaction with Tandor. Charley would make demands, taking over the operational aspect of the Resistance's fight to dethrone Dix and Dax. He would insist on information on who in the government knew what, what the next steps were, what the weak points were, and exactly where they could find Clarus and Sholto to free them—not to mention Onnser or any help that Tandor and his fifth column might be able to contribute. As Charley reached the door, he felt as though maybe *he* should have been the one to call the meeting with Tandor, and he was ready to run the meeting *his* way, dismiss Tandor, and return triumphantly to Wednesday. And things would be okay. Maybe even within a day or two. Charley formulated his first words to make sure Tandor knew that he was ready to fight. His mind made up, Charley bravely opened the door to the dockhouse and entered. It was dark, but when the door shut behind him, a lightfish lantern went on to reveal Tandor Ovenheat seated in a rickety chair in the back. Tandor stood up.

"Charley."

"Tandor. Where are Clarus and Sholto? We need to free them."

"They're dead, Charley. They've been dead for many years."

Charley felt all his recent warmth leave him through the back of the base of his skull.

"What? But we need them . . . we need to free them."

"That will be highly, highly difficult, Charley. Impossible even. They are dead."

"Are you sure?"

"Yes. I am sure. I am very sure. I have been very sure for a long time."

"But . . . I don't understand."

"Have a seat, Charley."

"Are you sure? How? What happened? Dead?" Charley said, taking the chair Tandor offered, the one Tandor had been on when Charley entered.

"Clarus and Sholto O'Friday are dead, Charley. They were executed long ago. Long ago. When they were taken, when the Resistance made its push all those years ago, Dix and Dax had them imprisoned and, of course, interrogated."

"How can they be dead?"

"That's why I needed to talk to you tonight, Charley. That's why I arranged this meeting. Onnser turned himself in for questioning—and I doubt he'll be let out anytime soon. If ever. And there's nothing I can do to help him right now. We have Grimfir, too, as you might know. Though he certainly doesn't have the kind of information or importance that Onnser does, or probably that Bellanca and your other rescuers did, it is thought that Grimfir might be easier to crack, and names are all they would be looking for from him."

"This *is* horrible. . . ."

"Yes, this is horrible. And it stands to get worse. I have done my best to deflect attention from Wednesday, but I don't know how effective that will be in a day or two. It may even be that I have to bring her in . . . and interrogate her myself. And I will have to do it, Charley. I will have to. I did not want to kill Gwenowit. Please understand that. I did not at all. He was a good man; he just didn't realize what he was doing was wrong. He was devoted to his family, and he felt that in doing his job he was making the world a better place. He honestly believed in it, and he really had no idea that the institution he was helping was evil. It crushes me that I had to do what I did, but at least we had the benefit of there not being any witnesses. That won't be the case with Wednesday, Charley. I won't be able to protect her once she is in custody."

"Her parents are dead."

"And now we have Onnser, and I can't guarantee how long he will live. I am glad that I myself do not have to interrogate him. And you, Charley. Had I not stopped Gwenowit, I assure you that you would not be alive in the morning. That's why I did what I did. Charley, I must impress upon you one thing: I am on your side. I am. No matter what I have to do for Dix and Dax and the Ministry, know that I want the overthrow to succeed."

"Are you sure Wednesday's parents are dead? Can't there have been some mistake? It has to be a mistake. . . ."

"No. It is not a mistake." Tandor stopped talking and started pacing. Charley, feeling dazed and windless, watched him blankly, feeling the hope that had been so strong in his chest rapidly receding. He noticed that Tandor looked tenser, more worried, and more frightened than he ever would have thought. Tandor stopped pacing and looked off at the wall, unable to look in Charley's direction.

"I know that they are dead because I was there. I was part of it, Charley." He looked into Charley's eyes. "I was part of it."

"What . . .?"

"I was there, Charley. This is why I wanted to talk to you. This is what I needed to tell you. I had just joined the Ministry—this is before it became what it is today. I was just out of school, eager to make a good impression, eager to get a good start on my career. When Clarus and Sholto were caught, it shook up the system for us. There was great reorganization across the board, and Dix and Dax consolidated departments and gave them broad new powers, especially to our Ministry. It was our job to keep track of every citizen, to root out possible terrorists and insurgents before they became active. To profile those rebels who were capable of taking on the government. And these particular people, of course, would be those who exhibited the ability to practice magic. It was all in the interest of national security, Charley.

Insurrectionists had tried to destroy the rule of the Orphan Lords. I worked for the Orphan Lords, for the government, for the country, so it was my duty to carry out their commands, and I did it with gusto. It was an exciting time to be involved, I have to say. When Gwenowit brought me into the newly formed Ministry, I was thrilled. It was though I had made it, and I was barely eighteen. We were doing what seemed to be the most important, most thrilling work imaginable—bringing down the bad guys, the evil wizards, the ones who held the Orphan Lords, and by extension the country, in disdain. Clarus and Sholto were the biggest imaginable catch. They always were, and they still are. Only you would be a bigger catch."

Reflexively, Charley was up and out of his chair, maneuvering so that Tandor was no longer between him and the door.

"No, Charley, I am not here to capture you. I assure you. I needed to . . . to talk to you. I've done some terrible things, Charley. I have such . . . regret. Gwenowit posted me to the interrogation team for Clarus and Sholto. It was unimaginable to me that I should ascend so quickly. I was a hard worker, a competent employee, a dedicated patriot, and to be rewarded so quickly with such an assignment went to my head. I was eager to prove my worth to the Ministry—to the legendary Gwenowit Husk himself. To Dix and Dax, the Orphan Lords. So. The interrogations, Charley. I was able not to let it bother me. It was torture. I mean, we used torture. We were extracting information from unwilling sources in an effort to protect the homeland. Do you see? Do you understand? And I was playing a direct role. I was there, Charley. I did what I was told to do. No, I did more than I was told to do. I showed unique initiative. I have so many regrets, Charley. I helped torture Sholto and Clarus. I thought I was doing the right thing. I really did. I didn't stop to think about it. When we got as much information out of them as we could, we imprisoned them. You found Clarus's cell today. Empty. It was empty less than a year after it became her home. It was too dangerous to keep her. To keep them. We knew it would only be a matter of time before the rebels regrouped and tried to free them. And that it would be time after time that they would try. We considered making a public spectacle of their capital punishment, but it was deemed more profitable to keep it a secret, as a dead-end lure for future rebel rescuers—such as yourself and your band today. So we killed them, Charley."

"Tandor—"

"I killed them, Charley. I killed them. The job fell to me, and I killed them. I killed Onnser's sister and her husband. I killed Wednesday's parents. I did it myself. Afterward, I was assigned to investigate Onnser, and more importantly, Wednesday. I spent a lot of time with them, working to overcome Onnser's well-founded distrust of me. Wednesday was young then, but already exhibiting signs of great magic. I convinced Onnser the best way to save her life would be for us to remove those abilities from her. Truth be told, it was the best way, given the circumstances and my willingness to advance the wishes of the Ruling Powers. But it was horrible and painful for her. And the more time I spent with Onnser, the more I came to respect him, and Wednesday was always a startlingly engaging child. I grew to realize and regret the magnitude of what I had done to her parents. I came to realize that what we did as a Ministry, as a government, was wrong. Of course it was too late. I know that. But it changed me. I think Gwenowit sensed that I had gone too far too quickly, and he was always very kind to me about placing me where I was comfortable, and I never complained and was happy to be out of the most covert work that the Ministry conducts. I've done well for myself, and I think for the purer ideas of what the public face of our work is, but I can never let go of what I've done. That's what drove me to the Resistance, to helping out Onnser as much as I could while still working within the system of my job. I still believe in defrocking fakes and charlatans, but I have been actively helping Onnser and Wednesday as much as I could. They do not know that Clarus and Sholto are dead—very few of us do—and they don't know the involvement I had in the events all those years ago."

"Why are you telling me?"

"I had to tell someone, Charley. I have lived with this inside myself for so long, and I needed to tell someone I could trust."

"What makes you think you can trust me?"

"I know you never liked me much, Charley, but I hope that what I did today, when you faced Gwenowit, earns me some respect, and some trust. I've fallen in love with Wednesday, Charley. I didn't mean for it to happen, I didn't expect for it to happen, and I fought against it. But I have watched her grow up, I have seen what a strong woman she's become, and I have fallen completely in love with her. And here it is that I am the one responsible for the pain and misery in her life."

"Why are you telling me all of this? I don't want this

burden."

"I know you are fond of Wednesday, too. Charley, I don't think you and I are so different."

"Tandor, I appreciate your need to find someone you can talk to, someone you can open up to, but I am not the one. Why not the Abbot? I have enough that I have to worry about—things that I never wanted to worry about. I don't want this! I never wanted any of it! It's not fair of you to tell me it! What am I supposed to do?"

"I don't know, Charley. I am sorry. But you are the one who seems to have to bear the troubles of this place. And I actually wanted to know from you what I am supposed to do."

"What *you* are supposed to do?"

"Yes. I don't know what to do."

"Tandor, can't you see that we have bigger problems than you being in love with Wednesday? I need to know what to do about saving Onnser and Grimfir, and taking down the Orphan Lords. I need to find the Talking Sword of Flassto. If Clarus and Sholto are dead, it is our only hope, and I need your help."

Tandor sat back down in the chair.

"I don't know what to tell you, Charley. All I can do is ask that you and Wednesday try to find a way to avoid being captured, and work on this on your own."

"That's it? How is that supposed to be helpful?"

"What more can I tell you, Charley? I wish I could do something to right the wrongs of the past decade, but there's nothing I can think of."

"What about Mr. Hiram Poison? Onnser mentioned him as some important figure in all of this."

"Mr. Hiram Poison? I've heard of him, but I've never seen him. I think only Dix and Dax have, and that he served or serves as some sort of a mentor to them, or an advisor, or something. I believe he is the one who told them they could be defeated by the Talking Sword of Flassto, but that otherwise they were nearly invincible. And it is only through the community of magic, according to Mr. Hiram Poison, that the Sword will be discovered. In all the years I have been involved with the Ministry, though, I have never come across any concrete evidence of what the sword is or where it might be. I don't know, Charley. I just want Wednesday to be safe. That's all."

"Tandor. Clarus and Sholto are dead. Onnser and Grimfir are in custody. Wednesday and I are being sought after by the Ministry. Nobody knows what to do. I need help. I need someone to help me."

Tandor sat quietly in the chair, looking from Charley to the floor.

"Tandor, please. Please help me."

"I can't help you, Charley. I don't have any help to give."

Charley looked at Tandor for several moments, feeling disappointment, anger, and pity all at once. He turned and headed for the door of the dockhouse, determined to shut as much of this out of his mind as he could. Which, he knew, would amount to nothing.

"Charley."

Charley had his hand on the door. He stopped, but did not turn to look back at Tandor. He waited.

"I can't tell Wednesday what I've done. I can't. But . . . I want her to know. Can you tell her? Somehow? Everything?"

Charley closed his eyes and leaned his face against the cold wooden door.

"No, Tandor. She has to know, but I won't be the

one to tell her. I refuse that responsibility. It's yours, not mine. I have enough."

He pulled the door open and slipped out into the night.

Chapter Thirteen

Charley beelined for the shrubs where he found Wednesday, still hidden and fully alert.

"How did it go?" she whispered.

"Not as I hoped. Let's get back to St. Orson."

He took her by the hand and they retraced their path through the dark. They picked their way silently through the woods, Charley feeling awful, feeling a headache spreading from the top of his head all the way down into his shoulders. For a moment, he suddenly wondered if he had meningitis. Then he wondered if he might actually prefer having meningitis to having the knowledge that Wednesday's parents were dead and the revolution was stalled. He felt sweaty and cold, and was trying to think about what he would say and what they would do once they were back in the safety of the hidden basement in the monastery. As they drew within sight of Lake Fritz, there was a rustling on either side of them and a flash of light.

"Look out!" cried Wednesday as she pushed Charley

forward.

"Halt! Halt! You are under arrest!" came the voices as a small band of soldiers jumped out from behind trees on either side and gave chase as Charley and Wednesday ran.

"We have to split up, Charley—you have to get away!"

"I won't leave you, Wednesday!"

"You have to! Make for the lake—use the water-walking!"

"Wednesday—"

But Wednesday had veered suddenly as they came to a thick stand of high bushes, and when Charley came out on the other side, he could see her heading off perpendicularly from his own path. He knew that turning to follow would get him caught, so he fled onward toward the lake. He could hear soldiers still after him, as well as some sort of dog that was gaining ground. As he ran, Charley began tearing at his shoelaces, and when he felt his shoes sufficiently loose, he began to kick at them. The right one came off, but the other was still too tight. In mid-stride, Charley clutched at his left foot, yanking at the shoe. He lost his balance and pitched forward, into a forward somersault. Miraculously, he came out standing up again, propelled forward by his momentum, and found his left shoe and the sock in his hand. He cast them aside and continued for the lake. He tore at his shirt to get at the Abbot's pouch, which he practically ripped open as he ran. He was about ten feet from the lake's edge, running with a bare left foot and a socked right foot. He scooped the waterwalking potion with both hands and quickly gunked up his left foot on the upswing. A step later, and he jumped as far as he could onto the surface of the water, landing with his left foot down. He splashed in, down to his knee, but the raging particles in the potion brought him quickly back up to the surface, where Charley managed to maintain his balance and hop another fifteen feet or so toward the center of the lake. He flung off his right sock and slopped the potion onto his other foot, and ran a bit farther. He turned to see the dog reach the shoreline and jump in after him, but the lake quickly got deep and the dog swam back to shore, barking. Along the right side of the lake, Charley saw Wednesday darting among the trees with her pursuers close at hand. He began to run her way, but the soldiers overtook her, quickly having her on the ground and tied up. Charley knew it was too late to help her, especially as his own set of guards had now made it to the water and were putting arrows into their bows. Had the moons not been out and so bright tonight, he thought, their getaway might have gone much more smoothly.

Charley turned and ran across the lake as the arrows sliced into the water around him. As he neared the far edge, he found himself overrunning his own legs, and he tripped and fell. His feet up to the ankles remained floating on top of the water, and the rest of him floundered underwater, in the cold and dark of the lake. Charley tried to right himself by swinging his legs under, but the potion was too strong and would not allow him the luxury of keeping his feet underneath his body. Arching his back, Charley sputtered to the surface. He knew time was critical—he had just gained maybe an hour's worth of time on his hunters, provided they scrambled along the edge of the lake in order to follow him. Deciding not to waste time by trying to figure out how to stand back up, Charley instead forced himself to swim, though doing so with his feet unable to go below water made it an exhausting—though ultimately effective—endeavor. He crawled ashore on the far side of the lake, wet, cold, and tired. Without even bothering to scrape the goo from his feet, he began running for the monastery. He of course avoided the footpath and took relatively the same course up the back of the hillside as he had previously, but even before the monastery came into sight, Charley knew the situation was not good.

In the direction of the monastery he noticed in the sky, dark plumes with flashing crimson under-colors. The closer he got, the more he could smell the acridity of many things burning. He considered running off into the woods, but he didn't know where to go once he did that. Besides, there was a chance that the fire was an accident, and that Deviz and the Abbot would still be around and able to help. So Charley continued, though as he got close he skirted among the thicker trees, in order to assess the situation. Sure enough, the monastery was in flames, and Ministry goons were detaining the escaping residents even as the fire spread.

Charley could see no sign of the Abbot or of Deviz. He snuck around to the back-door entrance, but it too had a number of soldiers, as well as some local firefighters who had cut down from the road that was not too far from this side of the building. There were conventional fire trucks hard at work, horse-drawn water pumpers standing off to the side, and some zippy one-man firefighting pods hovering here and there, attacking the flames from above. It appeared to Charley that the Ministry people were trying to prevent the firefighters from doing their job, instead forcing them to show credentials and answer questions. Again, no sign of the Abbot or of Deviz.

Charley withdrew back into the woods and made his way up toward the road from where all the fire engines were coming. He stayed within the darkness of the convenient trees, but close enough to be able to make out the faces and uniforms of the men, women, and creatures of indeterminate sex that were pouring back and forth, getting into each other's way. The Ministry officials were in the process of setting up some sort of a roadblock, leading Charley to the conclusion that not a lot of time had passed since everyone arrived on the scene. Perhaps here he would find a familiar—preferably trustworthy—face. But it was someone else who apparently spotted him. A dark set of horses drawing a dark carriage came as out of nowhere as such a large, bulky, and loud contraption can, lurching up suddenly to a stop right in front of Charley. The horses were whinnying in all the commotion of the evening. Charley took a fearful step back, looking up at the black-clad, angular coachman. It was Vang. Vang was looking at Charley with piercing dark eyes, visible in the light of the nearby fire.

"You there! You there! Come over here at once!" cried one of the roadblocking officers, apparently at Vang, as Vang looked away toward the voice. The angle was such that the carriage prevented the official and Charley from seeing each other. Vang motioned with his hand for Charley to step back into the darkness, and then brought his carriage at a trot over to the man who had called for him. Charley could hear only what the official said; Vang's responses, if there were any, were too quiet for him to hear.

"What are you doing here? Looking for trouble? Drawn to help with the fire, eh? A regular volunteer? Let's see your papers. Men, check the carriage."

Two soldiers searched on top of, under, and in the carriage, while the speaker looked through Vang's identification. Vang took advantage of their distraction to look back at Charley and make what almost looked like a hook shot, and Charley could just barely detect a glimmer of something arcing very high out of his hand, cresting a good hundred feet high, and coming down toward him. It was clear but noticeable with the smoke and colors behind it, reminding Charley of the shimmering heat waves visible rising off the blacktop on bright summer days.

"Your help is not needed here. Move on!" The official handed back the papers to Vang as the other soldiers stepped back from the carriage, and Vang snapped his reins, turning the great horses and driving them fast and hard from the scene.

A panic rose in Charley's throat as Onnser's servant rode off, but then the clear band he had tossed came down and wrapped around Charley tightly, binding him so that he couldn't move his arms or legs. It looked to Charley like one of those ribbons that a gymnast dances with, spiraling up and off, and connecting back to the departing carriage.

The head soldier who had dealt with Vang was looking at the area where Charley was hiding, and Charley was glad to have moved back among the higher trees. The soldiers, conferring quietly but not subtly, moved toward Charley's location. They were within a few yards of him, obscured by the front line of shrubs, when Charley felt himself tugged and then jolted directly upward, vertically along the trees until he was clear of them, and then even higher and higher. Below, he could make out the soldiers tramping around in the area he had been in moments ago. Charley was pulled through the air by this translucent ribbon, up and up, headfirst. The only way he was able to see anything below him was due to the increasing distance between him and the ground; otherwise, he was unable even to turn his head and observe the burning monastery or see if anybody noticed his soaring escape. As it happens, no one had.

Charley continued his trajectory upward, until he hit the crest of his curve, where he hung weightless for an instant, as though he were in an elevator that began a rapid descent. Then he was tugged gently across the brink and began his soft fall down toward Vang's carriage, which still continued at clattering speed down the road. As Charley approached Vang and his vehicle, he could see the ribbon coming into tighter and tighter spirals into Vang's outstretched hand. Vang looked up back over his shoulder to gauge Charley's distance and velocity, and then a few seconds later he gave a sharp jerk with his hand, bringing Charley crashing solidly onto the roof of the carriage, just behind him. Charley felt the warm ribbon uncoil itself from him, and then he couldn't even see it anymore. Charley lay on the roof for several minutes, processing what just happened, and instinctively holding onto the jolting stagecoach top to save himself from being thrown to what was surely a neck-breaking death. And then, for the first time since knowing him, Vang spoke.

"Get in."

The motions Vang made with the reins indicated that he was slowing the horses, but Charley noticed only the barest perceptible deceleration. He continued to wait, until Vang reached back and opened the left side door, and then looked at Charley. So, it seemed, this was as slow as it was going to get. Moving carefully, gripping each spot with knuckle-cramping intensity, Charley maneuvered his way over until his lower abdomen, waist, and legs hung down in front of the open door. Vang looked back impatiently, but Charley couldn't figure out what the next move should be. With something that looked like an exasperated glare, Vang brought the carriage into a sudden, sharp left turn, effectively throwing Charley into the body of the carriage. The carriage straightened out, and Charley regained some of his wherewithal to pull the door shut and not be a complete baby about everything. Still, he was soaking wet and cold and somewhat shaken from the last thirty minutes, the last couple of hours, the entirety of the day. Vang drove the horses on, and Charley shut his eyes to think about Wednesday.

To his surprise, he could not dwell on thoughts of Wednesday. This despite the kisses, despite the blossoming love. Despite her capture and imminent interrogation at the hands of the Ministry, Charley could not keep his mind on her. He could only think about home. He thought about Cynthia and Tabitha. The last time he had talked to Cynthia, his elder by two years, she had been upset because the guy she liked, Slade Autokankis, had stopped calling her and recently been seen in the company of a notoriously easy girl by the name of Jenilee Cristalbum. Charley and Cynthia had spent most of their lives clashing and disagreeing with each other. As he now thought about it, it seemed strange to him that so much of their time was spent arguing. After all, she was his sister and he loved her, and he was certain that she loved him, but they never got to that part of the matter. Maybe it was because they loved each other and knew it that they didn't waste any time on basic sentiment and instead spent their valuable time together engaged in petty bickering. However, when Cynthia shut herself in her room, in tears, over the fallen relations with Slade, Charley stood outside her door, overcoming his innate distaste for the mawkishness of the situation, and then entered. He saw her crying at her desk as she wrote in her diary. She turned and gave him a most evil look as she closed the diary and tried to hide the emotion on her face. He came in and sat on the foot of her bed, and she looked at him. Neither sibling said a word. Charley stood up again.

"Slade Autokankis," he said.

"Charley."

"His name is Slade Autokankis. Slade Autokankis. Slade Autokankis." Charley made a face that exuded the intelligence level that one who never met Slade (or perhaps one who did) might believe someone with such a name might exhibit when confronted with some dilemma such as nine times nine or perhaps even the challenge of naming the days of the week in backward order. Cynthia, with a slight smile, was still angry.

"Charley, don't be a jerk. . . ."

But Charley was already encouraged. "Slade Autokankis. Slade *Auto*kankis. Slade Auto*kankis*.

Slade *Autokankis*. *Slade* Autokankis. *Slade* Auto*kankis*.
Slade Autokankis. *Sladeautokankis*."

Cynthia could not suppress her laugh. Charley continued.

"My name is a disease of lameness. Sladeautokankis. I am incurable. Not even a shot of penicillin in the eye can change a damned thing about me. It's terminal."

Cynthia was now laughing out loud. Charley, who had been keeping not just a straight face but one of the utmost seriousness and professionalism, now could also not help but laugh.

"Jenilee Cristalbum."

"Stop it, Charley. She's a nice enough girl."

"She certainly is nice enough. Nice enough for anyone. *Nice enough* for *anyone*, if you catch my drift— and if you catch what she has to catch. Jenilee Cristalbum. A match made in heaven, Jenilee Cristalbum and Slade Autokankis."

The already emotionally drained Cynthia was now powerless with laughter, her hands holding her stomach. Charley, having had lifelong practice at figuring out the right time to exit a scene, took his cue and headed to his room. He got up late the next morning and ended up taking the bus after Cynthia, and by nightfall he'd been here on Nivalg.

With Tabitha, two years his junior, his last interaction had not been as pleasant. This was exceptional, as Charley and Tabitha tended to get along very well. In fact, their fights were so uncommon that when they happened they were of such rare vitriol that it even took the participants themselves aback, and within a day or two they would be closer than ever. In that way, it was almost the opposite of Charley's interactions with Cynthia. With his older sister, he fought so often that the fury never rose above a medium boil, but with Tabitha, those isolated disagreements were powerful enough to peel the wallpaper. And so it was that the morning after he had reduced his older sister to tears of laughter, he reduced his younger sister to tears of rage.

Tabitha and Charley were fundamentally different people, and he thought that maybe this is why he loved his little sister so much, generally without even realizing it. He had never put much thought into it before. He realized that he felt lucky to be in the regular company of such an interesting yet disparate soul. She was not someone who, left to his or her own devices, he would have been friends with; and therefore, having her as part of his life made it seem very special. Still, that morning before he was transported, she had done something or said something that so riled him that he was on the verge of screaming at her in anger. But now, in the bumpy carriage, he could not at all remember what the transgression had been. More than likely, Tabitha had done something like use up all of the milk before Charley had a chance to eat cereal, or maybe it was that she had been in the bathroom when it was understood to be his allotted use period. Whatever it was, it was minor, but he'd left the house that day murderously enraged at her, and he hadn't seen her since.

The carriage continued on its way to some destination that Vang had selected, and Charley continued to think about his sisters—both the times of happiness and the times of annoyance. By the time the carriage rumbled to a stop, Charley couldn't wait to see Cynthia and Tabitha Tooth (Teeth?) again. He half-expected they'd be waiting to greet him as he stepped out of the carriage. Of course, they were not.

When Charley did disembark from the black box, he found himself in front of a low cottage without neighboring dwellings anywhere in sight. The road itself was dirt, and Charley's bare feet stung from getting dust in the cuts he had acquired from running through the woods after getting out of the lake. He was still damp and shivery, certain he'd get some sort of cold or pneumonia, as that's what everybody always says when you are cold and wet.

Vang led him to the door and knocked on it. Presently, the door swung open into the warmly lit one-room layout of the house. At a table by the fireplace sat a short, heavy, clean-shaven man wearing a sort of long Nehru-jacket-type of garment. Charley noted that the door swung open on its own, and that the man at the table looked vaguely familiar. Vang led Charley in, and Charley saw in one corner a small bed, in another corner some chairs, and the rest of the room was lined with books. The man stood and came over to them.

"Hello, hello. Vang, yes? It's been a long time, my old friend. Welcome. And who are you?"

"My name is Charley. Charley Tooth."

"Hello, Charley Tooth, my name is Ganka."

"The Historic Ganka?"

"Oh, my. Yes, yes, I suppose that would be me. The Historic Ganka, formerly. Now, at best, An or A Historic Ganka—under house arrest and getting on in years. And what brings you to my company, Charley Tooth?"

"I don't know. Vang, I guess."

"Of course. And what brought Vang to bring you to

my company, Charley? I may be getting forgetful, but I do remember our friend's long-standing reticence. Tell me who you are and what you do, and what you might want with an old forgotten magician such as me."

"Oh! The Talking Sword of Flassto!" exclaimed Charley, getting not just to the point but perhaps somewhat slightly past it.

"I beg your pardon? The Talking Sword of Flassto? That's who you are?"

"What? No, I am Charley, and I am looking for the Talking Sword of Flassto."

"I see. Perhaps it would be easier on an old soul like me if you were to answer my questions in order. My goodness, you are wet and cold, aren't you? Come over here by the fire. Let's see if I can't fix things."

Ganka waggled his fingers and hopped up and down, and Charley felt a blast of heat from the fireplace sweep over him, immediately drying his clothes and hair into stiffness.

"I'm afraid I can't do anything about your lack of shoes, Charley. Mine wouldn't fit you. Now. Where were we?"

"I was asking about the Talking Sword of Flassto."

"Were you? Oh, yes, that reminds me. Tell me again what it is you do and what you want from me."

Charley was getting annoyed. "Historic" seemed to be a pretty euphemistic way to describe Ganka. Maybe "Antique" would have been better.

"My name is Charley Tooth. I am here because Onnser the semi-Magnificent and Grimfir Boldrock and a bunch of others think that I am a magician who can help save them and this place from Dix and Dax, the Orphan Lords—"

"Is that who you are?"

"That's what I'm saying, sir—"

"I mean, is that who *you* think you are, too? Or is this just what they think?"

"I don't know what to think, but I have come to think that, magician or not, I seem to be the only one remotely willing or able to deal with this."

"And how is Onnser these days?"

"The Ministry of Magic Investigation, Regulation, and Accountability has detained him. The Resistance is in shambles."

"Oh, dear! I have been out of the loop, haven't I? I'm not allowed out of the house, you see."

"And that's why I need the Talking Sword of Flassto."

"Can you tell me what the Talking Sword of Flassto is, if it's not you?"

"I am hoping—really hoping—that you can tell me about it, instead."

"How do you know about it?"

"Onnser mentioned it to me. As did Tandor Ovenheat."

"Tandor Ovenheat? Hm. Consider the source."

"Tandor is on our side, Mr. Ganka—"

"It's just Ganka—"

"And he said he's heard about it as something that Mr. Hiram Poison discovered or something."

"Mr. Hiram Poison."

"Yes, that's right."

"Tell me what you know of Mr. Hiram Poison."

"Only that nobody knows much about him. That he keeps counsel with the Orphan Lords."

"And so the confidant of the Orphan Lords has spread the word on how to overthrow them? Doesn't that seem a bit odd?"

"I never thought about it. I think it was to engage in a preemptive maneuver, you know?"

"Hm. I suppose it's possible. But be careful how much stock you put into what people say, especially if these are people who have a history or an interest in deceiving you."

"So what can you tell me about the Sword?"

"Nothing. I've never seen it or heard of it."

"What?"

"I've been in seclusion for many, many years, Charley. Occasional visitors, but I stopped taking much of an interest in what was going on out there because it was far too depressing, especially because there was nothing I was capable of doing about it. I mostly read and write all day long. It suits what has become my temperament."

Charley looked at Vang, who as usual was inscrutable. Charley looked back at The Historic Ganka, so astonished that he felt himself shiver.

"That's it? That's all the help you can give me?"

Ganka chuckled. "Well, I'm not a magician for nothing. Or am I? I am not. I might have something useful around here for you. I must."

Ganka moved boxes and papers around, looking through various trinkets and polished stones. Charley thought that maybe even The Dottering Ganka would be the most appropriate moniker. Ganka turned back to him, holding something small on a necklace in his hand.

"Here you are, Charley Tooth. Wear this. When you need it to help you, simply say, 'Orm eet eese way-hayplay,' and you will find its magic coming to your aid. Can you remember that? It would be most helpful to remember."

Charley slipped on the necklace. Hanging from the chain was an amulet—a simple round, smooth, brassy-looking piece of metal. It hung at about his sternum, and it felt good and heavy against his chest. While it was certainly no Talking Sword of Flassto, it was incredibly reassuring to have this talisman from The Historic Ganka. Charley felt better already, and in his mind he quickly revised his opinion of this wizard.

"Thank you, sir. I promise not to abuse its power."

"Do what you like with it."

"Thank you."

"And thank you for stopping by. It's so rare that I get visitors; I forget how nice a little human interaction can be. If that's everything, then, I should turn in. The older I get, the earlier my bedtime is."

Charley didn't think it was time to leave. In fact, he was reasonably sure that, with some coaxing, The Historic Ganka might be able to help him plan the next few moves for the Resistance, and then they—or more accurately, Charley—might have a chance.

"But I had some more questions for you. I was hoping we could talk. I need some advice on what to do next."

"Next? What to do next? Good heavens, how could I be expected to know what you should do next?"

"I just thought . . ."

"I am deeply flattered that you thought I would be someone of such power and sway to be able to solve your problems, but I'm just an old wizard with problems of his own. I'm housebound, and my elbow has been bothering me for years. I wonder if I must have dislocated it or something at some point. I haven't been active in decades, and the Orphan Lords had me restrained well before the Resistance made its first attempt and failure all those years ago. I'm afraid the time passes by rather quietly for me these days. If you are looking for someone to tell you how to know when to be rigid, when to be flexible, when to strike, when to lie low, how to pick battles, and how and who to fight them, I can tell you only that nobody but you can tell you that. I tell you what, though. Have a copy of my book. It's a thorough compendium of all things magical, *The Magic That Is and Maybe Isn't.* Here, I'll even autograph it for you."

The Historic Ganka did so, signing it, "Dear Charley Tooth, Good luck with the Revolution. All the best, The Historic Ganka." Charley took it without saying anything, hiding his overall disappointment with the visit.

"Okay, now, Charley, out with you. Let an old man get his sleep." Ganka came toward Charley, shooing him toward the door. Charley still hesitated.

"I don't mean to be a rude host, Charley, but unless you have something else pressing that you need to ask me, I really do request that you leave me so that I can get some sleep."

Charley turned to go, but Vang stood still, looming in the doorway. For the second time, Vang spoke.

"Is there no other question you have for him?"

Charley blinked and looked at Vang again. Even Ganka had paused. Charley wondered what question Vang wanted him to ask Ganka, as he was sure that Vang would not have said anything unless Charley were forgetting something. Forgetting! Of course! How could he forget the most important question of all? He turned back to Ganka.

"I do have one more question. Can you tell me how to get home?"

"Home? Back to Onnser's? Well, that depends—does he still live. . . . Wait, Vang should be able to take you there—"

"No, *my* home. Earth. It's a different world, a different planet. I don't know how I came to be here. But I need to get back, and I am not sure that it's going to happen by taking on Dix and Dax."

"I see. Charley, I have always been bound to this world. The kind of travel you are talking about is far beyond my powers, even when I was at my height. And that's saying something. I remember, ages and ages ago, there was a girl who came through. I don't remember a whole lot about her, but she was journeying from world to world. Nobody knew how she did it, as I recall. Other than that, though, I personally have never known of anyone able to do it. I do know, however, that the power does exist. It's just something beyond the realm of anything we here in Nivalg can do. I'm afraid I can't help you."

Charley felt as hopeless and as close to tears as he had felt in quite a while. "Maybe you can tell me this, then. When I do get back home, when I get back . . . do you know . . . if time will have passed? I mean, there are all these stories about people who find themselves on different planets and worlds and dimensions, but when they come back, it's as though they were never gone. And I figure if all these stories are like that, maybe it's because every now and then, at some point, there have been these travelers, like the girl you remember, and they come back and tell their stories and find that no time has passed since they left, and it gets into the oral histories, and passed down, and passed down. Do you know? Do you think this is possible? Do you think when I get back no time will have passed? My family? My friends? My life? Will I be able to find that everything is still the same?"

Ganka looked at him and smiled sadly. "Oh, my, Charley. No, I don't think so."

Chapter Fourteen

Vang took Charley for another long ride in Onnser's carriage, farther out than where they had been with The Historic Ganka. Charley wasn't feeling much like talking anymore, so he was grateful that his companion also was not given to chatter. Charley had been in enough cab rides back home to know that it's all nice and fine to have a gregarious driver, but only when you don't mind the intrusion. When you're in a bad mood or low funk, the last thing you want is some talkative stranger yammering away at you and trying to get you to yammer back. Charley was feeling sorry for himself, and I suppose he had every right to, so there's no need to rebuke him on it. It had been a pretty tough day, after all.

Vang eventually pulled the carriage off the side of the road and behind a hill that extended up into the mountains. Charley had never been out this far, and he noticed that the air felt colder out here, and there were more stars that shone brighter. Vang removed a box and a bag from the back of the carriage, and he motioned for Charley to follow him. Charley did so, and Vang led him on a walk up another hill, into a place of tall, thin trees that reminded Charley of pines. They walked for about twenty minutes, Vang picking his way here and there, Charley sometimes stumbling but not willing to create a light without Vang's invitation. Charley's feet, still bare and cut, felt like bloody blocks, and after Vang led him across a small stream they felt like bloody blocks of ice. They arrived in a small clearing, and Vang set down the bag. He opened the box, removing canvas and poles. In a short amount of time, he had constructed a roomy tent. From the box he also pulled several blankets. He unfastened the bag to reveal that it was full of food. He turned to Charley.

"I will return as soon as I safely can. Stay here and wait for me."

And without waiting for a response, he quickly vanished into the woods. Charley watched him go, watched his silhouette once he had gone, and kept his eyes on Vang long after Vang had in fact already been well out of sight. Charley sat down by the bag and picked at some of the food before realizing how hungry he was, and then he gorged himself. Once sated, he took the blankets into the tent. He wiped off his feet and wrapped them in one blanket, and with the other blankets he approximated a sleeping bag. Before his head hit the makeshift pillow, he was asleep. Upon his head hitting the pillow, he woke back up, startled, as falling asleep before your head hits the pillow is a surprising and ill-advised feat. After a few minutes of collecting himself, he fell back asleep again, this time quite deeply.

He awoke when the sun was high in the sky, and he

was again hungry. Charley got out of the tent and opened the bag of food. Looking through it, he calculated that there would be enough food to last him for five days, if he was careful. This fact surprised him—he had expected that Vang would return for him that morning, for some reason. Maybe Vang was just being overly cautious? Maybe half of this food was for Vang? Or maybe Vang was going to bring more people, the scattered members of the Resistance who had yet to disappear until the bad days passed? Charley decided, then, the best idea would be to hold off on breakfast and give Vang and whomever else a chance to join him. Charley passed some time examining his sore, battered feet, which today ached and stung pretty much nonstop. He could only walk gingerly, or on the softer patches of grass or pine duff (or whatever kind of duff it was these trees generated). Otherwise, Charley lazily rolled about or crawled, checking out the little area that Vang had made into his camp. Charley couldn't tell if this spot had been used for similar purposes before—he found no fire ring, no forgotten trash, no rusty penknife—but he got the impression that it must have served as a hiding place in the past. It felt safe.

A couple of hours after waking, Charley could not wait any longer to eat. He had bread and jam, and fruit and nuts. After eating, he dozed, on his back, outside of the tent. He kept dreaming that Vang was arriving, and so he kept pulling himself out of his half-sleep to greet him, but upon finding it was just a dream, he would lapse back into slumber, only to have the same dream, and the same experience, all over again. When he was awake again in the afternoon, it occurred to him that it was useless to project when Vang might return, and so he ate some more, lay on his back looking up through the tall trees, and daydreamed. He had not been this relaxed since entering this world, stinging feet aside.

Charley thought about his family for a little while, and how much he wanted to see his parents. It killed him to think that he knew where they were, and how they were feeling, but they didn't know where he was—that is, if time were passing back home. This train of thought led him to think about Wednesday, and how she was so looking forward to rescuing her parents, and Charley got so depressed that he rolled over on his stomach and buried his face in his arms, shutting out the solace of the trees. Everything was so depressing.

Charley lay like that for a couple of hours, until it was dusk. He then sat up and ate again. After dinner, he considered what was going to happen once Vang showed up again, conveniently ignoring any gnawing pessimism about the possibility that Vang might not ever show up. Charley figured if Vang brought another person or two from the Resistance, they together could come up with the plan. But then Charley thought about it, and he realized that nobody else had seen as much and knew as much about what went on recently as he did. And as Onnser's apprentice, Charley would be expected to take the lead. Everybody would be looking to him to make the plan and lead the attack. At first, this thought depressed Charley further, but then he came to the conclusion that at least he had reached a solid conclusion—that he, Charley Tooth, would have to be in charge from now on. It wasn't what he wanted, but at least it was something. Dwelling on what that meant, Charley crawled back into the tent and went to bed.

The next day, Charley awoke before the sun was completely over the horizon, and so he felt the chill of the morning and absorbed the peacefulness of the quiet light as it edged its way over the hill and through the leaves. Charley took a few ginger steps and found that his feet felt a lot better. Not that he would want to run anywhere, and stepping on the occasional twig or seed pod was an excruciating reminder of his wounds, but Charley could now actually amble around the camp. After a late breakfast, Charley actually climbed back up the hill to see if there was any sort of view, any sort of indication that Vang might be on the return. The top of the hill, however, was still in the thicket of trees, so Charley had nothing to see farther than a good thirty yards in front of him. Recalling Vang's words about "staying here," he then decided a literal observation of those words was a safer play, and so he returned to his campsite. He decided to work on his action plan.

Charley cleared a spot on the ground and tried to reconstruct what he had seen from the maps and from his own experience of the layout of the Ministry Building, from memory. He was drawing with a stick for about twenty minutes before he realized what a waste of time it was, as he couldn't remember much, and it wasn't as though he was going to lay siege to the place. And though it certainly felt like he had some time to waste, with no sight of Vang, he felt bad about wasting it on something that pretended to be important but went nowhere. Too much hypocrisy. He scratched out his feeble artwork and threw the stick away.

Sitting there, he went over in his mind the different possible plans that might arise. If Vang brought back lots of people, with weapons, an all-out battle could conceivably work. Of course, the magic of the Resistance would not be much in the face of what the Ministry controlled, and that put Wednesday, Grimfir, and Onnser in jeopardy. That would not work. Maybe if Vang brought back a lot of supporters, from them Charley could pick the most dedicated, the most valiant, the most capable, and have his own little roundtable, and use just them. But that seemed doomed to fail as well.

The more Charley thought about it, the more it became apparent to him that the best chance of success would have to be a secret strike from within, somehow. Maybe a band of two or three people could sneak in through the dockhouse, and with Tandor's help, come upon Dix and Dax while they slept or were otherwise unawares. And then . . . then they could slay the Orphan Lords, and maybe all the armies loyal to them would abandon their evil cause, like the henchmen to the Wicked Witch of the West. Hmmmm. Maybe. But that sounded increasingly unlikely the more Charley went over it in his head. He got up and began to pace.

Any move that he made put his three captured friends in danger. Providing that they were still alive. Charley reckoned that they probably were still alive, and not just because they were valuable sources of information, but because they were connected to Charley. If Onnser had revealed to the Ruling Powers that he believed Charley to be the one capable of their overthrow, perhaps they would keep his friends alive as insurance in case Charley showed up breathing fire and wielding the Talking Sword of Flassto, as some sort of bargaining chip. It was possible, and not altogether improbable. Charley had learned from Onnser that even the good guys will use the pawns they have to their advantage. That seemed to be the way of the world. Unfortunately, Charley couldn't think of anything that he had to play against Dix and Dax's pawns of Wednesday, Onnser, and Grimfir. There was Charley, and there was somewhere the Talking Sword of Flassto. That was it. And Charley realized, that was all there needed to be.

With a renewed sense of purpose, Charley went back to the bag of food and ate a lot of it. Somehow, deciding on his plan of action made him famished. He puttered about until darkness came, and then he spent a few hours just watching the stars. He went to sleep that night and dreamt of variation after variation of confrontation with the Orphan Lords. He often dreamt that he himself was one of the Orphan Lords, which concerned him greatly, even within the dream.

The following morning, Charley was again up early. He had just finished eating when he suddenly noticed Vang standing about ten feet away. Charley was so surprised that he rolled over backward in some vague idea of a defensive move. When he righted himself, Vang was still standing impassively. Charley stood up.

"Thank you for the tent and the food."

"I forgot to bring you shoes and socks."

"That's okay. My feet are actually feeling pretty good today."

There was a protracted silence between them before Charley spoke again.

"I thought you might be off gathering more members of the Resistance."

Vang moved his head slightly, just once, to the left, to indicate that there was nobody else.

"That might be for the best, actually. Well, I think I have a plan. Do you have a sword I could have?"

Vang pulled back his cape to reveal a decent-looking sword on his hip. He unbuckled it and brought it over to Charley. Charley was glad that he was as tall as he was, as Vang's sword was clearly designed for a taller gentleman. Charley unsheathed the blade and was struck by the beauty of the weapon. The hilt was ornate, and up the center of the blade ran a thin filigree of intertwining vines, worked in some sort of pearl. Charley looked up at Vang.

"You're sure I can have this? I can't guarantee I'll be able to give it back when all of this is over."

Vang stepped back a few paces and put his hands behind his back, indicating, in Charley's mind, a sort of "no backsies" mentality. Charley sheathed the sword and leaned it against a tree. He turned back to Vang, not knowing what to say.

"Do you want some food? There's still some in the bag."

Vang took one step forward and looked intently at Charley.

"Where do you want me to take you, Charley?" he asked.

Charley sighed and sat down, saying, "I was hoping to put off that question for a while. But you're right. Let's pack up; I'm ready to get out of here."

As soon as he had said it, Vang got to work taking down the tent with maximum efficiency. Practically by the time Charley had closed the food bag and picked up the sword, Vang was already off with the tent, leading the way back to the carriage. Charley followed, but this time did not feel quite the compunction about not following as closely behind as before. He was in no real hurry to get where they would be going.

When Charley reached the carriage, Vang had already loaded the tent, and he took from Charley the food bag, which was noticeably lighter. Then, with one hand on the open door to the carriage, Vang turned to look at Charley, to see where they would ride.

"Okay, Vang. Please take me to the Ministry, or as close to it as you can."

Slowly Vang shut the door and leaned back against the coach, regarding Charley with a mixture of inquisitiveness and skepticism that Charley had never seen on this man's face before. Clearly, Charley needed to explain.

"Well. It's like this. Everyone seems to think I am the only one who can take on Dix and Dax. I have never been able to figure out why people thought that, but they do. So, by now, perhaps even the Orphan Lords think I am the one. Maybe they think that I have the Talking Sword of Flassto. If I am the chosen one, and I show up and they are scared of me, the advantage is mine. However, if I am not the chosen one, they still will be scared of me—at least at first. And maybe I can leverage that to get Wednesday, Onnser, and Grimfir freed. If I do nothing, those three will probably die. If I try and fail, then they will probably die. So if I go in acting like I own the place, like I'm going to win, I might be able to pull off their release. Worst-case scenario is that everybody dies, which is going to happen if I sit around and wait. Best case is that I free those guys, or at least one of them, and they can figure out how to rebuild the Resistance for when the right guy comes along. I don't imagine the Ministry is expecting me to show up knocking at their front door, so I might as well do that and be as surprising and unpredictable as I can. And since it seems like nobody's seen the Talking Sword of Flassto, I might be able to bluff my way with your sword. Make sense?"

Vang grinned curtly and opened the door, gesturing for Charley to step inside. Charley got in, Vang shut the door and climbed to his stoop, and they were off.

The ride, of course, was a long one, and as Charley sat with the sword across his lap, he had plenty of time to reconsider, and then to reconsider his reconsideration, again and again. Which he did. Then, examining the scabbard to Vang's sword, he was again struck with the remarkable beauty of it, and how it looked like the handiwork of some ancient master. It made Charley wonder how old Vang was, which he had never wondered before. Vang certainly was older. Old, even. But beyond that it was hard to tell. Charley had never brandished a sword before, and he was wondering how professionally he would be able to do so. It was heavy—much heavier than he expected it would be—and he realized that he would actually be menacing some very powerful people with it. Maybe he should have asked to remain in the woods for another day or two, getting used to it and learning the basic ways to comport oneself with a weapon such as a sword. But at this point Charley was much more afraid of altering the plan already set in motion than he was of facing down his unasked-for nemeses.

Charley was surprised how easily he and Vang made it into town and toward the Ministry Building. He had thought maybe the Orphan Lords would have set up more checkpoints and be doing thorough searches of anyone entering or leaving the city. Maybe they believed the Resistance already to have fled? Or perhaps they didn't think the remaining rebels posed much of a threat? Whatever the case, it made for an easy enough journey for Vang and Charley. Sneaking a peak out of the window, Charley could see that they were approaching the headquarters of the Orphan Lords. It looked even more imposing on the outside now that Charley had seen the inside and knew from Tandor what kinds of activities had gone on in there over the years. And to see it now as the place that had all his friends locked away made his heart beat faster, and the familiar cool ring of sweat bead up along his hairline.

About one hundred yards from the entryway to the Ministry, at which four soldiers were posted, Vang drew the carriage to a halt. He got down and looked in the carriage window. Charley looked at him, and knew that Vang was asking him if he really wanted to go through with this, or if he wanted to turn back. Charley gripped the sword and nodded, and Vang immediately opened the door. Vang stood so that Charley was blocked from view of the gate. He held out a cloak to Charley, which Charley quickly put on. Then Vang fastened the sword to Charley's waist, and drew the cloak over it, effectively hiding it. Then he stepped to the side to allow Charley to pass. Charley began the walk toward what appeared to be his fate. He avoided the slimeway, not wanting to chance it, what with the sword and his bare feet and his occasional problems with balance. Vang got back up onto the carriage, and stood there, his arm poised in the way it was before he lobbed whatever magic it was that spirited Charley up out of the trees outside the burning monastery of St. Orson.

The four guards stepped forward as Charley neared. He was expecting them to say something like, "Stand and deliver!" or "Halt! Who goes there?" but instead they just sullenly barred his way. Their mute reaction surprised Charley enough that he also stood there, silently, for a second, not trying to pass.

"Excuse me. I'd like to get through."

The shortest one, who had long ears like a beagle that moved and reacted with startling dexterity, responded, "Nobody gets through."

"It's urgent."

"Nothing's urgent."

"I am urgent."

"Nobody gets through."

"I am here to see Dix and Dax, the Orphan Lords."

Three of the guards snickered at this, including the speaker. The one non-snickering guard in back put on a face of being tired past the point of exasperation, as though everyone in the world were conspiring to wear him out by asking to see Dix and Dax, the Orphan Lords.

"Seeing the Orphan Lords is a matter of invitation, not request. As in, only when they 'invite' you."

"Tell them Charley Tooth is here to see them."

"I'm telling you—"

The head guard was interrupted by one of the other guards, who improbably had the face of a flower, with a full mane of petals. This guard whispered something in the head guard's ear, and he blanched and turned back to Charley. The annoyed guard in the back remained as he was, but the third guard, who looked to be of a similar species as Grimfir, stepped forward, looking quizzical, but still deferring to the head guard.

"You are Charley Tooth?"

"I am."

"You know that the Orphan Lords are looking for you?"

"Yes."

"What are you doing here?" asked the one who looked like Grimfir.

"Yeah, are you crazy?" asked the flower-man.

"While Dix and Dax may be looking for me, I am also looking for them. So I am here to see them. Please bring me to them."

The guards exchanged glances. The head guard shrugged.

"Okay, if that's what you want." He turned to the morose guard in the back. "Lionel, you stay here, and we three will take him."

Lionel sighed and looked at Charley. Charley looked at him.

"Where are your shoes?"

Charley was surprised that Lionel had even noticed, let alone asked about it. The other guards looked down at Charley's feet, and then at each other, somewhat puzzled but also wary.

"You sure you're Charley Teeth?" said the flower one.

"Yes. Tooth. Charley Tooth."

The head guard shrugged, the Grimfir-like one opened the gate, and the three guards and Charley stepped into the courtyard of the building. They walked down the straight, dusty path that cut through the semicircular green. At the front doors to the building proper, there was another set of guards, all four of whom were of the buzzard-cum-lion variety, if you can picture it. They immediately began squawking about as soon as the incoming group set foot on the first of the marble steps.

"Relax," said the head guard. "Special meeting for the Orphan Lords."

The door guards kept up their racket, and one of them began pecking at a shiny vein of something like mica or maybe silver in one of the marble columns that stood on either side of the entrance. The band of gate guards led Charley up through the hysterics, which Charley had to admit were frightful, disconcerting, and annoying enough to drive a visitor away, had the fate of the free world not rested on his shoulders. When the gate guards tried to open the doors, though, the buzzard-lions freaked out completely, darting this way and that, screaming at the top of their lungs, and refusing to let the group pass.

Charley could see through the glass of the doors into the expansive lobby. It was cavernous, with amazingly high ceilings, but it was all cold, pale marble, with Byzantine staircases leading off in several directions to several different levels. Metal trim provided the only break from the sameness of all the stone. Charley felt a hand on his shoulder, and found the lead guard's face close by.

"Sorry about this, sometimes these guys are impossible. We'll go use a side entrance."

The group left the shrieking door guards and retreated along the left side of the building. The lizardy one walking on Charley's right turned to him.

"So if you're really Charley Tooth, do you know Grimfir Boldrock?"

"I do. He was my first teacher here."

"No kidding! He's my cousin."

"Really? Is he here? Have you seen him?"

"I understand he's here, but I haven't seen him. I don't know how he's doing, but let me tell you, I certainly don't envy him right now. Next time you see him, tell him his cousin Warfo says hello?"

"Warfo? OK. Hey, what's your full name?"

"Warfowarfowarfowarfowarfo-Warfeau. Can you remember that?"

"I'll just stick with Warfo. Are you two close?"

"Not very, though he owes me money. Remind him of that, too, will you?"

"Okay, if I get the chance."

Warfo laughed at this, then took a couple of quick steps ahead and yanked open a dilapidated-looking door on banged-up hinges. It revealed a dimly lit stairway, and the four of them marched on up. At the top of the stairs, there was another door that opened into a smelly, dirty hallway that looked like it had been abandoned as soon as it was finished being built. They walked down this dingy passageway to another door that looked down on its luck. Warfo put his shoulder into it, and the door gave way into a very fancy but austere-looking hallway of the same marble that Charley had noticed through the front doors. In fact, they seemed to have come in not far from the entrance, but a level up, as right in front of them, just past the railing, hung a huge lightfish chandelier that served as the main light source for the main part of the building. They went left down the balcony, and Charley marveled at the workmanship of the place, as plain as it was. It certainly could not have been easy to construct this place . . . unless, he realized, you had a lot of magic at your disposal.

After zigging and zagging down a few more hallways and up a few more flights of stairs, they came to a wide, low vestibule off of a main hallway. In the wall at the back of the vestibule was a yawning recess that was about as tall as Charley, and about twelve feet across. The guards led him to it, and he saw that there was no floor nor ceiling to it—just darkness where the vertical tunnel angled off, cutting off any possibility of light carrying through. The beagle-eared guard flipped a series of levers, nine in all, into the up position. The guards linked arms, with Charley in between the daisy and the lizard.

"Ready?" asked the beagle-eared leader.

The others nodded, and the daisy whispered into Charley's ear.

"Jump forward on 'three.'"

"One . . . two . . . three!"

All four of them jumped into the cavity, and Charley expected them to plummet downward. Instead, they plummeted upward. The arm-linking didn't last long as they were quickly blasted along through the pneumatic tube. Soon, they were just a jumble of bodies hurtling up through the vertical shaft. After several minutes of this, they clattered out of another fireplace-type of opening in a wall, sliding across the smooth marble floor.

Discombobulated, the group stood back up and straightened themselves out. The daisy guard helped straighten out the collar on Charley's cloak.

"It used to be like the slimeway, but it was a lot slower, and going up and down in all that goo was inconvenient and a little disgusting."

Charley was glad that his sword remained undiscovered in all the bumping and flying. He looked around to see that they were in some sort of big reception area, complete with a receptionist behind a large semicircular desk. The receptionist, a well-dressed cat with large glasses and bangs, was cleaning its whiskers as the beagle-eared guard went up to announce the intent of their presence. After a minute or two of discussion, phone calls, and calendar checking, he and the receptionist came to an agreement and he returned to the group.

"It'll be about fifteen minutes. Make yourselves comfortable."

In the waiting area were a number of chairs and end tables. The guards all went over to sit, and they thumbed through the magazines that were lying around. Charley wandered over to the far wall, where there was a table with hot drinks and food. It turned out that there was fresh hruckney, and as Charley loved hruckney, he had two plates of it. It was surprising to him, as he never could eat when he was nervous, like before an important soccer game. But here he was about to face actual enemies, and the hruckney really hit the spot. Charley did remain standing, though, as he just couldn't relax enough to sit down and look through magazines.

About twenty-five minutes later, the receptionist came over to them and purred, "You may go in to see the Orphan Lords now. It's just through the door."

The three soldiers and Charley went over to the huge metal doors to the left of the reception desk, and the doors swung open either magically on their own account, or by some buzzer that the receptionist controlled. Charley couldn't tell which. They entered a huge, clean room that had metal walls with a marble floor and ceiling. In the far end of the room were two thrones, made of marble with steel decorations. Off to the right, jutting out from the wall, were three large metal boxes about the size of telephone booths, each with a bunch of holes in them. There was nobody else in the big room.

Then, behind the thrones, part of the far wall came apart, as though rather than metal they were just curtains, and from a hallway revealed behind emerged two figures who entered and sat on the thrones. The beagle-eared guard stepped forward.

"Captain Uff reporting, sirs. A one Charley Tooth here to see you."

"Thank you, Captain. You and your men may return to your posts," said the shorter figure on the throne to the left. But it was hard to hear, as he was so far away, at the other end of the room.

"I beg your pardon, sir? I can't hear you."

"I said, 'Thank you, Captain! You and your men may return to your posts!'" shouted the same figure as before.

Captain Uff snapped his feet and turned, as did his men. The Grimfir-like one gave a quick, kind smile to Charley, and then he and the others left. The big metal doors swung shut behind them, and, as Charley saw, the seam between the doors disappeared. He turned his attention back to the figures on the thrones.

The one on the left said something again, but Charley couldn't hear him this time, either. It was a big room.

"I'm sorry, what?" he called out, taking a few steps

forward. He heard the two men on the thrones sigh, and they got up and also came forward. Both Charley and they stopped in the middle of the room, leaving a safe distance of about twenty paces between them.

"I said, come forward, Charley Tooth, if that's who you really are."

"That's who I really am."

"I am Dix, and this is my twin, Dax. You might also know us as the Orphan Lords."

"I do indeed," said Charley, feeling that this exchange was probably some sort of enemy dueling etiquette.

Though both of the Orphan Lords were elfin in appearance, and though they were twins, they looked quite different. Dix, as mentioned, was shorter, and he was particularly round. His nose was sharp and upturned, and his eyes sparkled with confidence and malice. This was offset by his pageboy blond hair. Dax, on the other hand was taller and thinner, and his nose turned down just as sharply as his brother's turned up. He had paler skin and the bad beginnings of a beard that thinly marked the outside of his face. He also wore a woolish hat that he had down almost over his eyes. Charley noted his bad posture, as well. Dax hung back, morosely, while Dix paced back and forth.

"So you are Charley Tooth. We've been wanting to meet you."

"Yes," was all Charley could think to reply.

"What are you doing here? I admit we were surprised to hear that you announced yourself out front. We didn't think you would come to us so easily. After all, let's face it: Our ideological principles are mostly at odds."

"I came here to seek the release of Onnser the semi-Magnificent, Wednesday O'Friday, and Grimfir Boldrock. I insist that you free them at once."

This time, Dax laughed and responded, "No way."

"But we would be glad to show them to you, Charley," said Dix.

The Orphan Lords moved back toward their thrones, but turned back to Charley rather than sitting again. Dix raised his hands to the three boxes on the right, and the metal smoothly reformed itself, withdrawing back into the wall. Where the boxes had been were Onnser, Grimfir, and Wednesday, bound tightly in body-sized cages made of bands of metal and marble. All three at once, upon being freed from the outer box, exclaimed, "Charley!"

"Hello," said Charley in return.

"Now Charley," said Dix, "a slight demonstration of some of the power that my brother and I yield."

Dax held up his hands, and from the floor rose a piece of marble, which he then coaxed slowly through the air to a point between himself and Charley. It was about the size of a basketball. Then Dix held up his hands, and out from the wall dripped a puddle of metal, which he then floated over to the marble orb. The twins, then acting in concert, wove their elements together into a single sphere of marble and steel.

"You see, Charley, that I control the metal, and my brother controls the rock. It can be quite dangerous for someone who sets himself against us." So saying, both twins threw their hands forward, rocketing the orb at Charley's head. Charley had been in enough lawless playground games such as Kill-the-Man and

Boom Ball to have developed lifesaving reactions when things were thrown at him, and so he ducked, and the ball smashed into the far wall behind him. Dax found this quietly amusing, and Dix smiled broadly before continuing.

"As you know, Charley, or at least as I assume you do, given the top level of instruction you appear to have had, Dax and me have powers that are more or less unopposed throughout the realm."

"Dax and *I*," corrected Dax, and Dix turned to him, ready to argue, but thought better of it and looked back to Charley.

"It would take a remarkable magician to get anywhere with us, Charley, and even the most capable magician might find that he is not fully prepared to be able to make demands of us and have them met. You do know that, don't you?"

"I do. And that is why I prepared myself as best I could before coming to meet you. How great a magician I am sounds subjective, so I decided the best way to convince you to release my friends was to equip myself with a certain advantage that you might be familiar with."

"*With which* you might be familiar," sneered Dax.

Dix shot a look at Dax and then said, "And what is this advantage, Charley?"

"I wield the Talking Sword of Flassto!" proclaimed our hero, throwing back his cape and brandishing in glory the sword that Vang had let him borrow.

There was some sort of "hurrah" from one of the boxed residents off to the right. Dix and Dax took a step or two back, and Charley was gratified to see a look of panic cross both their faces. Especially gratifying for Charley was to see the smugness momentarily disappear from Dax's face. He reminded Charley of a guy from high school who was a rude, intellectual snob lacking in social graces, who came to the realization that nobody much liked him. The Orphan Lords looked at each other, and then back at the sword that Charley held aloft but slightly back from his torso, not only to be coiled for battle but also to prevent the twins from getting a clear look at it. As it turned out, that part didn't seem to matter.

"But . . . but that's impossible. The Talking Sword of Flassto? You can't possibly have it. . . . It doesn't exist!" said Dix.

"No sword by that name was ever forged!" added Dax.

"And I'm a little dismayed that Captain Uff and his men didn't frisk you. We seem to need some security retraining," said Dix.

"Where did you get it?" asked Dax.

"I found it," said Charley, somewhat on the defensive.

"That's impossible. Really."

"I tell you, I bear the Talking Sword of Flassto. Disbelieve me at your peril," said Charley, gamely playing out his bluff, though somewhat nervous not only due to the twins' claim, but also because he wasn't sure that "disbelieve" was a real word, and he was somewhat distracted by the strange, cheap-novel phrasing in which he said those words.

"On top of that, your sword isn't even talking," pointed out Dax.

"Not talking now, but it will sing with your blood," countered Charley, grimacing inwardly at how he sounded.

"What?" asked Dix.

"Free the prisoners. Your reign is over." Like a pearl melting in vinegar, so went Charley's resolve.

"There is no Talking Sword of Flassto. It's merely a legend. Mr. Hiram Poison came up with it and said that there was no such blade. We created the rumor that the Talking Sword of Flassto was the only thing capable of destroying us in order to get enemies of the state to focus on searching for something they could never find. So, you see, your claim must be a lie."

Dix held his hand out, and Vang's sword tore itself from Charley's hand and floated over. Dix took it and held it at his side, not deigning even to look at it.

"And had it been the Talking Sword of Flassto, you would now be without it. I am a little disappointed, Charley. Overall, I thought you would prove to be a much harder adversary to best. Dax?"

They held out their hands again, and Charley saw steel from the walls and marble from the floor and ceiling coming at him, pitching him over to the left. Those years of cutthroat boys' play in the cement schoolyards had given Charley a sound sense of handling sudden onslaughts of irrational violence, but he had never had to face rock and metal conspiring against him. In practically no time at all, he was against the left wall, bound from neck to the waist in metal bands of about three inches in width and thickness, and with marble shackles covering his bare feet and ankles.

Dax was eyeing the captured sword in Dix's hand, and Dix was gloating over catching Charley so easily.

"Charley. Charley Tooth. I wonder if you feel guilty at having let down your friends. They had *such hope* in you."

Dax took the sword from Dix and examined it closely, and Dix continued to lord it over Charley.

"You realize you presented no challenge to us. No challenge at all. Look at you. Your friends were sorely mistaken. But I have good news—they won't hold it against you. They won't be able to. You see, now that we have you, there's not much point in keeping them alive and well."

"Where *did* you get this sword?" asked Dax suddenly.

"What?" said Dix, turning to him.

"What?" asked Charley.

"I know this sword. I know I know this sword. This is a sword from our past. This sword relates to our history. I know I know this sword."

Dix turned to Dax, who was holding out the sword. He looked at it, and also appeared to find in it something that sparked a long-dead memory. As Dix turned the blade over in his hand several times, Charley saw that he came to some important decision in his mind that he was not revealing to his twin.

"It doesn't matter," said Dix. "There is no Talking Sword of Flassto, the Resistance is crushed, and now we may at our leisure rid ourselves of these characters who have annoyed us for so long. However, Charley, I insist that you perform the honor of deciding who dies in what order."

"This is our crest! This is our family crest!" exclaimed Dax.

Charley felt helpless, and he suddenly remembered the talisman that The Historic Ganka gave to him. "Orm eet eese wayhayplay," he said quietly, and immediately he felt the amulet against his chest. It felt warm, and then hotter, and then hotter still.

Soon, the heat had spread throughout the core of his body, and Charley felt assured, confident.

Suddenly, Charley knew what he had to do. In a split second, it reminded him of a math exam he took in eighth grade, and a high school night of mischief in his hometown with Clint Ryder and some of his other friends who ran a little wilder than the average Connecticut teenager. On the math test, he was staring down the final problem (out of fifteen total), and though he could grasp the way he was supposed to attack it, somehow he couldn't begin. He looked at it and looked at it, and still he couldn't even begin to put down on paper the orderly scribbles that would earn him partial credit, if not lead him to the proper answer itself. Just before Mr. Howe, the neo-hippie teacher who always wore cords and a tie, called time on the test, Charley wrote down "7.34" as the answer. He couldn't explain it, couldn't justify it, and he certainly hadn't done the math, even in his head, to get there, but that was the answer he felt compelled to record. And, as it turned out, not only was it correct, but he was the only one in the class to get it right. When Mr. Howe, with his shaggy bangs and odd propensity to sing short refrains of songs as he talked, asked him how he arrived at his answer, Charley responded honestly, saying that it was a blind guess. With any other teacher, they would have pressed for more, or suspected him of cheating, but somehow Mr. Howe accepted his answer as it was.

As for the night of mischief, Clint Ryder had organized a late-night excursion of egging, toilet-papering, and mailbox-filling-with-whipped-cream activities in his neighborhood. Though Charley felt bad for the people who would end up greeting the morning only to find they had a major cleanup on their hands, he still took part in the activities, catching a ride with Clint, who was already driving. There were ten or so of them, boys and girls, and those who drove or biked had all parked in the parking lot behind the community center in the area. At about 12:45, Charley suddenly felt uneasy, and he took a break to go get something to eat. Not twenty minutes later, some neighbors came out on their porch to say that the cops were on their way, and may all the little bastards get what they deserve. Charley's friends all ran, skedaddling this way and that back to the parking lot, but that was where the police were waiting for them. Charley came ambling toward the parking lot just then, with a bag of food in one hand and a chocolate malt in the other. He saw the cop cars from a block or two away, so he put on his best nonchalant face and kept up his regular pace. He slowed just a bit as he passed the scene, and he saw Clint look at him and mouth the words "Get Out," so he just kept walking. The rest of the gang, caught, got personal police escorts home, and then had to clean up their messes and apologize to the victimized residents the next day. To a one, Charley's friends insisted that he take no part in the cleanup or apology, as he was "lucky enough not to get caught, and there must be a reason for that," as Clint put it. It didn't sound quite fair to Charley, but he didn't push the issue.

Here, in the clutches of the Orphan Lords, Charley once again felt the specifically vague intuition on what to do. He leaned into his bonds, and he felt the cold metal and cool marble against his body. He began extending his hands the way he had done to open locks, the way that he had to hit the lightfish tank just right in his room at Grimfir's. The same sensations of draining elsewhere in his body came up again, stronger, as Charley felt other parts of his body shifting instead of just his hands. He felt the flesh pressed against the twins' fetters begin to seep through the restraints. His forehead pushed through, and he closed his eyes as they were pulled upward and through the bars, as well. He felt his body, as it oozed out, meet itself past the bars, and begin to reform as it came in contact with itself again.

"Charley!" he heard Onnser exclaim in awe.

Dix and Dax had stopped their inspection of the mysteriously familiar sword to look at Charley, and they were petrified with amazement and fear as they saw him leak out of their little prison. When his upper body was finished its melding, leaning forward out of the restraints, he was shirtless, as the shirt and cloak were not able to pass through when his body did. He did not notice, but Ganka's amulet also failed to make the move, and it fell to the floor in Charley's shirt. The Orphan Lords then saw his bare feet escape their marble manacles, and Charley took a step forward.

"This is impossible!" said Dix.

"I am the Talking Sword of Flassto," said Charley, coming toward them.

"There is no Talking Sword of Flassto," replied Dax, though rather weakly.

"I am the instrument of your destruction," spoke Charley, coldly and authoritatively.

Dix reacted quickly, levitating the sword from Dax's hands and hurtling it directly at Charley's chest. Charley didn't even move, but just as the sword reached him, he opened up a hole in the middle of his body, no bigger in diameter than a softball. The sword passed through the gap in his body, crashed into the wall behind him, and fell to the floor. Charley sent one of his eyes travelling around his head to the other side, keeping the other one on the Orphan Lords. He extended his right arm behind him, and then just kept right on extending it until it reached the sword. He brought his arm and eye snapping back into place. He advanced another step on Dix and Dax, who now were both pale and trembling.

"Release the prisoners. Do it now and I will let you live."

Dix and Dax complied, but as Charley's friends fell to the floor, Dax held out his right hand toward Charley, and then clapped it with his left. The marble floor beneath opened up suddenly into a hole several stories deep. But just as he did so, Charley reached out archingly with his left hand, spanning the fifteen or so feet between them, and clutched Dax by the throat. Charley began to fall into the opening, but he poured the rest of his body into the direction his arm was going, and within very few seconds he stood right in front of Dax, still holding him by the throat, with Vang's sword pointed at his gut.

"Surrender now and beg for mercy," he said.

Onnser, Grimfir, and Wednesday had recovered themselves by now, and Dix, seeing this, moved to balance the playing field by quickly manipulating steel from the walls. However, before he could form it into something useful, Grimfir covered the gap between them with surprising speed and crashed into him, taking him down. Onnser was quick to respond too, coming at Dix with magic blazing.

Dax's terrified eyes were fixed on Charley.

"But . . . this is a mistake. Mr. Hiram Poison assured us. . . . This can't be. . . ."

Charley, disgusted, let go of Dax, who slumped to the floor. Within a beat he was back up, though, having created from the floor a sword of sharp, pearly marble, and he came at Charley. Charley held up his sword in defense, but Dax batted it away and it skittered across the floor. Charley didn't have time to grab it again, as he was ducking and backing up to save his life. Charley's ability to bend and shape himself proved an even match for Dax's marble manipulating abilities, and the two carried out a fabulous dance of obstacles and narrow escapes. Meanwhile, Dix was still fighting valiantly against Onnser and Grimfir, having been able to recover his feet if not quite yet his wits to battle them very effectively. Just as Dax had Charley boxed into a pretty tight spot, though, from behind him came Wednesday's voice.

"Dax. It's over for you."

Dax spun wildly, swinging his white marble sword at Wednesday, but she lightly parried it with Vang's sword, and then drove the metal blade home, deep into Dax's chest.

He dropped his sword and then dropped to his knees, unable to make any noise other than a gasp. He held the penetrating blade in his hands and ran the fingers over the design on the shaft.

"Dix," he called out, "I am finished, Brother." And he expired.

Dix turned to see his brother die, and he fought with a renewed sense of purpose. Understandably so. Wednesday removed the sword from Dax, and then she and Charley joined up with Onnser and Grimfir, hoping to encircle Dix. Wednesday lunged here and there with the sword, swiping at the remaining Orphan Lord, but he continued to dodge.

"Foolish Wednesday. Do you not realize that I cannot be hurt by metal? You may have been able to kill my brother with it, but metal is in my blood, and metal cannot harm me."

With that, he extended his hand and called the blade to him. Wednesday struggled to hold on to the hilt, but the magic was stronger than her grip, and the sword flew free. Just as it was arriving at Dix, Onnser leapt forward to seize it and rammed it full on into Dix. At first, Dix just sneered, but suddenly he realized that the sword indeed had caused him pain, and then he realized it had in fact caused him mortal pain. He looked bewildered more than anything.

"What is this?" he said.

Like his brother, he too traced his fingers along the sword, but seemingly to Charley with slightly more comprehension. He looked up at Onnser, and then at Charley.

"This is really surprising for me," he said, before falling over dead.

Wednesday hugged Onnser as Grimfir clapped Charley affectionately on the back. Then the room began to tremble, and Onnser held his hands up.

"The magic of the Orphan Lords is failing. We don't have much time to get out of here."

Charley withdrew the sword from Dix's body and resheathed it. The only opening in the room was the large hole Dax had made when trying to pitch Charley to his death. Though it was several stories deep, it cut through other floors of the building, so it was not a single shaft that would have meant broken bones and necks. Charley lowered himself, dangling his body into the hole. He reached out with his feet, and they quickly extended to the next floor, though Charley got to be quite thin in making the stretch. Wednesday climbed down him carefully, and then swung herself safe of the gaping chasm. Next was Onnser, who moved lightly and deftly, following the same itinerary as his niece. Last, heaviest, and most awkward was Grimfir, and he almost made Charley lose his grip, but Wednesday and Onnser were able to steady him.

Once they were all on the floor below, they saw that they were in some sort of general administrative offices, but that there were few workers present. In fact, the remaining people on the floor were all jammed up by the pneumatic tube through which Charley and his escort of guards had traveled. All the levers were thrown in the down position, and people were eagerly throwing themselves into the cavity, getting whooshed down, as the building pitched and trembled more and more ominously. The band of heroes made their way to the congregated people still waiting to jump, but a little bit of Onnser's magic, Charley's sword, and Grimfir's growl were enough to get them through the first thirty or so people. But then, as chunks of marble began to rain down, the crowd pushed forward, and Charley found that they were stuck.

"Lady coming through!" said Wednesday. "Lady and her elderly uncle! Make way!"

And people did make way. The workers in line were courteous, and they even let Charley and Grimfir escort Wednesday and Onnser to the airshaft. All four jumped in together, and a good tumble later they came out on the ground floor, in the lobby Charley had viewed through the front doors. There were three beings that looked like orange filing cabinets of indeterminate age or sex just past the opening, and to everyone who came out they offered a bagged sandwich. Charley and Grimfir each grabbed one as they picked themselves up. Just then the lightfish chandelier, which had been exceptionally bright and flashy due to the shaking of the building and the nervousness of the fish, broke loose from its anchorage in the ceiling and came crashing down. The lobby was pitched into darkness, and panic immediately overtook the hordes of people fleeing the disintegrating building. Onnser cast a light up to the ceiling, and the effect stopped people in mid-scream, and the scramble to safety resumed a more orderly attitude once again.

Out in the courtyard, the multitudes of the employees of the place were in various stages of fleeing, coping, gawking, and more fleeing. Charley and his friends joined in the rush for the front gates, but just before they got there, Tandor caught up to them, catching Wednesday by the arm.

"What happened? Are you all okay? What happened to the Orphan Lords?"

"They've been defeated!" she cried with elation.

Tandor looked at Grimfir, Onnser, and Charley, to see them all beaming but exhausted.

"Defeated?"

"Yes, vanquished! They are no more!" said Onnser.

"Dead as dead can be," said Grimfir.

"That explains the crumbling of their fortress. As it was constructed of their magic, which ended when they did. Only the main building will fall. But this is certainly an agreeable time to get out of here."

Tandor led them to an unmarked door not far from the left of the gates, and they trotted along a narrow passageway to another unmarked door. Tandor opened it, and they were outside the perimeter of the Ministry. The road was packed with people leaving, so Tandor led his group along the thin line of trees just past the road. Not too far along, however, Vang stepped out to greet them. He came forward and shook Onnser's hand, then Grimfir's, and then he gave a short bow to Wednesday. He nodded at Tandor, and then shook Charley's hand. Charley reached to his hip to undo the sword, but Vang put his hand on Charley's shoulder to stay him, for the time being. He then led everyone to the carriage, which was hidden just a bit farther off the side of the road. They loaded in and headed back toward Onnser's house. Inside the carriage, everyone was recounting the story to Tandor, interrupting each other, reenacting bits here and there, and so on. Charley remained quiet, though, still uncomfortable with Tandor and the secrets to which he had made Charley privy.

When the others were done recounting, Wednesday, flush with excitement, said, "Now that Dix and Dax are overthrown, we can find Mom and Dad!"

Charley looked at Tandor, but Tandor didn't break eye contact with Wednesday.

"I have some information on your parents, actually. I wanted to tell you in private, but it now seems to me that everyone here deserves to know, as well. I am sorry, Wednesday. Clarus and Sholto are dead. Onnser, I am sorry."

Onnser paled and Wednesday leaned forward.

"Dead? What?"

"Yes. I am so sorry. It seems that the Orphan Lords ordered their deaths many years ago. That explains why the rescue mission couldn't find them. It explains why I was able to give you so little information on them over the years. The Resistance was never able to find any of this information out. It was not until recently that any of this information was . . . revealed."

He shot a quick glance at Charley. Onnser and Wednesday were now consoling each other in the sudden, immediate, and unstoppable tears of equal measure in pain as the elation they felt seconds ago. Grimfir reached forward and put a claw on Tandor's shoulder.

"You did what you could for us, Tandor. Thank you."

Charley said nothing, and looked at his knees.

Chapter Fifteen

In the months that followed, there was a rather extensive change in the government. The defeat of the Orphan Lords was made widely known, and the date of their fall made a holiday. Though the fundamental aspects of the government remained in place, there was restructuring of the higher levels and the more abusive branches of the bureaucracy. Top-level people in the Resistance became the new lawmaking body, and it was up to them to bring to the people the new power structure for the world. The Historic Ganka was brought in as a potential successor to Dix and Dax, but it was clear that he had no interest in the position, and that perhaps he was just a bit past his most effective era to be taking on a job of such responsibility. Eventually, they hit upon the idea of making Wednesday the next head of state, and she accepted, naming Onnser (now Onnser the Magnificent) as her advisor. She appointed Tandor to head the Ministry, and he quickly freed all legitimate magicians who had been imprisoned in the old regime, and he rescinded the Containment Laws that had for so long kept magicians from achieving higher levels. Grimfir and Charley both refused positions in the government—Grimfir simply wasn't interested, and Charley kept figuring he would be going home any day now, as the mission was apparently accomplished, even though months had passed. At one point, Charley had asked Grimfir about Wednesday being named Head of State, especially at so young an age.

"Well," said Grimfir, "she's a smart one, and her family has been known for generations to be upstanding, just, and so on. Plus, she's got no magic, which people find a comfort. Also, as it's been established that she's an orphan, she meets that particular requirement."

"It's a requirement that the ruler be an orphan?"

"The constitution says that the ruler 'must be without undue direct influence from his or her elders and progenitors, as though orphaned and therefore able to make decisions on his or her own, based in common sense and the good of the people' and so on and so on."

"But that doesn't specifically mean the ruler has to be an orphan."

"People are irrational. It's the constitution. Sometimes, it is less taxing on people's brains and morals if they just stick to the words and not to thinking. And since it is a constitutional proviso, it would be a headache to try to change it."

"That's completely bizarre and somewhat unsettling."

"Yes."

"I have another question, Grimfir."

"How lucky for me."

"When the new government was installed, why did the weird time zone practice stay in effect?"

"When people get used to something that regular in their lives, something that isn't overtly bad for them, it becomes a matter of the path of least resistance. Much easier to let things go the way they are than to try to teach people to do something new."

"Easier, maybe, but that doesn't mean it's the best course of action."

"Of course it doesn't. But what ever made you think that people choose the best course of action? I swear, sometimes I don't know how you managed to live as long as you have."

For the first few weeks after the overthrow, Charley expected each morning to wake up in his own bed, or to fall into some multicolored portal that would suddenly appear, or see some spaceship or even an F-16 make a spectacular landing on the front lawn, come to whisk him back home. As time passed, he decided he would settle for something a little less instantaneous. Maybe it would be a fast horse. Possibly some sort of moderately painful operation. Perhaps he could convince Flossy the One-Eyed Jerk to punch him not into next week but into last year, or whenever it was that he left. Charley had to admit that these scenarios were unlikely. Even Flossy had seemed to let himself go. Still, Charley held out hope. He even kept his suitcases packed. Charley developed a reputation for being slightly odd, primarily because he was always reading innuendo into the slightest of remarks that people around him made. He thought that perhaps there was a password, a secret conversational exchange that would reveal the speaker to be the gatekeeper to the way home. Charley lingered over comments, making severe eye-contact and fishing around for possible rejoinders that would prove he was ready for the journey back home. Some of them bear repeating here.

At a dinner party at the house of The Sisters Yippie, Lips O'Leary had been talking vaguely about her thoughts on the safety of flying carriages. Charley said to her, "Sometimes the road home is the most dangerous," waggling his eyebrows and making such direct eye contact with her that she shifted uncomfortably and excused herself from the table to get two more drinks.

In the market, Charley overheard Beytore of Beytore discussing the origins of hruckney. Charley tapped him on the shoulder and said, "What if you could send hruckney back where it came from?"

"I don't follow," replied Beytore of Beytore.

"Sometimes we must follow blindly," said Charley.

"Um, that's why we have eyes—so we don't have to," said Beytore, somewhat bewildered.

"If only our bodies could follow where our eyes could see," said Charley, thinking he was getting somewhere.

"What are you talking about?" asked Beytore.

"I mean, if only our eyes could follow where our hearts would take us," replied Charley, with a measure of uncertainty creeping in.

"What is wrong with you?" asked Beytore, getting a little angry.

"Wrong? Blind! I'm following blindly? I'm not following my heart? I need to open my eyes! Eyes! I don't know!" he stammered back, panicking that he was somehow blowing his chance by not answering the question correctly.

Beytore of Beytore bought Charley a mild sedative and recommended he eat only tubers for the next two days.

For a few days, Charley was so convinced that Riboflavia Gumchewie knew how to get anywhere—he had overheard her say to an exiting Duke Riebald at a late-night afterparty that "she knew how to take him to a home he never knew he had"—that Charley actually waited at her doorstep each night until finally Riboflavia called the police, who took Charley to headquarters. He would've spent the night there, had Wednesday not stepped in to get him released. She never asked Charley any questions about the episode.

In time, Charley's hopes dimmed, but never faded completely, and he found himself slipping into a normal life devoid of expectation. It was only in moments of great decision that he found himself still counting on getting home at any moment.

Vang stayed on as Onnser's attendant, assuming a greater role with Wednesday in terms of acting as chauffeur, bodyguard, and steady hand to the young Queen. He was still silent as ever, but Charley did have an amazing conversation with him one more time, just after the fall of the Orphan Lords. It was that very night, as a matter of fact. When they got back to Onnser's after vanquishing Dix and Dax, the first thing Charley did was to get a shirt, socks, and shoes on. He also changed pants, as he had been wearing the same pair from one of his suits since the day the attempted rescue had taken place. The second thing he did was to go down into the kitchen, where Vang was getting a feast ready while the other occupants of the house were celebrating and grieving in the living room. Charley showed up in a clean suit, and he had Vang's sword in his hand. Vang turned to look at him, but he did not take the sword. Charley debated putting the sword on the table and leaving, but he decided Vang deserved more thanks than that.

"Thank you, Vang. This sword, though. There's something special about it. The Orphan Lords recognized it. Dax said it bore his family's crest. Dix said a metal sword could not kill him, and I figured out that the inlay is not pearl, probably, but marble. And that's why it was able to kill both of them. So I wondered, is this the Talking Sword of Flassto?"

"Did it talk?"

"No."

"I doubt the Talking Sword of Flassto even exists."

"Oh. Then, what is this sword?"

"As Dax said, it bears their crest. It is a sword forged with their elements. It has never been used against one of us, so I did not know if it would have any effect on them. I suppose it actually could have made them stonger."

"Where did you get it?"

"My mother. It was her father's before hers, and before that it was father's upon father's upon father's, and so on."

"Really? So your family has always been against the family of the Orphan Lords?"

"No. Never."

"Oh. Just a coincidence then?"

"No, not at all."

"I am missing something."

"The sword represents its family. I was an anomaly. I have powers different from generations of my family. It had to do with my mother."

"Your family? You are the same family as Dix and Dax?"

"They were my sons."

"What! Wait, what? What?"

Vang said nothing, forcing Charley to get more specific.

"Your sons? But I thought they were orphans?"

"They were, in a sense. Their mother died in childbirth. They turned evil and they ceased to be the sons that I had raised. They thought I was dead. They ceased to be my sons, their goodness poisoned. They were orphans."

"Does Onnser know?"

"No. Only you. And that is how it should remain. I am in debt to Onnser. I always will be. But he will never know. The line dies with me."

"I am so sorry. I can't believe they were your sons. I am sorry they are dead."

"It had to be done. I am . . . relieved . . . that it was not my task."

"I am sorry for your loss."

"An orphan is a child who has lost his parents. I do not know of a word for a parent who has lost his children."

Vang turned back to the food preparation. Charley left the sword on the table and then joined the others in the living room. It seemed to him there were so many secrets, so many things that would make this world a different and possibly better place if people would reveal them to each other. But he knew it wasn't up to him to perform this service for them. Onnser and Wednesday were giddy with laughter and tears, and Grimfir appeared dopey. When Charley entered,

Wednesday gave him a big but chaste kiss right on the lips and handed him a glass of something that looked like champagne and had the kick of champagne but tasted like fizzy syrup.

Before long, visitors called on the house, in similar throes of jubilations and libations. There was laughing and singing in the street. Charley recognized many faces from the party at Hololo Summersweat's all those months ago, including Flossy the One-Eyed Jerk, who later they believed to be the one who walked off with an unopened bottle of the drink they were having. The Abbot of St. Orson and Deviz showed up the next day, having successfully escaped the burning monastery. The party seemed to go on for a week, in fact, and Charley never again had a one-on-one talk with Vang.

Charley and Wednesday tried their best to date, but it was a difficult time with the restructuring of the government and the small matter of Wednesday becoming Queen of the World. Still, they managed here and there, and Wednesday had a point that they would probably have more success if Charley were to join her and take a position as one of her Cabinet. But Charley steadfastly refused, thinking that he would be going home soon, soon. One day, as they walked on the roof gardens of the new palace headquarters, Charley noticed that Wednesday had a small box in her hand, and he asked her what it was.

"Charley. Tandor has been pursuing me. He wants to date me. He wants to court me. I need you to tell me what to do with this."

Inside the box was a simple yet elegant necklace. It was a gold chain with an emerald pendant. Its shape and heft reminded Charley of the amulet The

Historic Ganka gave him before he faced the Orphan Lords, and he thought about when he gave the amulet back to the esteemed wizard.

In clearing the rubble of the old headquarters, workmen had come across Charley's cloak, shirt, and amulet, which they turned over to Tandor. Charley let the government keep the shirt and cloak as a sort of token memorial of the big day, but he took back the amulet, and one day, several weeks later, he paid a visit to The Historic Ganka in his secluded cottage.

Ganka actually remembered Charley on sight, which Charley took as a good sign. They passed some time talking about the day of the overthrow and what all had transpired since then. At a late break in the conversation, Charley pulled out the amulet.

"I wanted to return this to you," he said, handing it to Ganka.

"What's this? Oh yes, I remember. I hope you found it of service."

"I did. Just when I thought all was hopeless, I remembered it and said the spell. I immediately felt its power, and right then I knew how to escape my bonds. Interesting, though, is that the amulet fell off when I escaped the little prison the Orphan Lords had me in. It turned out that I didn't need the amulet anymore to defeat them."

"Well, I should hope not! Fat lot of good it would have done you!"

"What? Why's that?"

"Charley, this is merely a heating stone. All it does is generate heat. It's a beautiful thing in the winter, especially. For skiing and snowshoeing."

"What?"

"Yes. A nice little trinket."

"What? All you gave me was a heating stone? To face Dix and Dax?"

"Don't you remember how cold you were? You were soaked, and you didn't even have shoes or socks. You couldn't stop shivering. So I thought this would be something useful to give you. I certainly didn't think you'd need it against the Orphan Lords. If you really were the one sent to us to vanquish them, which apparently you were, then there wasn't much of anything that I could give you that would help. And if you were not the one capable of their overthrow, there was also not much of anything that I could give you that would help. So I decided to give you something that was really more of a comfort measure. Thanks for returning it."

Charley smiled wanly and stood to go. There was nothing more for him to say. The Historic Ganka pressed upon him another autographed copy of *The Magic That Is and Maybe Isn't*.

Remembering this, Charley again focused on the necklace Wednesday now held out for his inspection.

"It's a very nice necklace, Wednesday. Tandor must have spent a fortune on it."

"You need to tell me what to do with it."

"Me?"

"Yes. Tell me to return it to Tandor, and I will. Tell me to throw it off the roof here, and I will. Or if you tell me to accept it, Charley, then I will let Tandor court me. He's been very good to me, very good to the Resistance, very good to everyone. But you have to tell me what you want me to do."

"Well, what do you want to do?"

"Charley, I've told you. I want you to join us. I want you to join me. Together, I think we can make this world great."

"But I can't. I just can't. And it's not up to me—none of it is, none of it ever was. It's up to you, Wednesday. You have to see that Tandor is a better match for you." Charley hated to say it, but in the end it was probably true. Probably. Maybe not.

"But it is *you* that I want. *You* I prefer. But if you tell me you don't want me. . . ."

"It's not that I don't want you, Wednesday. I just can't. I mean, what if, in the end, after all of it, none of this is real? You know?"

"You know that's not true. And why, even if this all *were* a dream of yours, or whatever you think it might be, why turn away from me?"

"Because I can't stay. I have to go back. I have to go on. Whatever it is, I can't stay. You know this."

"But we all want you to stay. I want you to stay. It wouldn't be so bad, would it?"

"No. Yes. No. I don't know. I don't know anything. I just can't do it, Wednesday, even if I did want to."

Wednesday stepped to him and hugged him. He held her for several minutes, then he let go. He took the necklace from her and fastened it around her neck.

"I'm not saying I am telling you to marry Tandor or anything, but he's better for you. I don't know if I could ever tell you to do that. He just is."

Both of them had tears in their eyes, and they kissed once more, passionately. Then Wednesday walked away.

Over the next few months, Charley saw little of Wednesday and Onnser. He spent most of his time with Grimfir, playing parties and doing the social circuit. At first, Grimfir thought that it might be a little cheapening for Charley, the world's greatest magician (as people thought), doing parlor tricks and birthday parties. But Charley had nothing better to do, and once Grimfir realized the amount of increased business he was getting with a marquee performer such as Charley Tooth, he dropped the discussion.

Tandor, however, made it a habit to drop in on Charley, or to try to make it to see him perform whenever he could. He even would send invitations to Charley to join him for this dinner with these dignitaries or a nice informal lunch somewhere not far from the Ministry. Usually, Charley was able to decline these invitations legitimately, or at least seemingly legitimately, as he wasn't all that eager to spend more time with Tandor than necessary. He appreciated how solicitous Tandor was, but it was hard for him to think of Tandor with Wednesday, for they were getting along very well. What made it exceptionally difficult was that Tandor still hadn't told Wednesday his role in the death of her parents. Charley had asked him this point-blank one evening when Tandor dropped by to play cards.

"No, Charley, I haven't been able to bring myself to tell her. There's nobody left who knows. Mr. Hiram Poison, maybe, but there's been no trace of him. I don't know how, at this point, I can tell her—you know? Now that we . . . now that things are going so well for us."

"I think the longer you wait, the worse it will be. Because you do have to tell her, Tandor. You know that, don't you?"

"Yes, I suppose," said Tandor, looking back at his cards.

"I'm serious, Tandor."

"I know, I know. Charley. I know I have to tell her. But I can't right now, not when things are good."

"What, you'll tell her when things are bad? Brilliant."

"No, when things are . . . settled."

"Tandor—"

"I *know*, Charley." Tandor looked up at Charley, and Charley could see his eyes were wet. Charley looked down at his cards, and they finished the game in silence.

A few days later, Charley had ducked out early from a show that he and Grimfir were performing at Mucker McFlugle's home. He was in a new, sharp suit, and his performance had been dead on. On his way home and feeling good about himself, Charley decided to enjoy a stroll in the evening, along the sidewalk rather than the slimeway. He was getting close to town, out where there had been a recent sprawl in residences and fancy restaurants, and Charley was whistling. Darkness had just fallen, and stars were beginning to come out. Charley stopped to tie his shoelace, and when he stood up, he noticed he was in front of a nice, romantic, out-of-the-way Rosalian restaurant (Rosalian restaurants in Nivalg were like French restaurants back home) that was one of the new hot spots. In the front window were Tandor and Wednesday, enjoying a meal. Charley had successfully avoided seeing them as a couple, socially, out together on a date. But here he was, witnessing her laughing with delight at something Tandor had said, sharing food, toasting. As he watched, Tandor leaned in and kissed her.

Charley felt all hot and cold, and choked for air. He

walked swiftly for a block or two, and then he had to duck into some low, ornamental bushes just off of the sidewalk. He vomited. And then he vomited again. And again. After he had voided the contents of his stomach, he dry heaved for a little while longer. When he was all finished, he brushed himself off as best he could and stepped back onto the sidewalk. There, in front of him, just behind the reaches of the rays cast by the streetlight, stood a figure.

"Hello, Charley."

"Hello."

"Do you know who I am?"

"I don't, but please don't take that as an insult, or me being inattentive. It's just that I've met so many people over the past few months, especially since the overthrow, and it seems like far more people know me than I them."

"Oh, of course not." The figure laughed quietly and kindly. It stepped forward into the dome of light cast by the lamp, and Charley could see that it was a man in a dark suit with a derby hat. "My name is Mr. Hiram Poison."

Charley took an instinctive step backward.

"I imagine you have in the very least heard of me, Charley? Charley Tooth?"

"Yes. I have heard of you. But it's been rumors, mostly." Charley took another step backward and his eyes flitted for an escape. Mr. Hiram Poison remained where he was standing.

"I won't hurt you, Charley. Rumors. I am afraid that the rumors about me, the stories, have given me a most undesirable and undeserved reputation. It's very unfortunate, but I suppose that is the price of the privacy that I need."

Mr. Hiram Poison smiled, and Charley had to think to himself that he did look like a kind and perhaps even trustworthy man. He was fit, dapperly dressed, and had a small, kempt grey mustache. His pale blue skin was set off by his suit, which Charley even in his sartorial ignorance could recognize as expensively cut. His dark yellow eyes were likewise set off by his suit and his skin.

"You did some remarkable work here, Charley. Truly remarkable. It has been a long, long time since I have been that impressed."

"Thank you, sir."

"And so polite. My, you are a find, aren't you?"

"No, sir. I was just trying to help out so that I could . . ."

"Yes, Charley? Could what? What do you seek, my friend?" He took another step toward Charley, and Charley remained where he was, riveted by Mr. Hiram Poison's cool gaze.

"I was just hoping to figure out a way to get home."

"Home? I believe I can help you with that, Charley. Here, give me your hand. I can help you." Charley did not raise his hand, so Mr. Hiram Poison stepped forward again and with his right hand grasped Charley by the left shoulder.

"I can help you get out of here, Charley. It would be my distinct pleasure to aid you in that particular endeavor." He smiled kindly, but it felt as though a steel rod was boring straight through Charley's shoulder from Mr. Hiram Poison's thumb to his fingers. Charley's side began to go numb, and he felt like he was under heavy medication. But, as his gaze was captured by Mr. Hiram Poison's, he felt no alarm. Well, that's not entirely true. He was aware of some alarm, but it felt so buried inside of him, so far away, like a dull ache in the center of his already shuddery stomach, that he couldn't quite pull it up into his consciousness for any usable purpose.

"Relax, Charley, and let me help you. This will all go away. You've done a very good job, and you should be very proud." A flare of panic shot up Charley's spine. The thought came to him that he should find his own way out, or at least try to understand it. He felt his body get hot, very hot. He felt almost unbearably hot, except for his shoulder, which was stinging cold. He began to feel very light, and he saw in Mr. Hiram Poison's face a questioning look arise. "What are you doing, Charley? Where are you going?" And he felt airy, even, as though he were coming apart, fading. Which is what he was indeed doing. He could still see Mr. Hiram Poison's disarming eyes peering intently into his own. "Who's got you Charley? Where are you going?" Charley felt as though he were becoming flames, flickering and wisping into nothingness. "How interesting. Charley, are you all right? Can you answer me?" Charley tried to speak, but he felt that his mouth was hanging open uncontrollably as though he were asleep and aware of it but unable to spark himself to directed action. He saw Mr. Hiram Poison try to pull back from him, and he felt the steel rod in his shoulder grow closer and closer together—he could feel the pressure of Mr. Hiram Poison's hand become more concentrated and solidified, even as he felt it trying to tug away, as though it were stuck. Mr. Hiram Poison's face now showed pain, and it was clear that his hand was indeed caught in the dissipating Charley. Charley felt the fingers on his shoulder come together. Mr. Hiram Poison was now visibly struggling to free himself from Charley. "Where are you going, Charley? Heading home so soon? Can it be? Not to worry, Charley, I will find you again." He snapped free of Charley and stood there, observing, cradling his right hand.

"Safe travels, my boy."

And Charley vanished. Mr. Hiram Poison stood, looking at where he had been for a while. Tandor and Wednesday continued in their romantic dinner. Onnser was already at home, in bed for the night. Grimfir was still living it up as the focus of the party at the McFlugle residence. Except for Mr. Hiram Poison, none of them was giving any thought to Charley, and none of them knew where it was that he would rematerialize. And neither, for that matter, did Charley.